Girl Underwater

Dee Stokes

I spent that long night with the handle of my guitar case in one hand and my dad's old Marine duffle bag slung over my shoulder as I watched for headlights. A sloppy rainstorm had started just as I arrived at the abandoned train station on the edge of town well before midnight. I ducked under the sagging shelter of a broad but leaky porch just as a crash of thunder shook the rickety wreck and ushered in a deluge. I was early for the rendezvous knowing that she would not wait. We had both graduated from high school earlier that day and after the graduation ceremony she had kissed me secretly before saying, "Tonight we go. Midnight at the old train station. Don't be late or else." I knew that 'or else' meant she would go without me. She was desperate to leave town and I was desperate for her. Our plans had been plotted and I had saved money for the trip during the last few months. A heavy freight train loaded with anthracite rumbled past, shaking the ancient station badly and making me wonder if I would be safer out with the rain and thunder. The old railway station had been abandoned decades before when the nearby interstate highways loaded with semis and the cavernous trailers took over freight and cars took over passenger traffic. It was a miracle of structural stubbornness that it still stood. It was probably because it seemed to be held together by its own will power and a handful of rusting nails. The structure had long been ignored and abandoned. But the old train station was near the road that went west to California. We were going to head due west until we reached the Pacific. She was going to be an actress and I was going to be a rockstar.

At least that was the plan we had made together.

The rain picked up and I checked my watch. It was just five minutes after midnight. My gut told me something was wrong. I was not worried, at least not then. At least not too much. She usually was never even a few minutes late. Obsessively punctual would best describe her. She wanted out from under the oppressive thumb of her father in the worst way. But the rain was heavy and no one could criticize her for driving at a reduced speed. I watched for the headlights of her old Mustang but it seemed like only freight trains and idiots with guitars were the only ones out that night. There was no way to judge how much time passed with me standing there waiting for her. But eventually the chill got to me. The sound of the rain hissing down was relentless and deafening. I slid down to the floor of the old porch, hugging my knees for warmth. At six foot six and one fifty one I did not carry a lot of body fat. I kept thinking about our shared dreams of our future as my body started to shiver. The mental portrait of our future that we had painted together was of the two of us tan, on the beach, and gloriously happy. We knew our plans were crazy long shots but we told each other that we would never know if we could do it if we never tried. And we had each other for support.

And I waited. My body was cold and wet but I kept watch for those headlights. I must have dozed off because a passing semi-truck jolted me awake with its clattering diesel engine. My watch said it was now just after five. Five! Slowly the eastern horizon began to turn pink. Another glance at my watch to make sure I had not imagined the late hour told me my hopes and dreams were officially over, by a few hours. No California, no future, and most ominously no Rachel. I reasoned that she must have driven by while I was dozing and she probably could not see me tucked away in the shadows under the eaves of the porch.

Why didn't she honk the horn of her old Mustang to alert me? Eventually it sunk in that I had missed her and she was on her way to California to be an actress. I took the shortcut through a soggy field to her house. A large 'For Rent' sign from a local real estate company was in the front yard. Her Mustang and her dad's pickup truck were gone. The drapes were pulled aside and it was easy to peer into the windows into the empty void of the house. Normally at this time of day her dad was getting ready for work and she would still be getting dressed for school. But now their house was as empty as my future.

She was gone and probably not to California. Her father must have grabbed her as soon as she got back home after graduation and taken her … somewhere. And I had no way to reach her.

—

I hurried back to the old man's house. I changed out of my wet clothes and started breakfast for the old man. My guilt and shame about sneaking away in the middle of the night and the subsequent failure made me want to make it up to him. The very last thing my grandfather had needed was a sullen teenager when I was dropped off in his lap the year before. He had enough on his hands as a county sheriff with an underfunded department in a rural area of Texas the size of one of the smaller European countries that was being ravaged by the methamphetamine debacle while his wife was dying of cancer. But he took me in. Money was tight. He had to lease the old McDavey family ranchland to augment his meager salary to feed us and pay for the medical bills my grandmother had accumulated. The oil industry was in slump only exceeded by disappointing crop and cattle prices which combined to make the local economy dismal. The meager ranch my mother had left me was also leased out and provided just enough extra income to help us squeeze by financially. He usually came home for breakfast to check on me and make sure I went to school before heading back to work after a few terse words barked in my direction. The night shift was prime time to catch speeders on the interstate and those fines were a large chunk of the county's income. He also had two deputies with kids my age and he took their shifts to let them attend their graduation. He had said he would try to make it to the high school if things were quiet but his lack of attendance meant things had been anything but quiet in the county. I had just heard the toaster pop and was scrambling the eggs when he came into the kitchen. Bill McDavey was a large, muscular man with a basset hound face. I was named after him but did not resemble him in the slightest other than height. He had the arms and shoulders of a man used to rough and heavy work. There was something in his eyes that caught my attention. "I guess you heard about the accident," He said.

I think my heart stopped right then. It felt like the entire weight of the universe was collapsing onto me as I stood on the linoleum in that small kitchen. "No. What accident?" My knees buckled and gravity seemed to be wanting to drag me down to the floor. I wanted to add, 'Was it Rachel?' But for some reason I did not.

"Johnny Yarrow and his mom were driving home from a graduation party last night when they went off the road on the curve by Brumholtz's farm. Car rolled into a water filled ditch. They couldn't open the doors or get out of the windows. The walls of the ditch kept the doors from opening. Both of them drowned. I'm sorry, I knew and Johnny were close." The old man was sincere. Johnny and I hung out together a few times this school year until Rachel had arrived. My grandfather ate quickly. "So what are your plans now that you're a high school graduate? Marines like your dad? Your chemistry teacher said you really have a talent for science and told me about some scholarships we could apply for if you are interested. And you can get the prerequisite classes out of way cheaply at the community college, if you want to try that route. We really need to plan this out."

We? Until that moment and that two letter word it had seemed him against me continuously. Up to that moment it had seemed to me that he never missed an opportunity to ride my ass over anything that annoyed him. But there was something in his eye, a fear, I had never seen there before. It hit me like a bolt of lightning that we were the only blood family each other had left. Grieving for his dead wife and his dead son had to be curtailed to take care of me. I felt even guiltier about my attempt to abandon him without a word. He said, "I realized last night as we pulled the bodies out of the car and after the death of your parents and your grandma that I have been too busy with work when I needed to be busy with you. I have forgotten how quickly time flew with your father at your age and I am going to hate missing you as much as I hate missing him."

7

His own father had been the sheriff of McDavey County and he had grown up in an era of racial insensitivity where many of his age were called non-whites Niggrahs, Messy-skins, and worse on a regular basis. Someone had once joked that McDavey County has enough 'white trash' to be considered a landfill. But something in the old man made him treat everyone equally, at least until they proved to him they deserved less. He had spent a good part of his youth around farms working next to people from all over, knew their hopes, lived with them, and understood their fears. A few grumbled out of his ear shot that he was not very tolerant of the intolerant but all seemed to appreciate the fact that if you needed Big Bill he would be there for you.

His hands were still scared from picking cotton when he was a child helping his family with his labor and there was a raised scar on his right arm from a bucking horse's hoof. The scar looked hideous but his main complaint about it was that he never was paid for breaking the horse and that he had to pay a vet to stitch him up there in the corral. My grandfather always worked hard and always showed respect to all, working side by side with anyone else who also had to earn their way. He said there was nothing like bailing hay or shoveling horse shit all day next to someone to show you that neither of you are special. Especially if you are covered in dust, grease, and manure. He picked up Spanish working pecan harvests and branding steers. Big Bill McDavey was a paragon of virtue and public service in a county started by his great-grandfather in a time when North Texas was dominated by Comanche, rattle snakes, and scarcity. But my grandfather had earned a reputation of being fair, being stickler for the law, and being the moral bulwark for the community. It helped that his wife, my grandmother, was a doctor who spent extra hours on those who could not afford a regular office visit. He had started out as a deputy out of high school and earned his current position by hard work.

I owed him an answer for the plans for my own future. But I had none, or none that survived past the last midnight. All my hopes, dreams, and aspirations were gone after the missed connection at midnight. There was something hollow inside of me and this void was from having absolutely no clue about my future. "I don't know," I said honestly.

"Well, you don't have to decide right at this moment. Not many of we McDavey's around and we need to watch out for each other. The guy leasing your mother's land will probably re-up and you could use that money for school. Oh, that reminds me. Jackson says he could use a hand today in the motor pool as asked if you wanted to make some money today." Occasionally I helped out when the sheriff cars needed washing, oil changes, or swabbing back seats out when too many drunks yarked while being transported to jail. Or sweeping up, degreasing tools, or other odd jobs. Eric Jackson was an old friend of the old man's and ran the county motor pool. For me it was not fun work but it put cash in my pocket. The past few months the money I had earned was set aside for California. But for the past month Jackson had not had any extra budget funds.

I had nothing else to do, my dreams being shattered. "Sure, why not." I literally had nothing else going on with my life. Somewhere I had once heard a drowning man does not question where a life preserver had come from or who had made it when one arrives at the right moment. "Jackson has budget to pay me?"

"It is the end of the fiscal year and for him it is 'use it or lose it' time," he said. "Heck I may even have budget to paint the cells, if you want to do that too." My grandfather seemed to relax and for the first time began to speak to me on an adult to adult level. From there on we settled into a comfortable existence where he wanted to help me become a man while I had given up on my dreams. And Rachel.

Chapter 2

Twenty Years Later

"Sheriff McDavey?" A squat man asked as I went to unlock my office door. He wore a visitor's badge on his blue Brioni suit and his matching blue silk tie gleamed even under office lighting. He was severely under equipped in the chin area and had too much forehead which made his head look like a balloon. His hair, or what was left of it, was short, sandy brown, and slicked down. His clothes and shoes were expensive and he carried an expensive old fashioned leather satchel briefcase which clued me in that he had to be a lawyer, but not a good one. He was not a top defense lawyer or would have recognized him from courtrooms. The air around him smelled of sandalwood and limes. He stuck out his right hand and provided a perfunctory handshake. He wore a pinky ring that was cold to the touch and the shake itself was like gripping a dead fish. "Carl Owen, new Deputy Attorney General for the Federal District of North Texas." The local Feds changed DDAs on such a regular basis that there was a joke that their offices were equipped with revolving doors.

"Will McDavey, relatively new Sheriff of McDavey County," I said. I had been elected to office nine months before and was still far from hitting any sort of stride. "What can I do for you?" I waved him into my office and he took a seat in a visitor chair cautiously as if expecting it to collapse under his weight. A faint sigh escaped from the man in my visitor which told me he was either not happy about being in my presence or being in the county provided furniture. I had the distinct impression that he had better things to do and I was keeping him from doing them. And he had not appreciated one bit that he had to wait for me to arrive for work.

He cleared his throat and spoke in a rushed monotone. "A male Hispanic was found dead in a car at a rest stop a few days ago. I would like to know what you know about the case." He gave me a look that an upset father would give to a young man when returning his underage daughter well after curfew. I wondered why he was trying to browbeat me.

I had been the backup on that call and it was odd enough of an event for the details to still be fresh in my mind. One of my deputies spotted a blue Honda sedan parked in a rest stop off the freeway, away from the bathrooms and the vending machines at seven in the morning. Seven hours later the same deputy spotted the same car in the same place. It was not unusual for someone heading into Oklahoma to pull off and nap for a few hours. But on a day when temperatures were in triple digits the interior of the car would be unbearably hot. The windows were rolled up and it had to be like a sauna in the car. There is a certain look as the heat bakes a body in a car that you learn to recognize. The water leaves the body and the skin goes slack. The man in the car looked, well, cooked. My deputy knew that look and she called for backup after a quick glance at the driver. I was the closest available unit. My deputy explained the situation over the radio on what she had found. I made a radio request for the coroner to send their van. The coroner's crew arrived just before I did. The driver of the blue car sat reclined behind the wheel. When I arrived I noticed nothing special about the vehicle or the occupant. At first it looked like he had died of a coronary and the smell when I used a Slim Jim tool on the door to unlock the car told us that he was starting to stink. The coroner's investigator and an aid took photos and then carefully bagged the body. Oddly the dead man had no wallet, empty pockets, and no personal effects on him nor in the car. The trunk was empty and the car keys were missing. It was obvious that the car had not been hotwired so someone had to have taken the keys, but whom? I looked in the nearby trashcan and bathrooms but failed to turn up anything related to the man or the car. Dispatch sent a tow truck and I asked to have it taken to the forensic warehouse. The license plate belonged to a Chrysler minivan stolen from a strip mall in Plano two weeks before and the Vehicle Identification Number said the car came from a rental car agency. The rental car agency said that the car failed to be returned three days and the renter had been a woman who had reported it stolen from a hotel parking lot in Arlington. The next day I was informed that there were no fingerprints in the car as if it had been very carefully wiped down. The car being wiped down, the lack of keys, and no personnel effects heavily suggested that the dead man had not died of natural causes. It would normally take several days to a week for the body fluids to be processed and the tentative cause of death was listed as heart failure. There were more questions than answers about the entire situation. But life and the paperwork for my job marches on and I had forgotten about the case until the visit of the new Federal DA.

Owen took notes on his cell phone and asked a few questions on department protocols. It was pretty much standard procedure until he put away his phone. He said, "Off the record, would it be a problem if I claimed jurisdiction on this case?" This was an odd request to make. His request was on the level of the Loch Ness Monster and BigFoot were asking you to take a bag of gold coins from them as it is too heavy for their unicorn to carry.

"Off the record, no. It would neaten up my crime statistics. But I would like to know why?" The Feds wanting to take a mess off my hands rather than dumping one off was a big surprise. They had their own crime statistics to report and willingly take a bad case was not something the Feds were known to do. And in law enforcement very few will do a good deed for you for no reason.

He squirmed in his seat. "Still off the record? My predecessor was running a CI and something went wrong. I know that he should have given you courtesy notice but the majority of the case work was North and South of here. I think the dead man was the CI from the files I found. And you are sure there were no suitcases in the trunk of the car?" Usually the Feds were pretty good about providing a warning that they were using a Confidential Informant in someone's jurisdiction and usually it came in the form of a warning to keep your hands off or else. This was the first time I heard about the suitcases.

I said, "Could your predecessor identify the body?" If his predecessor could peek at some pictures posted online then we could have the identification wrapped up very quickly. But there was a sour look blossoming on Owen's face.

"He is dead too," He said. Owen produced a sheet of paper signed by a federal judge saying Owen was taking over the case with the judge's orders directing me to hand over any and all the case materials. I carefully read the paperwork to make sure all was in order and that the case would not boomerang on me due to a technicality. The order was short, sweet, and handed all responsibility to Federal DDA Carl Owen. I told him all records would be assembled and couriered over to his office. That news made him smile. "Oh, any video recordings at the rest stop?"

"Yes, sir," I said. "But there are cameras only in the bathroom area to catch vandals and on the exit. By the way I counted forty seven cars that left the lot during the time we estimated the man in the car as there and no, the resolution on the fifteen year old exit camera is not good enough to pick up license plates. There is not a camera on the entrance so the time he arrived is unknown." I did not add that with things so very dry it was not uncommon to find folks who missed the entrance simply driving over the dusty ground over what used to be the grass verge to get into or out of the rest stop. The country commissioners would have loved to cut out all the cameras at the rest stop but felt their presence reduced vandalism.

"And your officer who made the discovery? Deputy Greeves." Owen squirmed in the chair as if he was sitting on something sharp. He was clearly uncomfortable.

I said, "Lilly Greeves?" She was a bright, hard working woman, with the proverbial heart of gold, and dedicated to doing her job to the best of her ability.

He pursed his lips for a second and then said, "I would like a copy of her complete personnel file." There was something of an upset high school vice principal dealing with a distasteful failed student prank about the man that made me cautious. He was trying to extrude gravitas to intimidate but that was not working on me. And I wondered why he was trying so hard to brow beat me.

I shook my head no. "Subpoena me for her records. State law and department policy says I cannot just have it over for no reason." His suspicion of Lilly doing something wrong was not enough for me to give him a copy of Lilly's personnel file. I was on shaky legal ground here but I would rather fight than hand over the information on one of my deputies to the increasingly annoying man in my office. My worst case scenario was that it would take him most of a day to get a subpoena and deliver it.

"The reason I want her file is that I think she has the suitcases I am looking for," He said. His voice was flat and it was easy to tell he was both bored and frustrated. "They were in the car. I know they were. And those suitcases are very important case evidence."

"She does not have them. I have no idea what happened to your suitcases but Greeves did not take them." Lilly Greeves was scrupulously honest. In fact she had been a nun for a few years before becoming disenchanted with aspects of her order's politics and she had a scrupulous record as a deputy. I had seen her chase down a man who left his wallet at the diner rather than turn it over to the 'lost and found' box. It wasn't until after the wallet was returned and the owner counted the money in that the wallet did anyone other than the owner knew it had five grand in it. She then refused any rewards. Lilly was not a thief. "What is in the suitcases?"

Owen nodded enthusiastically, "Mainly, these suitcases contain logs of transaction details or some sort of activities. Nothing useful for anyone but my team. But it is all vital evidence for an important case."

I said, "May I ask how you know the suitcases *were* in the trunk of the car?"

Owen forced a smile. "You can *ask*. I cannot tell." He then let a Cheshire cat fill his face. The urge to defenestrate the man grew in me but my office was on the first floor of the building.

I shrugged. "Sorry, but I really have no idea who has your suitcases. It is probably the same person who took the keys to the car after wiping it down."

"Could someone knowing there was a camera at the exit of the rest area and not one at the entrance have evaded the exit camera by leaving by the entrance?" That was possible and I agreed with him that it would be fairly easy to leave the rest area via the entrance. The grass verge between the roadway was hard concrete and there was not fencing separating the two. And the video quality of the camera at the exit was next to useless. I reiterated all that for him and his sloppy smile grew wider at my distaste of having to admit all that.

I said, "We are at the intersection of the highways where they head north to Oklahoma, south to Fort Worth, east to Dallas, and west to Amarillo. If the person who took the car keys also took the suitcases there is a better than average chance they were long gone before we unlocked the door."

He looked like he wanted to argue with me for a moment but thought better about it. Sometimes two bulls in the same field will make the preliminaries to fight for dominance and then back off the battle, sensing there was a better time later for another opportunity. I could sense there was more he wanted to say but he was holding back. He wanted to confront me further but was not going to force things further. Owen thanked me for my time and left quickly.

After Owen left there was a knock on the open door of my office. "We need a SCUBA diver and everyone else on the list is out," Janet Polk said. She was standing in the open doorway of my office. "Jessie is in court, Uma just went off shift, and TK is on vacation. That leaves you." The petite redhead was my undersheriff, my unofficial chief of staff, and she managed to take a lot of the day to day operations away from my busy slate as she kept things running smoothly. The sheriff's department had changed since the old man took me into his house. The first female deputies were only allowed to work in the jail supervising women prisoners back then. But now a third of my deputies on patrol were women. And since the days of my grandfather the budget had increased modestly, we had grown from four deputies, and a sheriff to twenty position. Sadly I was trying to hire for three open deputy jobs. Speeders were no longer the main source of funds for the department or the county. But the population had exploded, the paperwork had expanded exponentially, the laws were more complex, and thankfully Janet kept the wheels from falling off my wagon. It took a minute to bring her up to speed on Owen and his requests. I asked her to assemble the paperwork and evidence to hand over to DDA Owen.

"The Feds doing us a favor? I know Hell hasn't frozen over as it is still a hundred and five outside," she said. She ran her right hand absently through her hair and let out an exaggerated sigh of exasperation. I told her about the missing suitcases and that Owen assumed someone in the department must have them. "So they take the case evidence and leave us with a can of worms for the shit they lost. Figures."

"By the way, let Lilly Greeves know that the Feds are looking into the case and they are sure either she or I took those missing suitcases. And you know subtle is not found in their dictionary." I turned away from the computer screen where I had been assembling the monthly statistics for a report. "Where am I going diving?"

"Cross Creek. With the drought the water is low and Victor spotted an old car sitting in the mud. He went to make sure nobody was squatting out there. It looks like the car has been underwater for a long time and he wants to get it towed before the kids get to it. Attractive nuisance. Last thing we need is some idiot crawling inside and getting cut or trapped. Oddie says he will tow it but he can't swim and needs someone to attach a tow cable."

I nodded and locked my computer screen, "Okay, I will grab my gear and be there ASAP." This was one of those days when I felt like a bureaucrat who also carries a gun rather than a law enforcement professional but I was glad for a break in my routine.

Janet smiled, "Why would anyone just drive a car into a creek?" I grunted knowing it could be a stolen car or someone forgot to set the parking brake or any of a dozen other reasons. Then Janet said the words that made my blood turn cold, "Victor says it is an old Ford Mustang."

My first thought was that Rachel had a Mustang. Could it be Rachel? Could the rain storm have caused a flash flood that pushed her car into the creek? The creek was just before the old train depot on the road west. Maybe half a mile at most. Could it really be Rachel?

-

Janet Polk had become my first friend in the sheriff's department when I re-joined after leaving the Federal Bureau of Investigation. And it was because of one moment on my second night of patrol. There was a radio call for backup on a dark farm-to-market road. I acknowledged the call and found Janet's SUV parked on the side of the road with four men learning onto that SUV with their legs spread and their arms supporting their weight. What was unusual was that the men were in women's bras, panties, and high heels. And it was not a pretty sight.

I got out of my patrol SUV and walked over to Janet but kept my eyes on the scantily clad quartet. The strap that kept her pistol in the holster was unsnapped which was a sign that she was prepared to pull her semi-auto HK pistol and fire at the first sign the men tried anything. We had only seen each other at roll call and had not spoken. I smiled, "Good evening, ma'am. What is going on here?"

She spoke up and pointed at one of the men, "You there on the far left. The fatty in the pink paisley granny pantties. Please tell the deputy what is going on here." Her voice was flat, unemotional, and perfectly professional.

The guy on the left told a sad tale. He wore a matching leopard spotted bra and panty set that did not go well with his extremely hairy chest and back. It turns out that four men were planning on having a bachelor party at a nearby hotel. One of them had arranged for a stripper not knowing that said stripper was a friend of the bride and recognized his name when he made the arrangements. So she showed up and started a dance of the seven veils. While she swayed she unlocked the hotel room door to let in the wives and girlfriends of the men into the room. After a loud berating of the gentlemen they were offered an opportunity at redemption. A one time chance to make amends for their foul action. They were told that if they walked down the road from their hotel to the hotel where the ladies were staying for their bachelorette party all would be forgiven. After all it was just over a mile away. The four men all quickly agreed. Then the women said there was one condition. And that condition was lingerie and heels. It would be an opportunity for the guys to understand what the female of the species experienced to look attractive. The guys were told they would be observed and that they had to keep their outfits, including heels, for the full 1.1 mile stroll. The men knew they were in deep trouble and quickly agreed to the conditions set forth by their significant others.

The women left the men with bags of lingerie but took the men's clothes, car keys, cell phones, and wallets. So at ten thirty in the evening the men were ready and started their walk, wobbling on heels and jiggling in the lingerie. Janet found them in her headlights not long after their start.

"So," She said. "What do we do with these … gentlemen?" I had listened to the tribulations of the men calmly, trying to maintain my professional decorum. I wanted to laugh but knew I had to be stoic. Janet looked at me in a way that told me that I was being judged also. I was the new guy and knew what ever transpired would make the rounds of the others deputies at shift briefings the next day. Between the two of us we could transport the men to the jail and spend the next several hours producing reports. I did not want to have to write this one up on very weak charges as men dressed in lacy clothing walking down the street was not illegal, not even in this part of Texas.

"I do not see they have the capability to have anything dangerous in their pockets since they do not have pockets. It is too dark out here for a body cavity search,"

I said, providing my reasoning out loud. "And they have no identification?"

"Correct."

"And if we put them in the back seat of our SUV's and drive them to check to see if the ladies are at the Stone Bridge Inn they will still be in trouble. Maybe we let them cover the little distance to where their ladies await?" The men suddenly went from looks of dejection and shame in their eyes to looks of a slim hope of redemption and not being arrested.

She nodded. "Safe to assume they would still be in the dog house for a long time. Adding an arrest to their records for disorderly conduct seems overkill to me." One of the guys started pleading with us to let them continue their task.

I smiled at Janet, "Code one escort?" Code one was no flashing lights but we would escort the gentlemen to their destination with our headlights illuminating the dark road. She smiled back and nodded. She was happy with my answer. So Janet led the procession and I brought up the rear. The men tottered on the heels and a few times I thought I would be treating twisted ankles. It was a slow, painful march and the women came out of their hotel when they saw the arrival of the caravan. The men looked truly pitiful and the women had a smug but pleased look on their faces.

Janet read the women the riot act. Their men could have been hit by a drunk driver, broken an ankle, or some other calamity. They were lucky to have sore feet, swollen ankles, bug bites, and severe chafing. She sent the men into the hotel and then high fived the women. "Good job, ladies."

Janet and I met up after at a late night café. I was informed that the look on the faces of the men as they marched into the hotel was still on her mind. She asked, "Well?"

"I am glad I will not have to go to court to give evidence on that episode. 'Could you please describe in detail the clothing Mr. Doe was wearing when you first observed him?' 'Oh, a scarlet thong, matching lace underwire, and Manolo Blahniks. And I kept waiting for a momma skunk with a half dozen little black and white stink squirters to be sitting on the side of the road to get startled and spray all of us."

"They were not Manolo's. More impressive is that his wife managed to find some really good Jimmy Choo knockoffs in his size." She laughed and relaxed. "So you are the old Chief's grandson."

"Yes, for better or worse." I knew a lot of the deputies loved the old man and several had chaffed under his management. And knew a lot of them were wary of me, to put it politely. I had yet to prove myself to them and my past employment at the FBI raised a few eyebrows.

"He was not a bad boss. But I think the acting Sheriff Bill Drake will get appointed to sheriff and then all hell will break out here." She took a sip of coffee and decided to add some artificial sweetener.

"Drake doesn't seem to like me but I was an easy hire since I have been deputized before." Bill Drake had worked for the old man for a few years after working in Wise Country for many years and was better known for his ability to run spell check on computer reports than his patrolling skills. Drake seemed to be a bit of a dilatant compared to my grandfather.

She smiled. "Drake will change things just to change things just to prove he is in charge. It will not matter if it makes things worse, it is his change and you had better like it or leave." She was reigned to her fate and the waitress brought us our food. She had a Caesar Salad with salmon and a diet coke while I tore into a burger.

"That bad? The changes, I mean." I had been grateful to get the deputies job but had wondered if my connection to the old man would count against me. I later learned that my having the same name as my grandfather made it look to the state that he was still on duty.

"'That bad?' She said in tone without mockery. "You learn to lump it or leave it." Then she said, "Welcome to the department. By the way, that was a nice touch making them walk the rest of the way in those heels. I was just going to run them into the jail and let them spend the night in those outfits." She gave me a big smile and I knew I had earned her friendship.

"I was the one who transported your grandpa to the hospital. The paramedics were forty minutes out and I did not think he would last. By all rights that ambush should have killed him but that old man leads a charmed life."

—

Cross Creek at one time was the old swimming hole for the town of Paragon. The creek had been a very rare body of water in the area where the populace could cool off even in the worst baking heat of summer. It was close enough to town to be a short trip but far enough away to not always be crowded. A city pool with bright blue chlorinated water was built in the 1970s and most people gave up on the rusty brown water with the occasional snake in the creek. Except for the occasional skinny dipper, we rarely got calls about activities in the creek. Technically it was county property and was properly posted with no trespassing signs that were mostly ignored by the few who visited. A chain link fence had been in place a few years ago after a cow drowned but it had sagged in many places. Anyone really wanting to take a dip could do so readily. In recent years the drought had reduced the water level and turned the pond into a pool of brown sludge that had very limited appeal for the naked or swimsuit clad bathers. The air seemed to be filled with a thin but permanent cloud of dry gritty dust the clung to clothing and irritate the eyes. I pulled up in the GMC Yukon patrol unit assigned to me and was glad to see Oddie and Victor learning up against Victor's own patrol GMC Yukon. Oddie Roberts was skinny, gray, and ugly as sin but had won the county vehicle towing contract for three decades running. Victor Phelps had been a linebacker for the Dallas Cowboys for a few years before a younger man proved faster and more willing to sacrifice his body for the job. I walked over to the edge of the creek where the hood and roof of an old Ford Mustang sedan poked out of the water. The water level was at the level of the window sill and draining quickly. The car was upright but coated universally in a brown muddy ooze. In the few moments that I observed it, the dark brown sludge that passed as the creek water dropped a few inches.

"The car looks like a sixty four, five, or six," Oddie muttered. He had a habit of wiping the end of his nose with his left hand while talking. "They got a new body style in sixty eight, or sixty nine."

"My dad had a '71 Mach I – bright red with a Cleveland 351 V8, and I remember how cool it felt when I was in elementary school when he would peel out after picking me up," Victor said. He made a fair imitation of a roaring engine and tires screaming for traction. Victor had been a deputy for about a decade and was as solid as anyone else on the force. But for a second I could picture him as a kid as a passenger in the car he described as his dad stomped on the gas pedal. He then smiled at me, "Need anything from Hawaii, Sheriff?"

"Hawaii?" The non-sequitur had me confused.

He nodded and said, "Naval Reserve Duty next two weeks, starting the day after tomorrow. If the United States of American ever declares war between now and the time I retire from the reserves, my duty is to head to Pearl Harbor and get ready to repair radios and small appliances. It used to be Puerto Rico but my unit was reassigned to the Pacific." His infectious shit-eating grin led me to believe that all of his time for the next two weeks would not be spent with a multimeter and soldering iron in hand. I was having trouble covering shifts as it was and I had forgotten Victor was heading off and I hope Janet Polk had not.

As I pulled off my uniform shirt in preparation of getting into my dry suit I asked, "Any ideas why the water seems to be draining so fast?"

Oddie chuckled. "The drought? There was probably an old beaver dam that caused the water to pool and that old wood finally rotted away. The water got so low that it must have dried up the mud and the wild pigs rooting must have damaged the dam. Lots of hoof prints down there." He clapped his hand together to pantomime the failure of the old damn. I looked at where the ledge used to hold back the water and had no reason to doubt Oddie's theory. And I realized that the drought was going to make it even harder for the local wildlife to hydrate with this creek disappearing. It seemed that all around me was being sucked dry, baked, or turning to dust. As I stood there shirtless I was aware of the sun baking me.

"So how do you want me to attach the cable?" I had realized there were no two hooks on the old car and I doubted the bumpers were secure enough to be used as an anchor point. I did not want to rip the car apart in any attempt to extricate it. Nor did I want to get cut up from torn metal. I was getting hot in the sun and wanted to get on with the task.

"You're going to have to loop the cable through a rear leaf string, loop the cable back, set the hook, and hope the spring is not rusted out." Oddie had unrolled cable from the winch from his tow truck. I went back to my patrol vehicle and pulled on a dry suit. The benefit of a dry suit was that it was sealed at the neck and wrists so that you were basically enclosed in a plastic bag. The bad news is that on a hot, dusty day the lack of airflow makes you sweat to excess. And the day was oven hot with no air movement. To keep them safe, I locked both my work cell phone and my personal cell phone in the glove compartment along with my pistol before slogging my way into the muddy bog. The car was shallow enough where I hoped I would not need an air tank and regulator. By this time the water level was to the top of the wheel wells. I did grab my mask and snorkel before pulling the cable into the warm, murky water. My feet seemed to sink into the mud and then stick. It took great effort to pull my feet free of the goop and sort of stride forward. It took me a while to fight my way through the ooze to get to the car. I held my breath, slipped under water, and used my hands to feel around the flat left rear tire until I found the rear axle where it met the rear brake drum. I wrapped the cable around the axle and left rear leaf spring before attaching the shackle to the cable. Standing clear of the cable, I raised my arm and Oddie used the winch to reel in the car. There was a rumble and the cable to the winch went. For a second the old car seemed stuck and then made slurping sounds before it slid out of the mud. Like a prehistoric monster slipping out of primordial ooze, the car inched along out of the mud. The car itself was an old Ford Mustang notchback, just like Rachel's, and coated heavily in mud. The windows were brown, barely opaque, but intact.

A white Ford van arrived just as the old Mustang came up on the bank of the creek. Laurel Hardy jumped out of the van and started taking pictures. She was the head of the county forensics staff and her work was often invaluable in making a case. When the car was far enough out of the muck, Oddie turned off the winch. I went to the rear of the car and tried to scrape mud off the rear in hopes of finding a license plate. But there were no license plates on either end of the car. Laurel grabbed the driver's door handle and gave a sharp tug. Muddy water sluiced out of the opening and I heard Laurel gasp. She said in a loud clear voice, "This is now a crime scene. You all walk away from it now!"

I walked around to where she stood next to the car and peered into the muddy void of the car's interior. There was muddy debris in the interior almost to the level of seats. Staring back at me was a skull sitting upright on the driver's seat and on top of sludge covered bones. And the skull had a small hole in the forehead just above the nose that looked like it was from a small caliber bullet.

I hoped that it was not Rachel. But part of me wanted it to be her. I wanted an answer to what happened to her.

Chapter 3

I cleaned my dive gear and then took a hot shower back at the station in hopes of feeling clean again. My mind buzzed with the possibility that I finally knew what happened that night so long ago. The reason she had not picked me up was because she was dying. She had not abandoned me! But part of me also hoped that it was not her. As I was putting on my last clean uniform when Janet Polk walked in on me. "Sorry to bother you," She said. "But did you know your friend, the new Federal DA Carl Owen, is a pain in the ass?" She leaned up against the lockers, crossed her arms, and gave me a dirty look.

"Federal District Attorney and pain in the ass are redundant." I had taken to disliking Carl Owen and was glad that someone I respected had somewhat the same opinion. Janet looked well past the point of being pissed off and on her way for absolutely furious.

She smiled, "You were not gone two minutes when he returned. He had FBI Agents grab the car from the impound lot, the body from the morgue, and everything else from the dead man we had in the evidence locker. The entire kit and caboodle. The FBI Agents were snippy and Owen his own smelly self was downright condescending to me. When I went to talk to him he turned away and jumped into a very heavily tinted Chevy Suburban before driving away." She then fluttered her eyes at me, cocked her head to one side, and smiled with obviously faked enthusiasm. In her hand was a printed page of information. "I guess he is too good to deal with a mere woman like me." 'Mere' was never a word I would use to describe Janet Polk. She held up the sheet of paper and rattled it in my direction. She batted her eyelashes and said, "Ta-daaa!"

"And?"

"And, I have a copy of the toxicology report in my hand for the DB in that car from the rest stop. You had the lab put a rush on it and it came in this morning right after you left. But before the FBI left. I tried to hand it over to the Deputy Federal DA but he ignored me. By the way the deceased had amazingly high levels of benzonatate in his bloodstream. Enough to put down a horse." The look on her face told me she was pleased with herself.

I was more than a little shocked myself with the news, "Death by cough medicine?" I read the rest of the toxicology screen and noticed there were trace amounts of alcohol and marijuana in the system of the dead man from the rest area. But both of those were low so it would be easy to assume he imbibed the day before his demise. But I had never heard of anyone ingesting enough couch medicine to send them into the great unknown.

"Cough medicine that kicks like Heroin. Basically Rohypnol on afterburners and nothing to do with date rape, at lease in this case. Lots of folks get hooked on what they think is a harmless cough medicine and end up on a quick downward spiral. It appears in this case it was orally taken. Could have been in a soft drink he had before he died. Probably well less than an hour to go from the stomach to bloodstream. He probably felt sleepy and went to sleep it off in the parking lot of the rest stop. The drug would have to be taken in fifteen or so minutes before it started taking effect. Bake in a warm oven for several hours and you get a very dead body. The doc said it should have been a fairly painless and easy way to go, if he was committing suicide. But where are the empties and the car keys if he was offing himself?"

"Is that drug tasteless?"

"According to what I read it would be undetectable in a sugary soda or sweet tea. I will have to remember in case I ever have to get rid of the husband when he gets past his prime." She forced a smile and asked, "Are you okay?"

I assured her that I was okay but the look she gave me told me she doubted my statement. I claimed it was from being packed in the dry suit and being dehydrated. We discussed asking the gas stations, fast food restaurants, and convenience stores within a thirty minute radius from the rest stop for their security camera footage in hope of finding someone spiking the dead man's drink. It would take a lot of time and we barely had enough deputies to cover the basics. My two detectives were already overworked. Janet said she would handle it. I reminded her that it was no longer our case after Owen took it off our hands. I could tell that she did not like that one bit and I would not have been surprised to later hear she did the footwork herself.

"Victor asked if I needed anything from Hawaii," I said. I hoped there were no sounds of frustration in my voice.

"We lose JT when Victor comes back for a convention in St. Louis and then Bekler goes on off on delayed honeymoon." She laughed that being a social secretary was hard work in her job. We had a constant flow of deputies off for court, injuries, vacations, or time comped for overtime. And then she said I should schedule some vacation time. "You look like you could use a few days away," She said. And I promised I would do so and soon.

-

Mike Buchwald had sent an email asking me to drop by the garage when I had a moment. After checking emails, I pushed away from my desk and made my way to see Mike in the country vehicle garage and not really paying attention to what was going on as my mind was still reeling over earlier events. I found Mike half hanging out of the engine compartment of a cruiser and he was clad in his usual dark blue overalls. "Bad news, sheriff. We are down to eleven patrol units and I will need to pull two of those this week for preventative maintenance." I had started the job of sheriff with eighteen functional cruisers most of which were two to three years old which is a long lifetime in duty.

"I will talk to the county board soon and replacements are on the agenda," I said. Taxes were down in the country due to the prolonged drought and it was not a sure thing I would be able to replace the out of service cruisers. Running the sheriff's department was expensive and costs had escalated since the old man ran things. Something as simple a new set of tires for a cruiser was bureaucratic operation of confirmations, requisitions, and audits. And the county board were getting more requests from everyone in every county agency for more funds from a shrinking pool of funds.

He pointed over to his desk, "They are having an auction in Rowlett next week and I want to grab some of their old units for spares. It might let us creep along a little longer." He walked over to his desk and passed me a flyer for the auction and it was suddenly it was obvious that many of the cruisers being sold for scrap by other law enforcement agencies were practically new by our standards.

I nodded. "You don't need my permission for that. But please do what you can. And I do appreciate that you do more with less than anyone." I knew the Yukon I used was the worst of the bunch and had been warned that any code three runs at extended high speeds could lead to my having the engine blow.

An awkward smile across his lips. "Well, while I am over there, they want to talk to me about managing their fleet. It is not much of a raise but it would help. And my partner's family is over there."

"Let me talk to the personnel folks and see what we can squeeze out of the next year's budget. And if you get that job, you will be missed. And you can use me as a professional reference." I forced my own smile and let him get back to work. Mike was a hard worker and it would be hard to replace him. The slight headache I started at the creek was flaring into a full migraine with Mike's news. The drought had reduced every one into tightening of their fiscal belts.

As I left he said, "There is only so much blood to be squeezed from a dry stone. They gotta loosen the purse strings. We both cannot be expected to pull off miracles forever."

I could not argue that statement.

Chapter 4

I knew better than to drop by the forensics lab the rest of that Monday no matter how much I wanted to go over there. I finished up my paperwork, returned my calls, and locked up my office at six. The local burger joint provided a mushroom Swiss special, fries, and an iced tea for my dinner which was consumed as I drove home. Too many law enforcement officers slowly kill themselves by bad diet, stress, and hard hours. I made a mental note to clean up my act with a better diet and some exercise before a coronary stopped me in my tracks.

Billy Gonzalvez and his son were surveying one of the local farm-to-market roads and I stopped to see how they were doing. "Not bad, considering," Billy said. "It's damn hot and dry which makes the land move and that means more work for me. TxDot is doing their twenty and fifty year plans for road expansion. So they send me out here in a rush to redo the survey lines. In a few decades they hope to have tons of road widening work out here for all the homes they are projecting. Whole bunch of us can get rich in another decade or two if we can hang on and the drought doesn't desiccate us." I had been hearing that eventually we will get rich if we can hang on long enough for the suburbs to consume us and talk for as long as I could remember.

The Texas Department of Transportation did not have to have a crystal ball or a deck of Tarot cards to know that the ever expanding creep of the Dallas / Fort Worth Metroplex would relentlessly shove more suburbs away from the centers of those two cities and the land we stood on would eventually get consumed. What was the middle of nowhere when I was a kid was now packed with zero lot-line houses, strip malls with nail salons, and mediocre fast food restaurants. "Do you wonder what the old timers would think if they knew you could be in Fort Worth in thirty minutes?"

Billy smiled. "And all without having to sit on a horse. Well, maybe in my kid's time my land may be worth a lot. Sure not worth a lot now without water. Hell, even the wild hogs on the northwest part of my property moved out; it was so dry."

"Where did they go?" Wild hogs did a lot of damage to farms, natural habitat, and pretty much anything else they could get into easily. They could tear up a lot of property and were damned hard to eliminate.

Billy shrugged and said, "Not my worry anymore. I think they went east and south which means they will be Willow's problem. Or maybe they went more to the northeast. But they will be back tearing up my land when and if we get any substantial rain." He waved goodbye as I drove off and then went back to his work. I drove aimlessly for a bit and then decided that I would make the next left turn.

I took a quick detour to drive past the house of one of the elderly folks near where I am at the edge of the city limits and was glad to see their shadow on the living room curtains as they transitioned to the kitchen. Some folks did not mind us checking up on them but others were a bit paranoid. Kids who had moved away worried about parents and we tried to be subtle. My department made several courtesy checks on our citizens to check on their welfare on a regular basis. In this case the couple had a grandson in the Navy who worried about them and had asked us surreptitiously to keep an eye on them. I had been worried that if I had not spotted them that I would eventually have to go to the door to enquire about them and blow any surreptitiousness. My deputies would prefer a little extra effort on a regular basis than finding someone who had needed help and went without tragically. McDavey County was the size of a small European country with the population of a modest city block in New York City. I felt responsible for and knew a good percentage of the folks who lived in my county, especially those who seemed to need a little extra shepherding. Something about knowing at least they were good at the moment reassured me. The petty problems of those we protect and serve often inject themselves in our lives. I drove around aimlessly for a while before realizing that I was just wasting time.

-

The old family ranch my mom had left me was just far enough outside of the town limits of Paragon that it let me calm down a bit as I drove. My maternal grandfather had been in a Navy construction battalion and had scraped together enough money on a good piece of land when his enlistment finished. His wife and he had a quartet of kids with my mom being the baby of the group. Her dad had tried to run steers on a section of land but found he made a more consistent living selling and repairing farm implements. The whipsaw cattle markets and fluctuating expenses had wiped out many who tried. But he found people always needed things fixed or made to specification and so my mom grew up with her dad always tinkering. The house itself was hidden from the closest road and the wrought iron front gate that would normally guide people to the house was very conspicuously padlocked shut. But there was a somewhat hidden back way that you had to know was there or you would not be able to spot it. The back way into my house shared a drive with the local naturalist resort. A sign proclaimed 'Sun-Ur-Buns Naturist Resort' with a cartoon of a blazing sun shining down on nudist stick figures below stood on guard by the gate along with a security camera that fed to the resort's office. There was a heavy iron gate with a hydraulic opener that was controlled by a keypad sitting on a nearby poll for visitors. Those of us who used the gate regularly could open the gate with a garage door opener or by entering a code on a free standing keypad. I had an opener. You also had to know where to drive blindly over a berm just past the gate to find the track to my place or you would miss it. Unwelcome visitors were thus highly discouraged.

A friend of my mom's had started the nudist colony while I was in the FBI and asked to lease some of the old farm. Her business plan seemed reasonable and her payments more than covered the property taxes. With no other potential renters on the horizon and no immediate plans to live there, we signed a long term lease for the property. At the time I thought I had many years before I would ever consider going back to the old house and my gut told me they would not devastate the land like a bad tenant farmer. There was a small spring fed lake and a long grassy slope that had been turned into a small village for the nudists. She put in the gate and carefully controlled who had access. Spectators and lookie-loos (as she called them) were not allowed, her business was fairly steady with a lot of repeat business from families or older couples escaping colder climates during the colder months up north. With the front gate to my place padlocked, the gate to the nudist colony was the only way in or out of where I lived unless someone wanted to vault some serious barb wires fences. Being overly cautious was part paranoia on my part and a fair amount of effort had gone into keeping people from just dropping by unannounced. I remembered some upset relatives showing up at the old man's house and pounding on the door while demanding he release their loved ones, which never ended up well for the unwelcome visitor. Seeing a dressed stranger on my land was a sure warning sign of something going seriously wrong. However the occasional nude hikers could be disconcerting but it was hard to pack a concealed pistol when stark ass naked.

The drought had made everything dusty and had covered anything that did not move in a fine brown powder. The air itself seemed to be more powder than nitrogen these days. I drove slowly so as not to kick up too much more dust. The patrol Yukon settled into its normal place by the kitchen door. The old house had been built right after World War II in a mock Queen Anne style to replace its predecessor that had been torn apart by a tornado. Nearby an old barn from the 1920s lurked as well as a workshop my mom's dad had used as his man cave/workshop. After grabbing a Pacifico beer from the fridge, I stripped off, climbed into my hot tub, and soaked while I remembered my short time with Rachel. The stars in their heaven wheeled over my head silent in their truth.

—

"McDavey, could you let the new kid copy your assignment sheet?" Mr. Kitchener was the English teacher at the central high school. I sat in the back of the class partly because I was already hard to see over six foot six in a class loaded with short kids and partly because I was not a behavior problem at school. I had been busy writing an essay on Othello and heard the chair next creak as a body sat in it. But then I looked over. Rachel had a wild mop of dark hair, wide dark eyes, caramel skin, and deep dimples that bracketed a beguiling smile. "I'm Will," I said to her.

"Rachel." Her voice was a velvet purr. She took my offered assignment sheet and studied it for a minute before handing it back. Her eyes had dashed back and forth and she lightly bit her lower lip. She had deep dimples on either side of her mouth and a pert nose. Rachel was not the conventional high school beauty but had her own ethereal exotic look that had captivated me. She was wearing old jeans, a stark white t-shirt, and old Converse sneakers but somehow she made them look glamorous. What caught my attention were her dark brown eyes with golden flecks around the iris and three of those flecks made a pyramid under the pupil of the left eye. Those flecks seemed to glow under the florescent lighting in the classroom. Rachel was a sleek, exotic feline in a room of sluggish hamsters.

"Don't you want to copy it all down?"

She tapped the side of her forehead with a ruby red colored nailed finger. "Got it." She flashed a little smile and those dimples made that smile light up even more. At that moment I knew I was smitten.

"Wow! A photographic memory." I said and she just smiled back. I was surprised to find myself smiling stupidly back at her. "Where did you move from?"

"My dad and I lived in the Houston area for a couple of years. Louisiana before that. How about you? You don't have the local accent."

"All over. Marine brat."

She smiled at me again and I hoped that I was not blushing. Other kids in the class sneaked peeks at her but she was oblivious to their actions the way a lion ignores Meerkats when hunting gazelles. She grinned at me and then turned her attention to Mr. Kitchener as he tried to imbue the entire class with a sense of the greatness of the iambic pentameter with poor success. He wanted us to feast on a banquet of Shakespeare when the kids at the school were barely able to nibble on Dr. Suess. Most of the kids in my class would never read for entertainment outside of a TV Guide or a People magazine.

The class proceeded and I had a hard time keeping my eyes off of Rachel. She was also in my chemistry, calculus, and history classes also. Usually sitting where I had to consciously not study her and pay attention to class. I noticed the girls in the classes eyed her suspiciously and the boys eyed her lustfully. The teachers seemed happy to have a new face that belonged to a kid who paid attention. At the end of the day I was pleasantly surprised to find her locker just a few over from my own. She noticed me and said, "May I ask a favor, Will?"

At that moment I was ecstatic that she remembered my name. "Sure." And the fact that she wanted a favor sent my ego skyrocketing. I could have shoveled Mount Everest flat in an afternoon if she had asked for that.

"My dad is getting Texas plates on my car but he is running late. He left a message with the school office that he can't pick me. Could you give me a lift home?" At that moment, if I had no car, I would have gladly given her a piggyback ride anywhere in the world. She wanted to spend time with me! With *me*! Damn!!! "I'll buy you a shake

at that old burger joint on Oak Street for your troubles."
She then smiled at me with those dimples and I knew I was
helpless to resist.

I felt myself smiling. I told myself to be cool. "You
don't have to buy me a shake." Frankly my heart was
pounding so hard I was surprised she was not asking about
the thumping noise.

She said, "I insist." Those dimples and that
devastating smile were again working their whiles on me.

She was impressed or seemed politely to be impressed
with my old Ford F-100 truck. "My dad and I rebuilt it.
He had one like it when he was in school. He grew up here
but went to Annapolis." She walked around the truck
admiring it and then climbed in the passenger door that I
held wide open for her. There were a lot of my classmate's
eyes on us at that moment. And I felt like a king.

"I drive my mom's old Mustang. Thirty over small
block with a Hurst four speed." We drove down the street
to the old burger joint. Officially the burger joint was
named Bucks Burger and looked like it was caught in a time
warp from the 1950s, filled with chrome, red leather
booths, and all sitting on a black and white checkered

linoleum floor. There was even a Wurlitzer jukebox but a local FM station played over the restaurant speakers. We sat at the counter and she leaned over to whisper, "We're getting a lot of attention from the flock of cheerleaders over in the corner." Out of the corner of my eye I could see Candice 'Candy' Bahr and her small flock of friends staring at us like chickens. It felt a little uncomfortable with being the center of attention. Rachel nodded slightly at Candy and asked, "Did I cut in on your girlfriend?"

"No. I've been the strange new kid for a year and never fit in with any of the cliques. No girlfriends and not too many friends here. It is like they paired up for life in Kindergarten and distrust any late arrivals." I smiled, "They are probably jealous of you."

She laughed, "Me? Why?" Her laugh was infectious. She was so easy to be near that I felt caught up in the whirlwind of her personality. We seemed to have what my dad had mysteriously called 'chemistry' and I wanted badly to spend more time with her.

"You are what my mom called 'drop dead gorgeous'," I was surprised to hear my own voice say those words. I had to tell myself to keep cool, again. She threw her head back and laughed again. It was a throaty, melodic laugh. A lot of the people in the burger joint began to look at us. We were not being obnoxious and Rachel naturally seemed to be the center of attention of any group. The waitress came over to us and she ordered two chocolate shakes to go. We chatted until our order was ready and she quickly slapped some rumpled bills on the counter to pay for it. I was surprised as we walked out that she took my hand and I saw a look of shock on Candy Bahr's face as we passed her. I saw a few looks of jealousy cast our way as we climbed into my truck and drove away to her house.

Her house was a small one story, two bedroom ranch style on the very edge of town. The house was neat and well-kept but it was obviously an inexpensive rental. There lingered an air of cheapness about the place but it was absolutely sparkling clean. It looked like a sad pile of bricks with windows as eyes. She invited me in and I was surprised to see most of her belongings were still in packing boxes. "My dad will not be home until midnight," she said heading down a hallway. "Follow me."

I followed her. She looked over her shoulder to make sure I was following and a sly grin crossed her lips.

She stepped into her room. There was a neatly made queen bed and a pile of unpacked boxes in the room. She pulled off her t-shirt while she was grinning madly at me. She wore a sheer bra that quickly joined the shirt on the floor. Her arms reached up and encircled my neck, pulling me close for a long kiss. Those magnificent breasts pressed into me. Her skin was so very soft and warm. We were soon naked and on the bed. Her legs entangled me and she let slip a low moan as I kissed the base of her throat. The bed squeaked as we moved. I was inside her and we moved together with a frenzied urgency that she controlled. This was exciting for me but she seemed to be really enthralled with our actions. Rachel arched her back, let out a soft cry, and then went limp with exhaustion. "Not bad. Was that your first time?"

I admitted that it was and she laughed. She kissed me deeply and we began all over again. Those joyous moments and the melody of her laugh have stayed with me all these years. The memory of the thrill of touching her for the first time still comes readily from the depths of my memories. I still remember laying with our limbs and torsos twisted together afterwards with the ultimate feeling of being so very close to someone for the first time in my life. The gold flecks in her eyes seemed to glow in the room as it darkened. I had hoped the rest of my life would be like that … but I was a fool.

And probably I am still a fool.

Chapter 5

The next morning I was eating breakfast at the Courthouse Cafe. I had been up at five to hit the gym hard in hopes of burning away the hamburger I had had for dinner the previous night and I was ready for a long day. The city of Paragon was the McDavey County seat and most people had some reason to be in town on a regular basis. The courthouse square was the center of the county's community and it seemed to have most things people needed for daily living. The town library, grocery store, post office, a pair of banks, the hardware store, and too many offices occupied by lawyers. The cafe was the only place near the courthouse that served more than coffee and cinnamon rolls for breakfast. My grandfather had been a regular there one or two mornings each week for years. He told me that someone dropping by while you are eating breakfast and mentioning something odd or suspicious was not being a stool pigeon or an informer but just a friendly neighbor mentioning things in passing. It was amazing what people would mention in passing to me as I sat in the small café. A breakfast at the café could quickly turn into a confessional that served coffee and waffles. I had just taken the first bite of my scrambled eggs when Dolly Wood slid into the booth opposite me. Dolly was her real first name and she gladly gave up her maiden name of Von Bluchstaffel many years ago saying her married name made people smile at her. And who would smile at Von Bluchstaffel? "Morning, sheriff." She usually seemed to be overly happy in the morning and the woman grinning at me seemed very perky.

"Morning Miss Dolly. How are you today?" The art of politics is pretending to be nice to those who are often not nice to you. Ms. Wood often required all of my political skill and patience. She was a lovely woman but never really took 'no' for an answer. Dolly could badger the strongest personalities to get them to bend to her will and, quite frankly, was a pain in the ass. A well connected and very political pain in the ass.

Dolly was nearly ninety but still walked miles every day with two well trained Belgium Malinois dogs. Martin and Lewis were fine looking animals and devoted to their owner. The dogs were tied to a bike rack outside and I could see them through the window as they lay next to a dish of water the cafe provided. Both dogs had been trained to understand commands in German and were totally docile until Dolly said

'Achtung!' Dolly said, "I wonder if I could ask you a question about the law." Her conversations with me always started that way.

"I am not a licensed lawyer," I said. "I may not give you the kind of advice a lawyer would." This is the way I always started my part of conversations with Miss Wood. It was part protocol, part ritual, purely choreographed, and God help me if she ever acted on anything I said. And it was the way my grandfather had started his conversations with her. It was a protocol to warn her that we were making no promises.

"Well, I heard about the car being pulled out of the Cross Creek, the old skinny dipping spot. Not that I ever partook of such activities. Are you going to search or dredge that old pond?" She cocked her head over to one side and leaned forward to hear me better. Her hands fluttered about the tabletop like nervous sparrows. I wondered how fast and how far the news of the car from the creek had spread.

The conversation had turned in a way I could never have predicted. "I had not planned on it. Should I?"

A waitress dropped by with a hot cup of black coffee for her. "Well, when I was a girl, there were stories that Bonnie and Clyde had not only camped out there but were seen in the altogether swimming there. They supposedly left a small, empty safe there but I doubt that. My granny said those two spent money as fast as they got it and she was friends with one of the Barrow sisters back in her day. But there is the Santa Rosa Cross." Her hands were now flat and not moving on the top of the table. This usually signaled the part of the conversation she wanted to emphasize.

"The Santa Rosa Cross?" She now had me confused, my full attention, and I guessed I was about to get an amazing history lesson. I was not disappointed.

She nodded. "My granddaddy Howard told me all about it. Lipan Apaches raided Our Lady of Santa Rosa outside of Austin and stole a large cross of gold back before the Revolution. The Texan not American Revolution. But as their band rode north they started having visions of God, Jesus, and the Virgin Mary. Then they all had horrible apparitions of Hell, suffering, and eternal torture. Finally one of the visions told them to toss the cross into deep water or they would be haunted for the rest of their lives. Trackers caught them near what is now Bridgeport and the Lipans told them about the visions. Riding back along their trail the only deep water they found was that creek. But it was winter and nobody wanted to dare the chill. The creek is the only logical place it could be."

I had never heard that story and told her that. I had heard the story about Bonnie and Clyde but had heard the main persons of skinny dipping ranging from Lewis and Clark, Martin and Lewis, Cheech and Chong, to Burton and Taylor. "If we have spare time, it might be worth another look in the creek." Finding the cross would be a nightmare with the diocese in Austin, the land owner, and others parties claiming title to it. Logically the Lipan Apaches also could have a claim but I was glad I would not be part of those discussions, if there was a cross in the creek. Maybe that was why it was called Cross Creek. But I made a mental note about the cross. It would be an ungodly bureaucratic nightmare if she was correct about the location.

Miss Wood thanked me and took her cup of coffee away with her. A moment later a much younger woman slid into the seat opposite me. "Remember me?"   Ayce Huggins was a strikingly beautiful redhead with a sprinkling of freckles on her nose and very high cheekbone. Broad in the shoulders and long of leg, her physical presence often intimidated others. I remember someone once remarking that she looked more like a comic book superheroine than anything else. Today she wore a black polo shirt with an embroidered FBI badge on the left breast. The woman was a world class triathlete and had a handful of pistol shooting championships on her resume. We had been classmates at the FBI Academy at Quantico, Virginia way back when.

"A man never forgets the first beautiful woman who uses a stun gun on him," I said. I was glad she smiled at my joke. "I heard through the grapevine that you earned some major kudos for your work overseas."

"To be polite it was fluster cluck. But some bureaucrat determines the assignment is over, declares victory, and hands out accolades to prove it was a success. And that was two years ago and you are only as good as your last review." She gave me a brief overview of looking into how counterfeit and real US military surplus parts were being delivered in Egypt from source or sources unknown and then used against US forces in Africa and the Middle East.

Some of the real military surplus gear had been listed as scrap and sent for recycling but never made it. Other parts were cheesy counterfeits that failed at the first opportunity. A fake bearing had failed causing a helicopter crash which was brought to the attention of a senator who had demanded action and that action sent Ayce to the Middle East. She was able to quickly identify the culprits and take them off the game board.

"So Sheriff McDavey in McDavey country? Coincidence?"

"No, my great-great-great grandfather was in the US Army during the election of 1860 and was posted to the American embassy in Japan. He had promised Winfield Scott, the head of the army, that he would stay for at least three years and fulfilled the promise. His ship was dismasted coming around the horn and he did not get back to Washington D.C. until after the draft riots in New York, the battle of Vicksburg, and the battle of Gettysburg. He arrived at the department of war with his resignation in hand and wondering how he was going to get back to Texas. Then he ran into Secretary of War Stanton and President Lincoln. Lincoln asked him a lot of questions about Japan, saying he wanted to visit there someday after he was out of office. The man my great-many-grandfather thought was a power hungry monster impresses him so much that they talked for quite a while about his travels. So my forefather was enchanted, tore up his letter of resignation, served in the Union Army for a little while longer, and was later named a Federal Judge for this area at the end of the war."

"Wow. And he came back here to a peaceful life? Sounds so very Disney movie-ish." She seemed impressed with the story.

"No, not exactly. He came back to the family ranch to find that his older son was a captive with the Comanche, his own father was dying of tuberculosis, and his younger son had run off to California, his best friend had been lynched in Weatherford as a Union sympathizer. The friend had been complaining that he was being drafted into the Confederate army but his rich, slave owning cousin could buy his way out. Add in that after the war all the Confederate veterans and those who had not signed loyalty oaths were forbidden to enter into contracts, vote, meet in a group, or pretty much have a business. Things were a mess, nobody had money, and like now a drought staggered the land. It was a very rough time and he really was a very rough man," I said. "They needed a stern man who could command the area and he was exactly the man they needed.

Things did not go back to anything like antebellum status quo for decades. He was charged with making this area a safe place to live and felt he had a duty to protect all who lived here. And I do mean all. He was not a popular man with a lot of people and the Klan tore down a statue of the judge in the 1920s. But I doubt you came here for a history lesson."

She smiled again for a moment and then let it slip off her face. "I am here on unofficial official business." She looked very uncomfortable as she spoke. I could tell she did not want to do what she was going to be doing.

"Unofficial official?" What the Hell was unofficial official business? I forced myself to take a drink of coffee to keep from asking that question and to give her time to answer. She had been sent as a messenger and I owed it to her to hear what she had to say.

She said, "The DOJ wants those suitcases. They are missing some serious money. And they think you or one of yours has it." Her voice had dropped to a whisper. She said the new Federal Deputy DA, Carl Owen, had asked her to speak to me. I got the impression that she was afraid of Owen and was here to protect her career. He evidently thought I was an unmitigated smart ass and sent Ayce to read me the riot act. She started by filling in some details, off the record. The dead man from the rest stop was a go between for money laundering between drug dealers, a few drug producers, and a half dozen small banks all over the southwest. The dead man would pick up cash, move it through some front businesses, and then deposit it into bank accounts. Drafts would be sent to other banks offshore or across the country and then back again in a confusing tangle. The dead man had been doing all this work for several years and the FBI had recently discovered he was keeping a secret ledger of who got what and when. The FBI had only recently confirmed there was a written log book with all the details of the operation. Many of the front businesses were legitimate operations co-owned by some politically well-connected folks. Some of those well connected she did not name but she implied that those very people would bring pressure to get their promised monies and keep their reputations in good order. The key to recovering that money was the log and other documents that were in the suitcases. But now the man who laid golden eggs was dead and the logical conclusion was that someone in the sheriff's department had scooped up the cash and the transaction log when they found the dead man. Owen had been very upset with my explanation that my county had easy access to all points of the compass and that the thief was long gone.

I said, "I have no idea what happened to your suitcases or the log books. I know my deputies and they would not take them. And you know I would not take it. Two months ago one of my deputies found a duffle bag with enough Fentanyl to keep Austin quiet for a month and fifty grand in cash but did not abscond with them. My folks are true professionals who live up to their jobs." I did not blink and locked eyes with her. After a moment she looked away and then sighed.

"Owen thinks you took the suitcases for the money and probably tossed the logs into the trash. He wants the money and the cash," She said. I then realized that the suitcases, which I had assumed contained nothing but accounting type materials, also held cash.

"You know me. And I know you know me. You do not think I am dishonest. Hell, you better than anyone know that the FBI reamed me out for being honest," I said. I force a deep breath to help control my anger and frustration.

"Doesn't matter what I think, or know about you. Besides, for enough cold, hard cash you or anyone would do anything. So my orders are to do a full court press on you and yours."

"No one. Maybe not you," She said. "But we are talking about a lot of cash." She kept the volume of her voice low but the desperation of her, and my, situation rang through her voice. This situation went from a situation that was a mere curiosity to a crisis in a blink of an eye. Ayce said, "Enough cash to temp just about anyone but you."

"That much cash?" I started to do some mental math – two suitcases could maybe hold somewhere between one hundred thousand dollars and a million depending on the size of the bills. And I realized I did not know the size of the suitcases. If there were more than one suitcase and the bills were large enough, they could be out several million dollars.

"Yes, that much cash. And the logs evidently have details on how to electronically transfer much more. Account numbers, account passwords, and mother's maiden name type stuff." And then she said, "And either you or someone in your crew have to be dirty."

I told her about the dead man having no
identification, the car he was found in had been wiped down
for prints, and that someone had taken the car keys. She
said that just showed that someone with knowledge of law
enforcement procedures had to be involved. I did not rebut
that anyone watching television or reading police
procedural novels would know about finger print removal.
Whomever took the dead man's identification did that to
slow down to stop his identification. And I hope that if
any one of my deputies was, unknown to me, dirty that they
would not be as sloppy as to grab the car keys. Ayce added
that 'FBI management' when they found out I was involved
wanted to immediately have me incarcerated as well as all
of my deputies. I shook my head and was about to quickly
reply but thought better of it. I took another mouthful of
my breakfast, chewed it slowly, and then put my fork down.
"So you are going to get warrants on our bank accounts, see
who shows up to work in a new car, and pester our
neighbors?" I kept my voice very calm. There could
possibly be someone in my department who had the ability to
figure out the log of where the money was kept and get at
that money but not any of my patrolling deputies. "I could
see how your new DDA would be suspicious of me and my

deputies. There are enough sticky fingers in law enforcement circles to give anyone pause." But as far as I knew my staff were painfully honest. "But *Molon Labe*, as the Spartans told the Persians"

"That is so last century. We already have all the bank records and stuff like that. Owen just got reassigned from DC where he did financial investigations at the highest levels and can get anything from any bank without working for it. I just wanted to give you a heads up that my bosses think you or someone you know is sitting on the suitcases. Owen thinks it must be you. He has a hard on for you after looking at your history and talking to Rafferty. Rafferty, by the way, is now the Deputy Director Operations and still wants your skull on a pike outside his office door. Rafferty evidently thinks you delayed his promotions and would love to see you screwed over so much that he is giving Owen free reign on you. You have until next Monday at nine am sharp to find those suitcases, hand them over, or there will be a Federal bench warrant out on your ass."

"With no evidence? You'll get laughed out of court." I was outraged and incredulous but kept my temper in check. But I was worried. The last thing I needed was a Federal investigator snipe hunting in a very public fashion.

"Not with a Federal DDA in front of a Federal Judge telling that judge the local yokel sheriff is a notorious malcontent and rule breaker. And imagine what will happen to you and your reputation living under a cloud for a year or three until you get before a judge for a preliminary hearing. If they ever charge you and just don't leave you to dangle in the breeze. Owen will make you do the perp walk in front of every news camera he can find and then slow walk the case. Every time you get to court he will ask for a postponement, continuance, plead other priorities, change of venue, or for a new judge. It will take years and he does not have to prove if you are innocent or guilty. He just has to taint you. Every case since you joined the sheriff's department will suddenly be appealed over the mere hint of the allegation of a scandal. You and each of your deputies will have to go to court to be asked if they are crooked. They will be asked to prove they are not crooks. Owen says he *knows* you have *his* suitcases. You cannot prove a negative but a negative can gather a lot of attention. You and all those that work for you will be smeared." As she said those words I thought of all the current cases in court or being ready for court that would suddenly have to start again from the very start. Any of my deputies looking for a new job would carry a stain on their careers for being part of a dirt department. And I would be dragged into court for years trying to explain that I was not dirty and not being able to prove a negative. And courts are expensive and the Federal courts are very expensive. I was glued, screwed, and tattooed.

I said, "You have to be kidding." It took everything I had to keep my voice calm and steady. The idea that I was being threatened like this was infuriating. The thought of my department being dragged down was making my blood boil. But I would not let Ayce see me upset.

"I told them you are too damn self-righteous to be the crook but you may know or suspect someone. With your history with the Bureau and the DOJ, there are a lot of folks who want their pound of flesh from your ass. But maybe I can help." She smiled and cocked her head to one side. "Anything you can give me that I can report up through my chain of command. You must suspect someone of having that log book, the suitcases, and all that. We're not really interested in the murder." I kept my mouth shut except to eat my breakfast. She was expecting me to say something but I gave her nothing to use against me. I finished my breakfast in silence while she watched.

She said, "Do you have anything else to say to me?" There was a pleading urgency to her face but she seemed very pleased with herself. She thought she had me.

"No comment." I usually took people who threatened me at face value, especially when I knew they had the ways and means to carry out the threat.

"Excuse me?" She had gone from quietly confident to fully pissed off instantly. The look on her face told me she had moved to calm and confident to ready for all-out war.

"The DOJ is shy of me because I caught them doing dumb things and doing them badly," I said. "Harassment will not be taken lightly. Using an old friend to tell me that the federal government was going to try and ream me a new asshole is not appreciated. Tell your bosses that if they try to run roughshod over me, over my department, or anyone even tangentially connected, that they will receive the full brunt of my collected attention." If the Feds were going to war with me and my deputies I wanted to be prepared. "I do not have your suitcases nor do I know anyone who does. And I know you have to fully report the full conversation in your report and I want to state for the record that your lost log book and your lost money is your problem. Please add that I am not exactly overjoyed that you were running operations and confidential informants on my turf without being informed. And I know you will put crap in your FD-302 on this … discussion today but please make sure that you note that I am adamant that I know nothing about the missing contents of the car and I am very concerned at the FBI's lack of concern in the matter of a murder of one of their agents."

She said, "You have no idea what you are fucking with, Will. You are in some serious shit now. Either give up the money and the log if you have it or find it. If you didn't swipe the suitcases then you need to get your thumb out of your ass and find the fuckers that did. Fast! Or else." Ayce Huggins gave me a rage filled look for a tenth of a second and then shook her head before sliding out of the booth, striding away, and was very quickly out the door.

I watched Ayce storm out of the café and sat back to ponder what she had told me. The Feds were out money, logs, and a confidential informant but where not worrying about the murder. They had grabbed all the evidence related to the murder. But they were really anxious for the log book and the suitcases. And she had implied there was a lot of money in the suitcases but more to be had from the information in the log book entries. On top of that they wanted me to do their dirty work and I would suffer if I failed.

-

The rest of the day was a blur. I sent an email to all my staff saying that the DOJ and FBI were investigating the Sheriff's Department as we were the ones who found the body of a confidential informant who was supposed to be carrying some suitcases with unspecified evidence inside. At no point did I say what the evidence was nor that there was cash involved. I warned them to be on alert and to let friends and family know all was good if they had someone show up and ask about them. My memo emphasized that they had to comply with lawful legal requests fully and quickly. I also asked that anyone with any information on the investigation inform me about it as soon as possible. I wondered if temptation had snagged one of my deputies for the first time but I quickly put that aside.

I called Lilly Greeves at home on my personal cell phone and gave her a heads up about the feds. She was incensed that she was considered a thief. I let her know she had some vacation time on the books if she wanted to use it but she said she knew the department was short staffed. As a favor I asked her to let her pets, Cuddles and Sparkle, out on the front pasture on her property after making sure the front gate was chained and locked. Two very large rodeo bulls patrolling her front yard would discourage damn near anyone. The bulls were also much more of a deterrent than any barking dog could ever be. After another reminder to be careful, I hung up the phone.

Paperwork, more emails, two performance reviews for deputies with upcoming work anniversaries, and processing several purchase orders. Part of the afternoon was with the County Attorney discussing a lawsuit by an upset citizen who was very unhappy at waking up in the drunk tank covered in his own vomit after previously crashing his truck into a bakery. The driver was found sleeping in the back of his vehicle with a pilfered doughnut in hand. The case should be an easy one, a slam dunk or lead pipe cinch, but the details had to be double checked and presented just so or the county could be liable for millions in damages. This was all very exacting and draining. So I walked out of the office into the hot, gritty air feeling much worse for wear. The air seemed to syphon the water from my skin aggressively. My life seems to be desiccating and giving me an inside view of the experience.

The messages on my work cell phone had piled up while I was in the office of the County Attorney. One of my deputies who was in Austin testifying on a case informed me that he gave evidence that morning but the prosecutor needed him to stay as they were planning a redirect the next day on an intricate point. One of our GMC Yukon patrol vehicles had a leaky radiator and was going out of service until it could be replaced in four or so days. Oddie had a billing question that I was able to redirect to the accountants. And Ayce Huggins said it was urgent that I follow up on what 'we' had spoken about. The last thing I wanted to do was talk to her again but I made a mental note to call her when I was damn good and ready to do so.

I left my office after seven in the evening, grabbed tacos on the way home, and wondered what else could go wrong. It would be a good evening to go to bed early. But something popped into my brain and I took a detour, forgetting about the tacos.

The parking lot of Miss Jane's Tea House and Chainsaw Juggling Salon was almost empty when I stopped. Parking next to the trash dumpster, the patrol unit was as unobtrusive as it could be so it would not scare off customers. It had started as a strip club ten years before going broke and reopening under new management a few years ago. The place was about as quiet as it was going to be. Miss Jane's had a niche audience but a good paying one from all over North Texas as the sun headed over the horizon. The building was a squat brick building with a neon sign portraying Jane Austen wielding a chainsaw over a tea kettle. I pulled a windbreaker over my uniform shirt to hide it before I headed for the front door. The bouncer knew me by sight and nodded at me without expression as I entered the bar. A slender woman with an orange colored buzz cut, large hoop earrings, and bright red pouting lips was bartending. She pouted when she saw me. She said, "What do you want?"

I said, "Can't a guy just drop by his local lesbian bar for a drink?"

The right corner of her mouth twitched as if she almost wanted to smile. "Ginger ale, Sir?" She knew my bar drink from previous trips.

I put a few dollars down on the bar. "May I have a Ginger ale, please Loretta. Is my cousin working tonight?"

Loretta poured me a tall ginger ale and then nodded over her shoulder. "She is in the office with Vince." She almost winced as I thanked her for the drink. I was never sure if Loretta hated me personally, my uniform, my job, my gender, or just my astrological sign but she always acted like a professional, if reluctantly. I headed to the back of the barroom and entered the proper code into the cypher lock to the office area. My cousin had once joked this place was her own Fuhrer Bunker as it was very well secured. There was a short hallway that was flanked by a store room on one side and an office on the other. The office was a mix of clutter and neat stacks of papers on a battered old metal desk. Seated behind the desk was a muscular woman dressed all in black and a skinny old man in a black suit. Both were peering at an old laptop.

My cousin, Elizabeth Izzard, had her name mangled to Lizard during the first day of kindergarten during recess. The abbreviated name had stuck. Her mother was my sister's older sister. Vince Izzard was her step dad and for many years he was a top defense lawyer in the state with many extremely rich clients and the ability to piss off most of the population with a snarky quip to the courtroom reporters after a day in court. The clients Vince's style attracted seemed to be a wacky collection of rich people with numerous quirks, psychological problems, bad habits, sexual peccadilloes, a dearth of sympathy for others, and large financial asset pools. He was now pushing seventy, semi-retired, but still on retainer for many big firms, and many of the truly filthy rich. Not that they wanted him in court for them any more as his style was now considered a way too brash. But having him on retainer meant someone else could not hire him to sue the person who paid the retainer as there would be a conflict of interest. Vince was part myth and part legend with a reputation of being the smartest legal mind for hire around. But Vince had to like you to let him be hired by you these days. He now had enough 'go to Hell' money to turn down new clients that he was less than enthusiastic about. The senior Izzard had been stymied by a system that keeps some from crawling to the top of the heap or getting too popular and he had spent the last dozen years doing pro bono work to afflict those who had irked him or raised his ire. His step daughter was smarter than he only in that she picked her battles a little more carefully but she had been nurtured to viscously savage the legal jugular with a ruthless efficiency. Where her stepfather was an alpha predator in the courtroom, she was a predator of alpha predators. Vince was a brawler but she was a scalpel slicing viscera.

Lizard and Vince kept a more formal office in town near the courthouse but their working office was in the back of the bar. A few years before Vince got suspicious of one of his legal secretaries and suspected her of spying for the opposition so he set up office in the back room of the bar. It also let Lizard keep an eye on the bar and the bar was much more of a fortress than the other office. Anyone armed with a search warrant would need a team of battle engineers to get past the bouncers, waitresses, bartenders, and customers to get into this office. I was glad I was a) their friend and b) related or I had the distinct impression I would be road kill on the road of justice. We had done small favors for each other over the years and I trusted them completely. I also knew a few of their clients consulted with the pair to conceal their activities from me. Twice they had arranged the surrender of clients who wanted to quietly and peacefully give themselves up for arrest. They both looked up when I walked in and Lizard quickly tapped the keyboard to blacken the screen despite the fact that I could only see the back of her monitor. They were working on something that raised my professional curiosity but I knew that I personally did not want to know about. I smiled and said, "Good evening. Can I get a few minutes of your time?"

Lizard got up to give me a hug and Vince had his typical steel bear trap grip handshakes. "What's up?"

"I need some advice." I put a dollar bill from my pocket on the desk for my legal retainer. Since they were my paid legal advisors anything we said fell under attorney-client privilege laws which meant they could not talk to others about this conversation. "We found a DB in the car not long ago. Feds are now telling me he was a CI and that he was supposed to be transporting account information on drug deals. The suitcases with the records are missing and there is a large possibility that there is a large amount of cash in the same suitcases. The Feds are now looking at me and my department. Supposedly there will be a Federal warrant with my name on it if the money is not in their hands Monday morning. They say either stand and deliver or face an aggressive smear campaign. I told them to be very careful not to buffalo my department or the friends and family of my staff. Then my past as an FBI Agent was brought up as a warning. A nemesis from back then still wants to nail my hide to the door for past perceived slights and has given the Dallas District DDA free reign to bring me down. So, how fucked am I?" I took a seat in a visitor's chair.

Vince grabbed the cash and pushed my dollar bill retainer into his shirt pocket. "It is the considered opinion of the Law Offices of Izzard and Izzard that you are about to get screwed up the ol' bung hole pretty well." He forced a smile and let it drop. "Rumor has it the new Federal DDA for Dallas has been given a head hunting license by the FBI. He lobbied hard to get the job which is very surprising that someone of his level would want a job at that much lower level. His predecessor not only screwed the pooch every which way possible but the very ugly newly born puppies are not being adopted." The old man had a gossip grapevine that provided him with details to an amazing extent. "And you know your friend who ruined your breakfast probably already said you were evasive or lied in her FD-302 report and now they have grounds to go after you? Those forms are institutionalized perjury tools. Her word is now the official record and you are now a schmuck, in the eyes of the law." He did not add that he thought I was a fool to talk to Ayce either formally or informally.

I nodded and said, "That is why I am here."

Izzard asked, "How much cash?"

"At least two suitcases are missing but I do not know the size. They said suitcases not suitcase so I am assuming two or more but have no idea of the total value." I leaned back in the chair. "And the Fed claimed jurisdiction on the DB."

My two newly hired lawyers looked at each other and then back at me. Vince wrinkled up his forehead causing his eyebrows to look like battling caterpillars. "So their informant ends up dead, all the records that want to use to build a case are gone, they are missing a shit ton of cash, no provable linkage to them, and they grab the case? They should have dusted themselves off and scurried away. Something is rotten in Denmark and it is not a brooding prince Hamlet." He muttered something else unintelligible and then pointed an index finger at me. "If you have any desire to see a country with an extradition treaty with the

United States of America, now would be the time to consider an immediate trip." Then Vice threw back his head and laughed at my predicament. "And you may need to go one state north in the next few days too, if my sources are correct."

I said, "I have the impression that the FBI only recently learned of the logs. I could imagine that such a meticulous record keeper would also keep a record of any meeting with the feds." When I said that Vince touched the end of nose to indicate that I was correct with the old charades gesture. His grapevine had given him a lot of information that I did not have and the idea that these logs could be used against the FBI as well was unsettling. I took a sip of my ginger ale and asked Vince to give me some possibilities. But he was suddenly preoccupied scribbling something onto a legal pad to pay attention to me.

Lizard asked, "So that could be a log of meetings, bank records, meeting notes, and maybe something the informant would use to make a proffer. Anyone with that level of accounting skill probably also had enough business law training to know how to turn it into a neat package, a real get out of jail free card, so to speak. So they are

trying to clean up their mess and they want their money."
She picked up a bright yellow pencil and twirled it between
her fingers. "Something is missing in the equation. I
don't like this, not at all. Something this big should be
generating whispers but I have heard nada." Lawyers had a
gossip grapevine that was astounding and she was tapped in
as well or better than anyone. I could tell I piqued her
curiosity as well as frustrated her by bringing her in on
somethings she had no clue about at all. And it appeared
Vince was being cryptic to both of us for some reason known
only to him.

"May not be their money," Vince said. "Maybe it
belongs to druggies who as a general stereotype are not
known to be exactly gracious over lost capital. I would
love to have a peek at those logs." Years before a dirty
drug agent busted a dealer and the cartel in question
wanted: a) their dealer back, b) their drugs, and c) all
their payoffs to that agent. The dirty agent refused and
the evidence against the agent was presented by the cartel
anonymously to the agent's boss along with a picture of the
agent's boss's daughter's dorm room with a sincere note of
'I hope we can end these amicably and not involve actions

that may negate returning the damage & cleaning deposit on your daughter's room.'.

I let them know that Ayce had let me know that some politically well-connected folks had financial links in the schema. How or why I have no details to give them. Maybe that fact was tossed in by Ayce to rattle me. Vince said he really wanted to peek at those logs now that he knew that and added it was just for personal, not professional, curiosity.

Lizard had been a Dallas PD street cop but got stuck on assignment as a decoy hooker with the vice squad. She kept requesting transfers to other duties -- any other duties -- but superior officers refused. Her commanding officer demanded she wear ever skimpier outfits until she filed a formal complaint. That complaint got her a reprimand and a brief suspension. She had just passed the bar exam and went to the union telling them to sue for her or she would name them on her own suit. The union balked and the DPD's mahogany row painted her in the press as a simple minded, pretty to look at but dumb as a rock malcontent. The dean of her law school was offended that their most recent valedictorian was considered anything less than stellar and came to Lizard's defense. Lizard decided it was time to pull out all the stops, including battle plans I suspect were written by her step-father. She sent copies of her supporting case documentation to the city attorney's office and drew blood. The first page was an email from her commanding officer telling her to show off more tits and ass and denying a request to take vacation for law school finals. The idiot commanding officer then suggested she vacation with him at a clothing optional resort in Florida. The second page copy of a handwritten note from a senior vice lieutenant saying it was such a shame Lizard was a lesbian as she could really get a career boost by spending a weekend riding his penis while his wife was away. And if she wanted that career boost she should call his home number, not DPD supplied cell phone number, and he carefully wrote down that home phone number. The city attorney made three large financial offers before Lizard accepted an early retirement accompanied with a large cash settlement. Supposedly the city attorney refused to read past the first two pages of documents where the really damaging information lurked. Part of the settlement went to the purchase of the bar and rumor had it the cash flow from liquor sales were not bad at all.

Lizard took a sip of something out of a mug and then pursed her lips. "Let me do some digging." She reached into her desk and pulled out a cheap burner phone with a charger. Tossing them to me she said, "I will call you after I dig. Remember the old man's advice if they do show up with handcuffs?" She jerked a thumb at her stepdad.

I said, "Mouth shut, eyes open, trust nobody, and remember names." Vince had a legion of stories about how clients had been tricked or put into worse situations while incarcerated by not following his advice. Anyone on the inside of the jailhouse acting like a friend was most likely willing to repeat any statement or exaggerate or makeup stuff to make my situation worse.

Vince had a creepy smile and shined it on me. "If that money shows up you had probably, hypothetically better burn it. And if that log book shows up, you can retire to your own private island in the South Pacific from the proceeds and I will be your literary agent to boot. That book is the real McGuffin they want. The money would be nice but that log is a trove of treasure. A million or two is a rounding error for them. The white whale these Ahabs seek is the documentation."

Vince had reminded me of Napoleon exiled to Elba as he sat in the back room of a bar and the last thing I wanted was my own island too. He had a long career and during that time he had made a lot of folks in and out of law enforcement look like fools. Luckily he never sank his fangs into me or my grandfather but I knew of plenty of others with incisor marks in their posteriors. But he had an ability that I needed badly if I did not want the FBI to chew me and my deputies up; Vince went for the jugular like a hungry vampire.

Standing up, I thanked them and promised to follow their rules. I put my half-finished glass of ginger ale back on the bar while nodding to Loretta and headed to the door. I was walking out when a call made my work cell phone buzzed and I somehow knew it was bad news. There was a bad accident a few miles away and I quickly went code three to the location. A semi-truck hauling metal I-beams for a build stopped to make a left turn while the Dodge Challenger behind plowed into the trailer at well over ninety miles per hour. Truck driver was unhurt while the occupants of the car were killed. An eighty thousand pound semi-truck against a two thousand pound car is not much of a match and the interior of the car was a bloody mess. I recognized the car right away as belonging to Mollie Fenton, a recent college graduate. She had just started work at a local CPA's office and seemed to be a happy go lucky young kid. The passenger was too broken and bloody to recognize. But Mollie was too easy to identify with her bloody face and vacant eyes up against the driver's side window sitting at an odd angle on a broken neck. She was not wearing a seatbelt and the airbag probably snapped her neck when it deployed.

I was directing traffic around the accident and making sure the passing traffic was not rubbernecking when an old pickup truck roared around the line of vehicles and stopped. A tall man flew out of the driver's door. Walter Fenton, Jr. was a welder by trade with a craggy face. He cried his child's name with anguish in his voice and I wrapped him up in a bear hug. I said, "Wally, no. You don't want to see her like this!" He made a surge to get past me and then collapsed, crying in my arms.

"How bad is it?" His voice wavered in pitch. Wally Fenton was tough as nails but it was visibly obvious he was shattered and hurting.

"Bad." I kept my arms around him, and felt his body shake. "You do not want to remember her like this."

"My baby girl," He whispered. His wife had left when his daughter was in elementary school and he had made her the center of his life. Wally sobbed for a moment and then pushed himself away from me. He stumbled around for a moment on unsteady legs before stopping dead still. He had made some sort of decision but I could not tell what it was. His eyes ran over the crumpled car as tears welled up in them. Wally then glanced at the truck driver who sat on the rear bumper of the paramedic's van being examined. For a moment I worried he would attack the driver but as I watched Wally seemed to visibly deflate. Then he walked deliberately to his truck and reached into the cab. A pitch black Colt Python was now in his hand. A cold chill ran down my spine.

My own hand went to my pistol. "Wally, no!" I thought he wanted to kill the truck driver and pleaded with him to put the gun down. My steps in his direction were slow and measured. "Wally, there has been enough pain tonight."

His eyes locked mine, his Adams apple bobbed a few times. "I …," He said and then stopped. Tears flooded down his cheeks and I felt so terrible for you. "I have nothing now." His gun hand dropped to his side and he shook his head. I could see tears rolling down his cheeks. He was only a few arms lengths away from me and I tried to creep closer. His sobs wracked his body and covered the sounds of my footsteps. Another step closer and I could reach for the Colt or wrap him up with my arms. But I was not close enough. His arm flinched upwards. He put the barrel of the gun under his chin, there was a bang, and a spray of his blood and brain rained down on me.

Chapter 6

That night I soaked in the hot tub when I got home, heated up some leftover Chow Mein, and went to bed early. Wrapping up the traffic accident, suicide, and supporting reports took several hours to complete, leaving me past the point of exhaustion. Just before midnight I heard car tires rolling on my driveway and then a car door slam. My right hand slid between the mattress and box spring to find the old Colt 1911 I had placed there. I lay with my fingers on the butt of the gun as footsteps went around the back of the house. Someone was rattling the old potted plant with the barrel cactus in it that sat by the back door where I kept a spare house key underneath. Only a few people knew about the hidden key plus the code for the entry gate and those people I trusted. So my fingers withdrew from the pistol. I heard the door unlock and then the sound of her kicking off her shoes echoed from the kitchen.

She arrived in the bedroom doorway and said, "I know I said I wouldn't be back." There was just enough light in the room from the windows to see her outline silhouetted against the darkness. She reached up to remove a pair of dangling earrings that were dropped on my dresser. In a smooth movement her blouse and bra were lifted over her head before being released to fall on the floor. She shoved down her jeans in a fluid motion. The moonlight through the windows reflected off her skin with a fuzzy glow. Crawling up on the bed, she kissed me with lips that tasted of salt, lemon, and tequila. "I was having drinks with my friends and I could not concentrate on them because my mind kept thinking of you. They yammered on about their petty little problems and I was remembering that first time in your hot tub and your tongue circumnavigating my body." She shifted position so that she was straddling my face and I attacked her most sensitive area with my tongue. Sliding two of my fingers into her wetness made her catch her breath. Her weight bore down on me and she ground her hips with gusto. She trembled after a short time and then gasped before falling back on the bed spent. "Whew!" She collapsed on top of me with a giggle.

My work cell phone rang which made me curse. Bad timing was becoming my middle name. After explaining that it was the work phone and that I was on call, I answered and the gravelly baritone of Dr. Preston Warehouser III barked, "Got a minute?" He was a night owl and loved

carrying out his duties as county coroner in the middle of

the night when most would find his clientele at their

creepiest. He liked to work what he called vampire hours

and found it much more relaxing when others were not around

to interfere or interrupt as he worked. Plus he found the

dead much more to his liking than most of the living.

I looked up and saw that my visitor was shimmying back

into her jeans. I said, "I do now."

"That car in the creek had two skeletonized sets of

remains. Female about twenty to twenty five and a male

about fifty. She was in the passenger compartment and him

in the trunk. Gunshots were the cause of death for both

and I was able to recover three slugs. The female was shot

just above the crest of the brow line smack in the middle

of the forehead. The skin is long gone so no sign of

stippling and now way to estimate just how far away was

shot was made, but I would estimate it was point blank or

damn close to it. The male was shot twice behind the right

ear with the trajectory pointing upwards. Both were shot

with a very low velocity twenty two that scrambled brains

as it rattled around inside the skull. Not enough velocity

or power to exit the cranium. Extremely effective. Whoever

killed them was most likely a professional." He let that sink in for a moment. "There was no tissue left after God knew how long in the mud and water and fish but it preserved the skeletal remains very well. We may get some DNA out of the bones and teeth but no promises", he said.

I asked, "Any idea how long they had been there?"

"Nope. They could have been there a decade or more." He went on to explain that what he had been given was a puzzle with most of the pieces gone. The doctor explained that there were gouges in the inside of the skulls where the bullets ricocheted around that documented his claim of low power rounds being the cause of death. The slugs had been recovered but were soft lead and too damaged; therefore useless for ballistic analysis. There were no shells from the firearm used but that could be for a range of reasons including the possible use of a revolver to the shots being fired elsewhere and the bodies placed in the car later. And he added that it was hard to find a gunman with a head start of ten years.

I had to ask a question as my mind pictured Rachel shot between the eyes. I said, "Could the female be younger by a few years."

"Maybe.   Maybe late teens but not much earlier than that. Do you have a possible matching missing person case that may match?" He explained about growth plates in bones and how they provided details about age. He repeated, "Maybe eighteen, nineteen or so. And that would be pushing things. She could have been a late bloomer. So do you have a missing person in mind?" The doc really seemed to only get excited about gossip about the dead and I could tell he was intrigued.

"Maybe. One back from my high school days." After a moment of silence where I did not add any details, the good doctor promised to have his report uploaded before he went home. He wished me a good night and as I ended the call I realized that I was again all alone.

As I hung up, I heard a car startup and then drive off to leave me as lonely as I have ever been. My visitor and I had been off and on for a while with protracted efforts to keep things quiet for the sake of both our careers. I could still taste her margarita on my lips. And the moon light shimmered off her earrings that were left behind on my dresser.

-

Two months after Rachel vanished, I was washing a sheriff's car when my grandfather showed up with a gun belt in one hand and one of his old uniform shirts in the others. "Put these on while I deputize you," He said. It was obvious he was in a hurry which meant there was a big problem.

"What's going on?"

"Betty Lew Hollister was chased off her parent's property and up the canyon by Donny Welk. I need you to drive up to Parker Ridge and look for her. We'll be coming up the canyon and should find her but I need you at the far end to block it just in case." He quickly swore me in and made sure I knew his old forty-five had a round under the hammer. "Cock it and pull the trigger. You've used this pistol before." I had shot this gun and his others a few times.

"Where is Donny?"

"Probably still chasing the poor girl. Her mom saw him in the yard taunting the girl but by the time she got outside, he was chasing her down the street. They ran into the woods and the mom called up. If you start at Parker

Ridge and walk down the canyon we might trap Welk between us."

Betty Lew Hollister had Down's syndrome and in her ten or so years of life had never caused anyone harm. Donny Welk had dropped out of high school a few years ago and that would be the sad peak of his soon to be very short life. Welk wanted to be the street smart, wise cracking cool guy like the ones he enjoyed watching on television but ended up a dumb hick with a foul mouth who picked on anyone he thought he could get away with it. The old man said he expected Welk to chase the girl for a bit and then try to use the woods to escape. My job was also to make certain that Welk did not walk out of the far end of the canyon as the slopes on the wide were generally too steep to climb. And if I spotted the Hollister girl I would take her home.

I drove to Parker Ridge, a small butte overlooking the area at the south end of the residential area where the Hollister's lived. Odds were that Welk would chase Hollister into the wooded area at the end of the neighborhood but not get in too deep but there was a slight chance they might use the trails to get to the ridge. Betty Lew and her father hiked the area extensively and I hoped she had a good place to hide from Welk. I parked the car, turned off the engine, and listened to the birds. The area was still and quiet for a few moments and I tried to come up with a plan on how to walk the two miles to the Hollister's house when I heard a scream. It was the scream of a young girl. The radio handset was instantly in my hand and I thumbed the transmit button. I concentrated on enunciating clearly, "Unit 12 at Parker Ridge. There is a girl screaming up here". A moment later I was out of the car in a flash and heading deep into an old thicket while putting the handset radio back in the gun belt. There was a second scream and a wet thud. I rounded a grove of cottonwoods when there was shriek. Welk was waist deep in a large mud puddle and was holding something down as he wailed painfully. He was fighting hard to keep what was in his hands under the surface and for a split second the thing he was holding bobbed up in the water and turned into a human face. It was the girl! Betty Lew was wild eyed and fighting for her life.

I screamed out, "Donny stop!"

His head twisted around to look at me. By now I had the gun out and the sights leveled on him. As he turned, his arms came up and I could see he was holding the

Hollister girl by the neck. She was clawing his arms in an attempt to get free. Donny Welk looked at me with pain in his eyes, "I can't"

I said, "Let her up!" Betty Lew was kicking and clawing at her attacker and she started to wriggle out of his grip.

He said, "No!" His hands again clenched tightly around her neck. Betty Lew kicked, arched her back, and tried to roll away from Donny. But it was obvious she was getting weaker.

I had not shot anything living before larger than a squirrel up to that moment. My one trip deer hunting did not bring me close to any sort of deer and I kept doubting if I could drop the hammer on Bambi's mom which made me glad I never had the opportunity. Pushing my arms forward, I set the sights on his center mass and then squeezed the trigger carefully. The pistol jerked in my hand and the bang seemed to happen a long time after the gun bucked in my hand. Donny spun, released the girl, and he landed hard in the mud. I took aim again but he rolled away and disappeared into the nearby thicket without me knowing if I had hit him or not. I did not think I could miss from about ten yards but my heart was hammering in my rib cage. I plunged into the water and grabbed for the girl. She had sunk under the muddy brown water and at first started to fight me, probably thinking I was Donny Welk, and then her body went limp. She felt slick and incredibly heavy. Her dark eyes were wide and staring at me. I pulled her out of the muddy water and took a quick look around to make sure Donny was not sneaking up on us. The handset radio that had been on the gun belt was nowhere to be found. If the Hollister girl was to be revived, it would have to be by me. My fingers found her neck but no pulse. Using my index finger, I checked her airway and mouth for obstruction. By dumb luck I had placed the pistol between back in the holster when I went to grab Belly Lew and I felt for it in case I had to shoot at Donny Welk again as I got ready to perform CPR. But I had lost track of where Donny was while I was trying to clear her airway, hoping he was not going to circle back and attack. Things had turned into a disaster with me losing the radio, almost losing the gun, and with a dead or dying girl.

Betty Lew Hollister's eyes seemed to look past me in a weird unfocused fashion and I feared she was dead. And then her eyes focused on me before she vomited what seemed like gallons of muddy water all over me. I clung to her and she clung to me as she cried for her mother. Finally I heard someone calling my name and I answered weakly. Two deputies appeared and one took the girl from me. The other asked me what happened and that was when I realized Donny Welk had managed to escape. It was obvious that Donny Welk was still a menace and he could have been both Betty Lew and myself while I tried to aid the girl. I felt like a failure and a stumbling idiot who was only alive by dumb luck.

More deputies arrived and one found a small puddle of blood and they searched for Donny. "He won't get far," He said. "There's blood splatter on the ground over here." He called out in a loud voice for Donny to come out of the brush and get medical treatment. In a low voice he muttered, "The bastard is probably watching us. He will get light headed soon from the loss of blood and by then it will be too late."

The paramedics showed up a little later and transported the Hollister girl who was still crying for mama. Later a doctor would perform a preliminary physical and blood work and found her battered, scratched, and upset but otherwise fine. My grandfather arrived on the scene and took back his gun and gun belt. The radio was found in the bottom of the large mud puddle along with a Raggedy Andy doll the girl often carried with her.

"So what happened?" The old man's eyes seemed to bore into mine. He was much calmer than I had anticipated, almost clinical and sterile. We talked through the 'what happened' twice before he smiled and said he was glad I was alright. He examined the gun and gun belt carefully before securing both in his car. He said, "Tell me one more time. But slower, more detail this time." He had me pantomime how Welk had spun and said it sounded to him like I put a round into him all right. "Now tell me one … more … time."

My voice sounded muffled and far off to my own ears as I spoke. "I parked, heard a scream, and found Welk holding something under the water. I told him to stop and he refused. I saw it was the girl, he refused to let go of Betty Lew, and I fired. I was ready to start CPR but…"

"I'll need you to write a report. I'll help you write it. Are you okay?" He put a hand on my shoulder and looked me in the eye. "You did a good job. Are you sure you are okay?" x

I nodded. "Better than Betty Lew." How he could say I did a good job was beyond me as I had fumbled the situation badly with too many mistakes that could have resulted in both the death of Betty Lew Hollister and myself. I fought back my emotions. One of the deputies got a camera and took pictures of the area, gathered the shell from the round I had fired, and asked if I was okay to drive the car I had used back to the station. I then realized that I would have to clean up the car again from the muddy clothes I was wearing and chuckled to myself at the irony. I was escorted back to the car and was very aware the deputies were watching me to make sure I was okay. The old man told me to shower at the station before he drove away. The deputies nodded to me stoically before they too drove off in their vehicles and I sat behind the wheel listening to the birds for a few moments. I was exhausted, covered in puked up muddy water, and mentally reeling but I had saved a life. There was pride in that. It was not a gold medal performance but I had done it. I was euphoric for a moment.

Then I spotted movement in the brush. A head popped up and then disappeared from a thicket. It had to be Donny Welk. I had no pistol because the old man had taken it as evidence. I felt around under the front seat and came up with nothing I could use as a weapon. The gun belt had holders for handcuffs and mace but were empty and in the old man's car with the old man. There was a holder for an Ithaca riot gun but no shotgun. In the glove compartment was a book of unwritten tickets and I doubted possible papercuts would put fear into Donny Welk. In the trunk was an old tire iron which felt sufficiently heavy and mace-like in my hand. I walked into the brush and soon found Donny Welk collapsed under a bush. I wondered why he was covered in barbeque sauce until I realized it was dust and his blood. My shot had hit him to the outside of his left nipple and sliced its way between two ribs. If treated right away it was not a life threatening wound but by now over an hour had passed. He was cringing behind a pucker bush, "Help me, please."

"Why did you hurt Betty Lew?" I squatted down with the improvised weapon resting on my shoulder just far enough away from him to be out of his reach. I expected him to leap up and attack me with the same fury that he used on the girl so I kept my distance.

"I … I … think I may have gotten her pregnant," He said. He was obviously weak from the loss of blood and seemed to be going into shock. He was fading fast from the exsanguination.

The idea that he had hurt harmless Betty Lew Hollister greatly shocked me. She was a sweet, innocent little girl. "You raped her?"

"She said she wanted to be nice to me." I could not tell if he laughed at what he said or if he was wheezing. He muttered something I could not discern and shook his head. There was a sly grin on his face as if he was proud of himself. "So, she was nice to me, very nice."

Anger boiled up within me. I said slowly, "She is ten years old, Donny." She was a kid! How could he molest a little girl?

"She *wanted* to be nice to me." He chuckled and seemed to be very proud of raping an underage mentally handicapped minor. He smiled and then giggled as if what he did was something he was proud to have done.

"And you tried to drown her?" I felt my anger and disgust at Welk beginning to well up from deep within me.

"Tried to," He said. He examined the scratches on his arms the girl had made defending herself from her assailant. I pushed my hips back and went from squatting to sitting. Donny Welk was a monster and I was shocked how normal he seemed and how calmly I was handling the situation. I was still angry but I could not bring myself to action against him. The tire iron was heavy, resting on my shoulder, and I would not take much effort to swing it down on his skull. It would be so very easy to crack his head like an egg. That would put an end to him and his raping little girls.

"Take me to the hospital. I'm losing a lot of blood. I need to see a doctor. I don't feel so good." Donny Welk was a mess and I should have taken pity on him. Then I thought of the frightened, brave little Hollister girl. And then how Welk would be treated so kindly at the hospital, by the public defender's office, and finally at a trial. A trial where he would claim Betty Lew Hollister wanted to be nice to him and offered herself sexually to him to prove it. Or had he simply grabbed her while being a bully and things got out of his control. I doubted that she was a willing participant but he would give a great performance on the witness stand before a jury and her parents. Every easy smile that Betty Lew gave would be turned into a sexual enticement that Donny Welk could only cope with for just so long. Her parents who would forever hear the echoes of his slanders in their ears about their little girl who never harmed anyone. Donny would put on an academy award level performance painting Betty Lew as a seductress whom he could not resist, slandering her and ruining the rest of her life. I could imagine her being confused and frightened in court being barked at by a defense lawyer who would delight in tearing her down. I did not think Donny Welk would not be convicted but the damage would be done and the community would remember the salacious parts of his testimony. Then there would be appeals and probably television stores about the case where Welk would repeat his claims. Even if Donny received a very long sentence and sent to Huntsville the Hollister's would forever be scarred by the actions and the testimony. After a few moments of thought, I said to Donny, "I am going to be nice."

"You're going to be nice to me? Take me to the hospital?" It was obvious the exsanguination was having an effect. He tried to stand up and ended up flopping on to the ground.

"No," I said. "Not nice to you. And I am not taking you to the hospital." I forced a smile. "I am going to be nice to the rest of the world and watch you bleed out right here." I could have driven off and risked someone else coming to his aid. But if I was going to be judge, jury, and executioner for Donny Welk I needed to see the entire thing through to the bitter end.

"What the fuck, man?" He simpered. He started to cry and after a few moments he was lying face up with shallow breaths. It was hot under the sun while I waited.

And it did not take long for him to die. He had tried to plead with me, then cursed me, and then resigned himself to his fate. He grew weaker and weaker before the end. I left him there making sure he was not breathing for nearly a quarter hour. After covering my tracks, I drove away. One of the deputies asked what took me so long and I said I had to stop a few times to puke on my way back to the station. Two days later a local farmer saw the buzzards circling and followed their aerial dancing spirals to the well consumed corpse. Various animals had done an amazing job of reducing the corpse. I never told anyone about finding him or his death or how I let him die. And no one ever asked me about that afternoon. I did suffer a little from jokes about puking that day but they soon faded. But the memories of Donny Welk's eyes slowing turning glasses have never faded in my memory. But something inside me told me I needed to be in law enforcement.

Chapter 7

Deputy Juan Soto had an eggplant colored set of black eyes and a swollen lower lip. During the early morning hours he had stopped to aid a motorist with a flat tire when a drunk driver arrived on the scene, clipping the left rear corner of his car and then Juan. My notification call came at four in the morning on a sleepless night and after he was already being transported to the hospital. I stood in the doorway of his hospital room leaning against the door jamb while he assured his very pregnant wife that he was okay and that she should go to work. She was a nurse in the hospital's NICU unit and due to go on shift shortly. They spoke in Spanish and I pretended not to understand to give them some privacy. She finally relented but shot me a dirty look as she left. Soto said, "She wants me to quit. Again."

"It would be safer selling insurance at her daddy's agency and about as exciting as warm buttermilk." Soto was a good deputy and his loss would hurt the department. But so many good law enforcement personnel burn out, get burnt, or self-immolate. It was not uncommon for an hour

in the field to require four or five hours in the office
with paperwork and other offerings for the bureaucracy.   I
had seen many talented individuals leave law enforcement
and wondered if Soto was destined to follow in their
footsteps. An unhappy spouse is highly motivated to make
changes. A new baby would be extra motivation to do another
job. I suddenly felt very old looking at him and listening
to him recount the accident.

"I had just taken off my seatbelt and was opening the
door when I got hit. My Tahoe is destroyed, the guy I
stopped to help is still in surgery. His car is totaled. My
patrol unit is scrap. And I hear the drunk that hit me is
sleeping it off in the drunk tank." Soto seemed to get
more than his fair share of bumps and bruises. He was a
very good deputy but he seemed a little accident prone. It
concerned me as he did not seem overly macho or reckless.
Some deputies are like goats ramming their heads into
obstacles they could easily go around and others had more
sense. Juan seemed to be a mix of those two and I hoped he
would grow out of his butting goat period. As his superior
I had to take note of all this. He was a good deputy but I
wondered if he would be able to scrape by to retirement
without serious injury. Maybe he would do better selling

whole life insurance policies. I could not remember hearing of an insurance salesman getting two black eyes while at work; it probably happened but I had not heard of it.

Soto being in the hospital was going to be a hit to the department. Not only was it going to hurt the ability to patrol the county with Soto out recovering but the loss of the vehicle also hurt. I had to force my mind back on the flesh and blood man before me and not my administrivia.

I told him not to show up at the sheriff's station until he was well knowing damn well that he would be back much sooner than was good for him. "You'll have to ride a desk until you're cleared for duty. If you want to use some of your leave time…"

"Gotta save that for when the baby arrives," He said quickly. They had been married for just over a year and anxious to have kids. Juan seemed like he would be a good father but something about him seemed to be wanting to rush into full adulthood with afterburners on full. I wondered if school teachers felt the same way with students who wanted to be adults too soon.

I smiled at him. "Well, when you are feeling a little better, come back to the station and well give you some light duties until we are both sure you are ready. And meanwhile get ready for the baby. Try to get some extra sleep in the bank because that little one will be here very, very soon." We shook hands and I headed out of the hospital parking lot and drove over to the impound lot. Soto's GMC Yukon was badly wadded up. And my budget would not cover a new vehicle. The driver with the flat tire had an old Jeep that was next to Soto's Yukon and it looked like the Yukon had tried to mate with it. Nearby was a new Camaro that had most of the front sheet metal compacted into a two foot bundle of metal mess. The windows were down and the car reeked of pot and Jägermeister. I assumed that this was the car of the drunk driver as there were no other new cars in the lot.

"I just ran that car," Laurel Hardy said. She had snuck up and surprised me. "Frat boy heading back to SMU after visiting his brother in Bridgeport. He was not wearing his seat belts when he hit Juan and was doing forty eight miles per hour in a twenty five zone. We now have plenty of teeth, blood, and tissue samples from the steering wheel. And I just love that cars come with black boxes that record all the data. He had half an ounce of marijuana, four unopened beers, two opened beers, and an empty fifth of Gentleman Jack, some Jager, and a HK nine. "

I said, "You're in early, aren't you?"

She gave me her lopsided grin. "I have a court appearance this afternoon and too much paperwork that needs to be done before that. So I came in early to write up the results of the old Mustang you helped drag out of the mud." She was wearing a baggy set of overalls and boots that were part of her field uniform. "And that Mustang is very interesting."

I said, "Can you give me a quick summary on that car?" I fought to keep my voice sounding calm, professionally disinterested, and under my full control.

"No license plates, the VIN number on the fender was for a car wrecked in 1967 and the number on the engine block is for a later car. The car was probably pieced together from a few wrecks. In the driver's seat were the skeletonized remains of a female and in the trunk was the skeletonized remains of a male. I found two slugs when I removed the male and I heard the ME found one inside the skull of the female. All clothing save for a set of male penny loafers had rotted away. Good leather tanned well rots slowly. I did find a small silver necklace with a heart pendant with the female." She paused for a moment before saying, "And there were no car keys in the ignition or with the car. The automatic transmission in neutral which would make me think someone rolled it into the creek. It took forever to sift all the mud from the car." She shook her head. "Funny we had that car last week with no car keys and then this one. And before you ask the Mustang was not hotwired. No personal effects left intact after some time in the muddy water.

I shook my head. "What is it with dead bodies in cars around here anyway?" Between the car from the mud and the car from the rest stop, it seemed like too many bodies were ending up in cars. But in an area where you have to drive to get to anything it was just the normal reality.

"Do you remember when we met, Sheriff?" Laurel had a very stoic professional look she used most of the time but now she was grinning at me.

It took me a moment. "North side of the courthouse?"

She nodded. "I had just interviewed for this job and I was about to drive off when you lit up the lights and hemmed me in with one of the old Crown Victoria cruisers. I thought 'Hick cop about to give some macho bullshit ticket' and was ready to bitch to high heaven. But what do you do? You take the coffee cup off the roof of my Volvo and hand it to me while saying 'have a nice day'." She laughed. "And that was when I knew I wanted to work here, in this county."

"We are glad to have you."

"How is Soto?"

"He looks like he went for a ride in a rock tumbler," I said. She knelt down to show me where the chassis of the Yukon was twisted beyond repair and they pointed out that Soto was lucky he got only a glancing blow. She went into detail on recovering the evidence from the Camaro and then looked at her watch as seeing she was running late. "Thanks, Laurel. Enjoy court." She told me to have a good day and it almost looked like she was skipping back to her office. Laurel truly enjoyed her job and her enthusiasm was just a little contagious. I had gone from feeling old looking at Soto and not feeling ancient watching her disappear.

Janet Polk had not arrived in the office yet so I started a pot of coffee and headed back to my office. There was more than a morning's work for me to do and I felt better knowing I had an early start. I had almost finished my email for the morning when she arrived with two mugs of coffee. "How's Soto?"

"Good, considering. He is banged up pretty good. His wife wants him to quit," I said. We discussed how hard it was to replace lost deputies with our relatively low pay scale and the remoteness of McDavey County. We both knew losing Soto would put additional strain on the department and our limited staff. We had some potential recruits that we discussed but the prospects were not good. And the loss of the patrol vehicle would hurt us more. We had made plans for his vacation time off when his baby arrived but the potential of his being out long term with an injury was disconcerting. As was his wife wanting him off the department.

"My husband was worried about me getting shot. My mother thought I would go all Dirty Harry and then shoot innocent civilians." She laughed. "Families do not understand. My niece wants to do a civilian ride along as soon as she is legally old but does not want my brother to know about it. She is the only one in my family excited by what I do. Everyone else thinks I am nuts." She was sitting in one of my office guest chairs and leaned back. "Maybe we are nuts," she said in a flat voice.

"My grandfather has a scrapbook that my grandmother made for him. His third day on the job two idiots from Ada tried to hold up the Farmer's Bank while he was in there on his lunch break trying to make a mortgage payment on the ranch. They yelled 'this is a stick up' and fired their guns at the ceiling. He drew his gun, shot both dead, and then wanted to get back to the counter to get his payment in on time."

"Your grandfather is one of a kind. How is he doing, by the way?" She had worked for the old man and then for the idiot who came after the old man. In a fairer world she should be the sheriff instead of me. Before I ran for the sheriff's position she had confided to me that she really did not want to be the front dog in the sled team. At least not at that time. She said doing very public work in front of the county board was not her cup of tea. And that she really enjoyed what she was doing as the executive officer but not the commanding one.

"I need to go see my grandfather today," I said. "I still have the feeling that he resents me having his old job." Since I had been elected I had been too busy to spend too much time with my grandfather. The few times I had tried to set up something spur of the moment – diner, a quick beer, or watch a ball game – had been politely spurned. There was an undercurrent from him that suggested that he was a little jealous of me being sheriff. Or maybe he just wanted to get away from any fragment of his old job. I had been too busy to dig into the rift with the amount of time the job took. There was not a small amount of guilt on my part about neglecting the relationship.

She laughed, "I doubt if he really resents you. He probably cannot believe that either of us have stuck around this long. And he had it rougher in his day. My guess is that he does not want to seem to be bossing you around by adding his two bits worth of advice." She held up an index finger, "And we both know how busy his new wife keeps him. Maybe you need to work on her to get to him."

I admitted out loud that she could be right but internally I still had a sense he resented me taking over for him. Maybe he resented me for more than that. Maybe Willow resented me more.

"Well, give Willow my best if you see her. Oh, I almost forgot. Lonnie Kondowski said wild pigs came off the hunting lease next to his farm and killed his dogs. The heat is driving more than just the humans crazy." Polk left me alone in my office with my brain rattling with too many thoughts. I closed my office door and went digging in the databases. For years I had resisted putting Rachel's name or her dad's name into the computers for fear of hitting some sort of virtual tripwire on their records. I had spent too many hours over the intervening years wondering why she had left me at the train depot that rainy night and came up with hundreds of theories. By the time I was in the FBI Academy, I had done as many indirect searches on Rachel and her dad on publically available resources as possible. But I also hoped that every new Hollywood starlet would turn out to be Rachel. Maybe she had made it to Hollywood and was living out her dreams. I honestly hoped that she had made it. But in my darker moods I knew that maybe she was in the morgue taking up space in a plastic bag sitting on a shelf.

With great trepidation I logged onto the computer. I ran the name Rachel Marie Lopes and Rachel Marie Lopez through the various databases and found dozens of matches on the name alone. She had been Lopes in high school but sound alike names often make it into the databases. It was often amazing to find out how many misspellings one could find in reports, records, databases, and court records. Filtering the results I had by the approximate age and height reduced the matches to a handful.

The Texas Driver's License Database had eight matches. With the high Hispanic population of Texas and fairly common first and last named had made me assume that there would be many more matches. The first record was from twenty years ago and it was her. The picture was from around the time I met her in English class. Deep dimples lined her smile like that of the teenage girl who had just passed her driver's license exam. And the same hairstyle! Could she be older as the skeletal remains from the car suggested, if that was indeed her? But there were no renewal dates, updated photos, or other entries. I had hoped that a notice from the state of California that Rachel had surrendered her Texas license as part of getting her one from California. The other seven records were for other women. The national databases had dozens of women named Rachel Marie Lopes but none were her. There were several possible matches in California but none in Los

Angeles or the surrounding counties that matched. It was like being at the bottom of a mine shaft when the daylight fades and darkness consumes all.

Richard Lopes was a very popular name and I got very lucky. I knew they had come from Houston the first month of the year that I graduated high school and previous he had been in Louisiana. That shallow toe hold let me climb upwards. His driver's license photo from my graduation year beamed from the terminal. Richard Emmert Lopes's eyes in that photo seemed to stare at me with haunted eyes from the computer screen. He had received two traffic tickets for speeding within a month of getting his license and I am proud to say one of those was from my grandfather. There was a note that he had surrendered his Louisiana driver license to get his Texas driver's license and there was the records for getting commercial driver's licenses right after they disappeared. He had renewed his license three times and it was still valid. I put the listed address on an internet mapping program and found it was a store and forward mailing service in Fort Worth.

It was getting close to lunch and I could not put off calling the old man any longer. I dialed the number and a sweet female voice answered on the second ring. "He's in the shower. How are you doing?" Willow Montgomery McDavey had married the old man half a dozen years ago and it was obvious that they really loved each other. He was the land rich but penny poor rancher who paid the bills by being the county sheriff, as had his father. She was the daughter and granddaughter of wealthy oil men who seemingly as part of their genetics did not like my grandfather. LaMarr Montgomery had found oil on his land as a teenager and seemed to have the Midas touch with any investment. Sadly the oil was all over McDavey County except in the areas actually owned by the McDavey's. The old man went to work after high school as a deputy for his father and she went to Harvard to become a doctor. She spent many decades practicing surgery at Brigham and Women's Hospital in Boston before returning home. She had been the one to diagnose my grandmother's cancer. Willow was a lovely, gracious, warm, and loving woman but for some reason I did not like her. I had no reason not to like her but I never warmed to her. And she had been the one to convince the old man to retire. "I've got brisket and beans if you are hungry."

"That sounds wonderful. I need some advice on some old cases." I could tell as soon as I said the words that she was wishing that I would not dredge up old, bad memories for her husband. I was not sure if she was trying to manage him or shield him. Either way without saying a word she let me know she was not pleased with me. "Well then, I'll pack some sandwiches and let you two head out to the old barn to watch the elephants." Willow was always sweet acting towards me but something made me hesitant around her. She was great for the old man and they really loved each other. They booth seemed genuinely happy around each other which made me happy for them. But something about her put me on edge.

When I arrived at the Montgomery Ranch, I was met by an armed guard at the entrance who carefully noted my license plate and my badge before letting me on the property. By the gate was a sign that proclaimed 'Saving Texas Elephants since 2017'. I passed the new office complex and parked by the old ranch house. My grandfather sat in a rocking chair on the veranda with a glass of lemonade in his hand. He stood up and grabbed a paper bag that had been sitting on the floor by his rocker. I got out of the patrol unit and we wordlessly nodded to each other in a silent greeting. We walked in silence until we came to a new corral where a small set of bleachers sat under an old Live Oak tree. An old but meticulously cared for barn was off to our left. In the old corral was a pair of female Indian elephants quietly eating from a pile of fodder on the ground? Willow had started rescuing elephants after hearing about some circus elephants abandoned when the ringmaster went broke and fled to Mexico. She sent a good deal of money turning old steer pastures into something suitable and safe for the elephants. There were now at least a dozen of the beasts wandering around the old ranch. I wonder what the previous generations of her family would think of the large animals on land they fought so hard to keep. Or what a Comanche hunting party transported from two centuries before would think if they suddenly discovered the pachyderms on the edge of the plains. The beasts seem content to ignore us as we watched them from a short distance.

From his body language I would tell the old man was not in a good mood. He and the senior dowager elephant had the same sway to their walk that telegraphed to the world they would stomp you to a pulp if pushed either in the slightest. For a moment I wished that I had not asked to meet him but there were answers that I badly needed.

"Willow said you had some old cases you need to talk about," The old man said. He sounded like more than reluctant to answer my question but felt duty bound to discuss them. Since I had taken office he had become tight lipped around me. I could sense he was disappointed in me but he had never said so. And today he spoke in a way that told me that getting information out of him would be like pulling teeth. Everyone has bad days and would get grumpy occasionally but he seemed to be well into having a bad decade.

"That's right. One in particular." He pulled a barbecue brisket sandwich out of the paper bag and handed it to me. "The other day we pulled an old Ford Mustang out of the skinny dipping pond. Inside were the skeletons of a young woman and a middle aged man." There was no reaction from the old man and he bit into his own sandwich. I could be discussing the weather or the economics of Australasian communities for the lack of reaction from my grandfather. "Professional hit. Her between the eyes and him behind the ear angled up with a pair of low power twenty two rounds. Not enough powder to push the rounds through the skull but enough to scramble the gray matter. Very professional assignation style. The car was pushed into the creek."

He seemed more than a little annoyed at me. "And?"

"And. I remember Rachel Lopes had an old Mustang and she disappeared right after my high school graduation. She fits the profile for the female skeleton and her dad the male. So what can you tell me about them?"

He stopped chewing as if the sandwich had lost all flavor. For a split second I thought he would spit out his mouthful but somehow he resumed chewing and then swallowed it. "How much do you want to know? And remember that somethings are better carried to the grave without being conveyed." He had always been a serious man but today he was beyond his norm.

The question I had wanted an answer to for so long was finally going to be asked. "So tell me about Richard Lopes and his daughter -- why were they here and where did they go?"

The old man took another bite of his sandwich and carefully chewed it until he swallowed. My grandfather was stalling. I knew him well enough to know he was stalling and I could tell that he knew that I knew he was stalling. He then took a long swing of his lemonade as he watched the elephants. "First thing. She was not his daughter." He turned to face me, "She was his wife."

Chapter 8

"His wife?" I was surprised to hear my own voice say those words. Was he remembering her wrong or mistaken her for someone else? I wanted to correct but he never let me have the chance to do so.

The old man nodded. Then a smile slowly grew on his lips. "Lopes was a confidence man and probably the best I have ever seen. Slick, really slick. Usually worked on those who could afford to be taken or needed to be taken. But I caught him on a Chicago Shuffle on a vacation trip to San Antonio. I wanted to haul his ass to SAPD but your grandmother, well, she insisted that I let him go. Over the years there were amazing stories floating around him about him. Big scores on long plays. Boy was very good. Some of his marks never knew they were taken. One day his brother drops dead, leaving Richard a rather large pile of money earned on the stock market somewhat honestly. Enough money for him to say 'go to Hell' and never work again for the rest of his life. That money really impressed him and he decided to go straight. And he did go straight. Then Richard called me out of the blue after being off the game for many years. He wanted help building up a new legend for his wife because she was in trouble. A young woman with a bad past. She had tried to run a con on him and he fell for her. "

"Rachel?" My heart was in my throat and her name came out as little more than a horse croak.

"Rachel Maria Flores was her real name. Born in Galveston to a drunk dad who left when she was three and a mom who cleaned toilets for a living." The old man took a long pull of his lemonade and then fixed his gaze on me. "Rachel was a beautiful woman with the spirit of a rattlesnake. Richard could never see the real her and did his damnedest to get her set right. He thought she had – promise. And he wanted her to have a future."

"But why send her to high school?"

The old man smiled. "Rachel needed to be reinvented. The man she had worked for wanted her dead when the con on Richard fell apart. Her boss thought Richard was an easy mark but he had spotted them a mile off and knew what they were up to probably before they did. But she enchanted him.

Or more like bewitched him. So, he had the idea of building up a new identity for her and himself. He got a birth certificate for a baby killed in a fire but the dead child was a bit younger than his wife. She had never finished high school and they thought it was a good way to kill time. Things were much different before everything got computerized. A fake birth certificate and a real high school diploma could go a long way back then. And I promised to help them both as long as they kept their noses clean and moved on when they had her new identity established."

It felt like I had been slugged hard on the chin and I was just short of being knocked out. I was dazed and lost. For a long time I could not say anything and he just continued to eat his sandwich.

"Where did they go?"

The old man shrugged. He said, "I know he was in Houston for a while you were in Quantico. The money he had inherited was mostly still in the stock market and the economy whipsawed on him. He did a lot of things after that. Driving trucks for the frackers in Andrews County. Then El Paso where he ran a taco truck. He would send me

Christmas Cards with handwritten letters in them. He never mentioned her in the letters. I assumed they split up or she ran off or he kicked her to the curb. The Christmas Cards stopped arriving a few years ago and I assume he either got tired of writing or he died."

"Did you keep the cards and letters?" I had hoped to run the addresses against old records.

But he shook his head. "Burned 'em. I did not want them found so I burned 'em. There were several things I decided that I did not want around after I was gone and could not explain them. Those letters among them." He took another bite of the sandwich and chewed carefully. "I took the job of sheriff to protect and serve. You took the job of sheriff to protect and serve. That is protect and serve your community. Sometimes you do something to protect or serve that is not exactly by the book, kosher, halal, or legally correct just to keep them safe. Sometimes you have to make a bad bargain for the greater good. Rachel was one of those bad bargains for a good reason. And I made that bargain, not you."

I said, "And what bargain was that?"

"You have to remember that you see a young woman dealt a bad hand in life but you also see a spark in her that gives you an inkling that with a little help drawing cards from the deck that she just might overcome a bad start," he said. "Her husband wanted help with her. He begged me for it. He convinced me but she was the real persuasion." He then proceeded to finish the sandwich. "She fooled her husband, she almost fooled me, and she really fooled you."

I thought hard for a few moments and then said, "There are no prints or records in any of the databases for her. And not much for him."

"So what does that tell you?" He gave me his best flinty glare and said, "To me it means Richard was doing something for someone who could wipe the slate clean. I told you he was really good and he probably caught the attention of someone who could use him for their purposes. Someone who would do things to protect him. Someone who can do that probably does not want them found still. It takes a bit of power to get someone's records removed. And you should keep your nose clean of it. There are some old echoes from long ago battles that you need to avoid at all cost. Do your job but not to extraordinary lengths."

"What if it is Rachel in that car from the creek?"

"Then we will know what happened to her." He stood up and walked back to the house without speaking further. He had answers and I knew then I would not get them. At least from him.

-

I was on my way back to the office thinking about what my grandfather had told me, or, more correctly, what he had not told me, when dispatch radioed me to go to Juan Soto's house. His frustrated wife was on the front porch arguing with Ayce Huggins and two FBI agents. Soto's wife kept her hands on her very pregnant belly and said, "This is fucking bullshit!"

Ayce handed me a copy of the search warrant. The document gave the FBI permission to search the Soto house and confiscate all computers, papers, and other items they deemed worth collection at their discretion. It was as wide open as any search warrant I had ever seen and few judges gave carte blanche for such a fishing expedition. I handed the warrant back to Ayce, "You're serious?"

"As a heart attack," She said. Her head dipped, indicating for the marshals to push past Mrs. Soto. They rammed past her not noticing her condition. Ayce added, "I told you not to fuck with us. Sheriff, this is all on you." She said the last part loud enough to be heard by Mrs. Soto.

Mrs. Soto exploded. "What!?!" Her eyes flashed from me to Ayce and back again.

Ayce said to her, "Your friend here, the sheriff, is not playing nice. When does not play nice with us, we do not play nice with him. Or the peons who work for him."

I escorted the wife to an understanding neighbor's house and then returned to Ayce. "Her husband was hit by a drunk driver a few hours ago and she is eight months pregnant. And he was on a trip to El Paso escorting a prisoner when your car was in the rest area. This is out of line."

"You're out of line. We need to know who in your department is dirty. If we paint with too broad of a brush and smear everyone that works for you, it will reflect on you. Not us." She put on a fake smile, "And you pick the softest target to hit first, to send a message. You must remember that from the academy. You remember they taught us the procedures that produce the results quickest with the bad guys." She had an evil smile on her lips, "We will find something, probably not the suitcases. Someone who works for you has something to hide – pot, porn, or something – and we will use that to flatten you."

Two FBI agents came out of the house with heavy document boxes and had to walk around me to get to their vehicle. I felt useless. They agents went back and I stood with the very pregnant Mrs. Soto as they tore apart her house and removed box after box. They even took packages of diapers for the baby and baby shower presents. She called her parents and they took her to their house. A few hours later Mrs. Soto went into premature labor and the doctors had to heavily medicate her to keep her calm. And Juan passed the word through the chain of command that she and the doctors thought it best if I did not drop by the hospital to see her.

Chapter 9

Larry James Proctor needed to go to the bathroom and shared this information to his two traveling companions as they pulled into the gas station. The trio were driving across the country and swapping off for driving shifts. But the young man with the full bladder was still reeling from the effects of three beers several hours before. Proctor had been in the back seat of a 1973 Chevy Caprice Classic and woke up as the car came off the interstate for a refueling stop at a gas station. He told his buddies he was going to pee and climbed out of the Chevy. Proctor did use the men's room and when he came out he opened the back door of the nearest car, climbed in and went to sleep.

Lourdes McGuire needed a pack of cigarettes and stopped at the gas station. She ran in, paid, and headed back to her car in a big hurry to not be late to her job as a receptionist at a radio station. McGuire was just pulling onto the freeway and lighting up a menthol when she heard snoring from the backseat or her Ford Crown Victoria. A quick look over her shoulder revealed the sleeping stranger in the backseat. Her call to 9-1-1 came in a whispered voice -- "There is a strange man sleeping in the back of my car!" The dispatcher realized she was near the McDavey County Sheriff's office and directed her there.

Meanwhile Proctor's traveling companions were wondering what had happened to him. They checked the bathroom, the store in the gas station, and had walked around the property without finding him. Proctor was many things including being very dependable so they called 9-1-1. "Our friend went into the gas station bathroom and disappeared," One said. They did not know if he had been kidnapped, taken by space aliens, or somehow got sucked into the sewer system.

The dispatcher asked one question. "Does your friend snore like a water buffalo?" Larry James Proctor had been found.

Fifteen minutes later Lourdes McGuire was back on her way to work and Proctor was still not fully awake. One of my deputies ran his Florida driver's license and found outstanding warrants for drugs, battery, and domestic violence. His two friends had clean records and headed off as soon as they were told they could leave. Proctor glowered at me from his holding cell saying, "This is bull*SHIT*!" He stomped around the cell like he was hoping to find a reluctant land mine. I had been checking with the jailors about schedules when he was brought in. He threw a fit and kept screaming that he was going to sue everyone.

"I just wanted you to know the Orlando PD is sending someone to transport you back," I said. "Don't be a jerk here and you will be treated well. Got it?"

He nodded. "Man, two more days and I'd be in California living the dream." I felt my stomach lurch. I had once wanted to live the dream in California.

Back in my office I dry swallowed two aspirin. Carl Owen had sent me an email asking me to call him. I made sure to drain my bladder and grab a fresh coffee before settling in behind my desk to make the call. I thought I would be in for a long chastisement. With a clean pad of paper next to me, I reluctantly called back. His secretary answered his line and asked me to please wait.

"Sheriff McDavey?" It had taken a few minutes to track him down and I was about to hang up when he got on the line. He said, "I need to pick your brain about something.   First, do you know anything about a group that was called the Blue Dogs?" No mention of the raid on the Soto house. Or a mention of the suitcases and the money. The situation had gone from odd to strange.

"Yes, they were some Choctaw kids from just across the border in Oklahoma that got into the crystal meth business many years ago. They bought the chemicals in Fort Worth and drove them back to the reservation where they brewed up their product. One of them had been a chemistry major at Texas A&M and learned the business down in College Station supplying his buddies. From what I remember they spilled some red phosphorus in a car while swerving to avoid an accident and set their vehicle on fire. One of my grandfather's deputies caught a lung full and had to take a lot of time off to heal. That was well before my time, twenty five years ago minimum. I have heard the stories but do not know the details."

"Twenty seven years to be exact. Do you still have files on them archived someplace?" The Federal DDA seemed much nicer over the phone than in person. "One of the original members of that gang is boomeranging back. One of the members of the old group is requesting a new trail and it looks like he is going to get it. His name is Wilson

Birdsong. And we think he may have restarted the Blue Dogs. At least that is what I can gather from the information left by my predecessor."

The name Wilson Birdsong did not set off any of my mental alarms. "Give me a few hours and I will call you so you can have a courier come get them."

"Second question. More recent history. Marlene DiGenova." The man must have been looking at a list of dumb and illegal things that happened even tangentially in my county and was finding the big incidents.

I let out a low whistle. "Marlene the Texas Terror? She grew up around here but did all her … projects down in Austin. She was a year behind me at high school. She went to the University of Texas on a full ride academic scholarship." DiGenova had been sexually assaulted at an off campus party and nearly killed. The Travis County District Attorney did not want to go to court with a 'he said – she said' case and dropped the matter. She got her revenge by luring a string of horny men to her apartment above a garage off Congress Street. Her modus operandi was to bring the men into her place, give them a drink laced with a muscle relaxant, and then 'neuter' the men before dumping what was left of their bodies in a chroming tank of the auto repair shop downstairs. The acid in the tank dissolved flesh and bone. She was only discovered when her landlord came to inspect the premises and found the collection of removed male genitalia in Mason Jars in the pantry.

"We have a theory that she was involved in a cold case. A storage unit in Plano was opened after a ten year lease expired and we … found items belonging to DiGenova. Does she still have family in your area? If so we'd really like to talk to her."

I said, "No, her parents moved to Montana after the news of her crimes made the news. She had an older brother who ironically was an urologist in Fresno and her grandmother was moved to an assisted living facility in Bridgeport a few years ago but I do not know if she is still there."

I could hear him scribbling notes with a heavy hand over the phone. Finally he asked, "Could you ask your grandfather to call me?"

I felt myself smile. "I will pass him your number. But he may not be quick to call back. He is retired and does things on his own sense of time these days. By the way, that was a bad move on your part to search Soto's home."

"Can you explain how Juan Soto just deposited twenty grand in his account at Wells Fargo? In cash? I want your answer in writing by close of business today." Owen hung up on me, leaving me to sulk. I called the bank and the assistant manager refused to bend any rules to give me the information I wanted but she did give me the number for her manager who would want a warrant for that information. I called Soto's hospital room and found him in a bad mood with his wife as they were getting to check out. He said the deposit was for two grand not twenty and was for a college fund for the baby from his grandmother. I apologized and told him that I would straighten out what I could with Owen. But I could tell he was not interested in what I was saying. Soto was not in the clear but the evidence would not be enough to stand up to a review by a decent judge or prosecutor. But Owen was playing dirty.

It turned out the deposit was for two grand but it took me nearly a day to get the warrant and then the information. I wondered if this is how a fish hooked through the lips feels when it is being reeled into shore.

Ben Mentzer was at his desk tapping a report into a computer with only his index fingers. He was the senior of two detectives I had and looked more like a serious accountant than a detective. I told him I needed to have the twenty or two grand deposited in the Soto account looked into as soon as possible and told him about Owen's pressuring me to deliver suitcases of money that we supposedly had. I then asked about the Blue Dogs.

"Blue Dogs? That's a name from the past. Making one bottle meth is a lot simpler than the new synthetics. The guy who was the cook for the Blue Dogs bought the farm not long after getting out of Huntsville." I watched as he opened a new window on his computer and pulled up the record on a John Wayne Scott. He laughed, "Ever notice guys with three first names are all assholes?"

We read the file on the late Mr. Scott had been diagnosed with stage three liver cancer about the same time as a parole hearing and the parole board, being conscious of taxpayer funding, decided it was easier to cut him loose than pay for his medical treatment. Scott was released to a half-way house and got a job in a restaurant as a dishwasher. Sadly he was crushed between a trash dumpster and a wall when a car bumped the dumpster while he was smoking behind the dumpster. That was four years previous.

I said, "Why am I looking at Mr. Scott's records?"

Mentzer smiled. "Because he was the brains of the Blue Dogs and when he died his followers scattered."

"What about Wilson Birdsong?"

He said, "Now that really is a blast from the past. I do happen to know right off the top of my head where you can find him. The medical unit at Huntsville Penitentiary. He mouthed off to one of the brothers and got his head banged off the concrete floor, snapping his neck. He is a quadriplegic but the system will not turn him loose. Evidently he is still keeping his finger in things, so to speak."

"Could that include restarting the Blue Dogs? Or would that name have enough recognition to attract customers? The Feds tell me he is looking for an appeal while still running things from behind bars."

Mentzer shrugged. "Maybe, by accident. He doesn't have the smarts that Scott did. And I doubt anyone old enough to recognize the gang name Blue Dogs would be a serious threat. It's not like a brand name that people would associate with a product." He then got a funny look on his face. "Can I ask you a personal question?"

Hesitantly I said, "Sure." I assumed he was trying to make a point but I had no idea where he was going with this vector of questions.

"When you were at the FBI, I assume that you pissed off your fair share of people, judging by the way you work today. But for the Feds to ream everyone who works for you to get at you shows an advanced level of upset that is well past their normal. So what are they really trying to drag out of you?"

I had no answer.

He continued. "You are in a no win situation. Let me check on something about that DB you found at the rest stop. And let me check on the Blue Dogs."

I got ready to leave when something else came back to me. "Have you ever heard of the Cross of Santa Cruz?"

He grinned. "Dolly Wood got to you too, eh?" He told me that he was having a historian at Southern Methodist University look into the lore of the cross.

—

Mentzer was right that I did seem to 'piss off' my fair share of folks when I was at the FBI. It started on the first day in the first class at the Academy. After getting a computer science degree with a criminal science minor I had applied and was surprised they actually wanted me as a computer geek. Five minutes into the first lecture, the instructor was telling us that witnesses are notoriously unreliable and a group of eyewitnesses often report contradictory details. I was sitting in the front row by the door (seats were assigned alphabetically) listening to the lecture when the door swung open and a man in a baggy black jacket and wearing a black baseball hat pulled low on his head walked into the room with a shiny chrome pistol in his right hand. As the hand rose, I was already out of the chair, heading towards the doorway, and quickly slammed into the gunman, mashing him into the doorframe. I performed a *kote gaeshi* wrist lock on the hand with the gun and used my hip to leverage the gunman off his feet, into the air, and then gravity did the rest, sending him to the floor with a heavy thump. I still had the wrist locked with my right hand, the gun in my left hand, and my foot on the throat of the gunman when the class instructor demanded that I stop.

The problem was that the 'gunman' was a senior FBI instructor who was supposed to rush into the room, fire four blanks, and then retreat out of the room. At that moment the instructor would have every student in the class write down exactly what they saw. Usually a class of fifty would hand in fifty different descriptions of the gunman with each differing in respect to the clothing, the number of shots, hair color, and height. Thus making the point that eyewitnesses are often mistaken, unreliable, and anything they say is to be taken with a grain of salt.

Instead, I had screwed up the demonstration and badly bruised a senior instructor. Some of my classmates started calling names like Ninja, Killer, and Psycho. Most of them just avoided me. The instructors all gave me funny looks. I decided to keep my head down, ears open, and mouth shut from that time forward.

That worked for about a month until we were in a self-defense class where another instructor, a buddy of the 'gunman', picked me out in class. "Attack me with a knife from the table." We were in a gym with wrestling mats and nearby was a table with a plastic Marine k-bar style knife. Shrugging I went over to the table and grabbed the fake knife with my left hand blade down and approached the instructor. He was smirking at me and he told me to make a serious attack. I raised my left hand and took a wide looping swipe with the pretend knife at half speed. The instructor dodged out of the way of my swing, avoiding the blade and he stepped directly into my other hand. He was wearing a polo shirt (with the FBI Academy logo embroidered on the breast) and I grabbed the collar and yanked him off balance as he stepped away from the pretend knife. As he stumbled, I moved in behind him, snaking my right hand under his chin and using my elbow on his chest and leveraging his chin backward with my forearm. My biceps and forearm made a perfect clamp over his carotid artery and it would have been easy to put him into a 'sleeper hold'. I then drew the plastic knife down inside the front of his polo shirt. The old adage about knife fights is that winners drip while losers hemorrhage and this guy was lucky this was only play fighting.

My classmates were impressed. The instructor much less so. He had me attack several times with his best results being him able to pivot away from me. His poorer results seemed to make him more frustrated. Finally he called an end to the class but asked me to stay behind.

"You think you're hot shit, McDavey, don't ya?" He waited until we were alone and the others were out of the gym. I could tell he was trying to gauge me and was not just out to take off some hide, as the old man would have said.

I said, "No, Sir."

"Where did you learn your skills?"

"My dad was a Marine -- Force Recon," I said hoping he would not dig further. My dad had me learning Judo, Jiu Jitsu, and Aikido as soon as I could toddle.

"Out in the field, that sort of crap you pulled today could get you or your partner killed." He puffed out his chest and I had to suppress the urge to ask how many knife fights he had had out in the fields. I knew he had never had someone come at him with a knife with serious intent to hurt him.

I wanted to say that if I needed to attack someone with a knife while in the field for the FBI then things were pretty desperate. I kept my mouth shut and then noticed a man built like a bull wander into the gym. He was wearing gym shorts and a t-shirt that were soaking wet and I assumed he had been running. Ben Ruggles had been the head of the FBI Hostage Rescue Team and had also been rumored to have a long history with anti-terrorism work. He walked up to me and looked at the plastic knife that was still in my hand. He gave me a lopsided grin, "Come at me hard."

"Sir?" I could tell he was serious and knew what he was doing.

"Are you fucking deaf as well as stupid," He barked. "I want you to really try to get me." That was a direct command and I knew I had to act.

I nodded, "Yes, sir." He took a wrestling stance with his feet spread, his arms akimbo, and leaning forward. His eyes watched the plastic knife carefully. I exhaled and gently lobbed the knife so that it landed flat on the mat between his feet. His eyes tracked the knife on its long arc and not me. He did not notice me step forward. I grabbed the front of his shirt and let my ass fall backwards. I put my right foot into his gut as I rolled and he catapulted over me. Our momentum carried us over and he landed on his back. I landed astride his middle with the tip of my elbow at his throat.

Ruggles started laughing. "That was slick," he said. He worked on knife defenses with me for the better part of an hour before he dismissed me. A week later I was leaving an evidence class when Ruggles took me by the arm and guided me to a quiet room. "If you are angling for a spot on the HRT, I am here to tell you that you are not going to get it by showing off to me."

"Yes, sir. I am not looking for a spot on the HRT, Sir."

He seemed disappointed that I was not angling for a spot on the Hostage Rescue Team, "So, is that what you really want?"

"Permission to speak freely, sir?" He nodded. "My grandfather is a county sheriff in Texas and my dad was a Marine. My dad wanted to take over as sheriff when he retired from the corps but he was killed in an accident. His dad was a Pacific Theatre and Korean War Marine before becoming the sheriff. His forebears were mostly law enforcement. I guess it is an inbred gene disorder. They all taught me that some people need to be sheep, some need to be shepherds, and too many others need to be wolves. I want to be a shepherd, metaphorically speaking. And they made sure I studied Aikido, Judo, Jiu Jitsu, Kendo, and Hojo Jitsu." I told him I was sharp with computers and wanted to work cyber security which seemed to surprise him.

He grinned, "Well, I am glad you do not want to be a wolf. I'll be keeping tabs on you, McDavey. So keep your nose clean." He actually shook my hand before he wandered away. I guess he passed the word about me as my instructors seemed to be less upset with me.

—

When I returned to Paragon after leaving the FBI, I was able to get a job with the sheriff's department. I was driving down a quiet residential street when a car jack rabbited away from the curb. I did not catch the license plate but I radioed that I was code three (lights and sirens) following a late model, black Chevy Corvette. I managed to read the license plate. The Ford Crown Victoria was no match in power or handling of the Corvette but I

159

hope local knowledge would aid me. "Car turning West onto Hickory and approaching Washington."

"Two-five, I will block Hickory at Jefferson," One of the other deputies replied. And up ahead at the last moment another Sheriff's department Crown Victoria blocked the street, bottling the Corvette. I slid to a stop behind the Corvette and got out of the car. The other deputy and I approached with hands on the butts of our pistols but with the pistols still in the holsters. If the driver did anything quirky we were both ready to draw our weapons.

But the driver, a white male aged about forty, smiled at us. He waved us over. I walked over to the driver's side window, ordering him in a loud voice to turn off the engine, and lower the window. He turned off the car, lowered the window a crack, and pushed out the ignition key. He laughed at me like a mad man as he rolled the window up. Then he held up a bottle of bourbon and took a deep pull. He burped and then drank some more.

I reached for the door handle and found the door locked. Picking up the key that he had dropped onto the street, I shoved it into the lock and opened the door. The driver looked surprised for a second and then he started laughing hysterically again. He was still laughing when I pulled him out, cuffed him, and put him in the back of my car.

"Are you going to try to get him for drunk driving?" The other deputy was grinning at me. He explained it was an old trick. I had seen the driver drive recklessly. But he stopped and turned off the car as ordered. We had no evidence that he was drunk driving and could argue any alcohol ingested was well after he was stopped.

"But we saw him drinking," I said.

"We saw him drink after we stopped him. We have no idea if he was driving while under the influence. That is up to a blood test for blood alcohol content and/or a field sobriety test." I was getting treated like a school kid on things he thought I should know about.

"Then why was he doing that?"

"What address did you first spot him at?"

"About one seventy Durango."

"See any other vehicles around there?" The other deputy said, "Moving van? Pickup truck?" I then realized that this jerk had tied up the only two patrol units on duty while his buddies stole everything not nailed down at the house where I had first spotted the Corvette.

"He is a decoy?" It turns out the driver was a decoy. His brother was going through a nasty divorce and the driver used the jack rabbiting car as a distraction to tie up the only two patrol units while others emptied the house of valuables. The other deputy watched me arrest the driver and then drove over to where I had spotted the car racing away from the curb. The house at 172 Durango had the front door open and everything worth taking was gone.

This was the first time I had been made a big fool of while wearing a deputy's uniform. And it was also my first run in with Larry 'Rocket' Hamilton. He laughed and smirked the entire time I was processing him into the jail. He was polite and asked for a lawyer. The breathalyzer test showed he was just under the legal limit. It took me two hours to do the reports and Hamilton was happily eating a meal in jail when I checked on him. He was released on his own recognizance and a two grand bond the next day. And four weeks later the judge would fine him five hundred bucks along with six hours of picking up trash on the side of the freeway.

His brother's soon to be ex-wife Kim and her lawyer asked to dispose of me in the traffic incident. The poor woman was destitute after having her hubby spend her money and a small inheritance she had received. The hubby was fighting the insurance company for the items taken from the house. The insurance policies were all in his name so she would get nothing. The lawyer was a friend of hers from college who was working pro bono. The one thing the wife wanted back was a mahogany box with her mom's cremated remains inside. That box was made by her father who had craved the name Abigail lovingly on the lid. Off the record the lawyer said the both the Hamilton brothers were scum.

Then the wife took me aside. "Ever see a white chalk mark on the side of the mailbox on Oak Street and Second? Big diagonal slash? Well, if you do that is a sign that the Hamilton's are holding. Meth, grass, pills, or whatever. Larry marks the mailbox before dawn and you would be surprised who drives up to his doublewide."

I said, "And you think they are going to be selling soon?"

"They took my stuff for some reason and the reason is always drugs with them," She said. "They probably had a big deal going down and I know they have another big deal almost ready to go." I passed the tip on to my superiors and two days later I got a call just before dawn. One of the deputies saw Rocket Hamilton marking the mailbox with chalk. Did I want in on the raid?

Thankfully it was a cold morning and we could hide our uniform shirts under winter jackets. We wore jeans instead of uniform pants. We rolled up in a battered crew cab pickup that had seen better days. I was worried Rocket would recognize me or one of the others but he was amped up on some of his own product. His face hung out the open door to his double wide with a suspicious look. Then he saw the cash in my hand and he opened the door.

The rundown trailer sat out in the middle of an open field and I could see no electrical lines into the place. They had a generator for when they wanted electricity but it was not running when we arrived. I guessed there was no running water and the possibility of an overloaded septic tank seemed rather high. Trash was strewn around what passed for the front yard. We knocked on a door that hung slack on old hinges. A voice called for us to enter. The interior of the trailer was dark and lit by two windows without curtains by the thin light of dawn. I kept my jacket collar up around my ears and a ball cap down on my head, thankful that it was hard to see inside. The place reeked of old beer, pot, and perspiration. It looked like it had been decorated with furniture found at the county landfill and the shag carpet had to be many decades old. On what passed for his dining room table was a smorgasbord of drugs. I held up a bag of pot and muttered it looked good when Rocket said it was the best shit ever. I asked, "You grow this shit yourself?"

"I got it off a friend over in Frisco who has a grow room the size of a barn," Rocket said. He seemed to wobble a little as if high or drunk. The advancements in antiperspirants seemed unknown from him from the stink that radiated off his body. Rocket wore grimy jeans and a t-shirt with food stains interspersed with holes.

One of the other deputies said, "He grew the crank his-self, too?" We laughed and the brothers joined in with us. One of the other deputies I could tell was counting up pills as if he was an accountant for a pharmaceutical company and I wished he was not so damned obvious about it.

Rocket laughed, "Nah. I know someone who knows someone." He wiped his nose with the back of his hand and told us he was the prime seller in the area. We told him we were from a fracking crew from Lubbock which seemed to please him. I said we need things to help us keep awake for long hours and then things to help us take the edge off when we were off shift. Both brothers really seemed to like the idea of new customers with fists full of cash. But they grew tense when one of the other deputies asked about the pills.

The other Hamilton brother said, "You fuckers are asking a lot of questions. Now buy or get the fuck out of here." He was sitting on an old recliner and was propping his feet up on a small wooden block. Nearby to him on a coffee table was a chrome plated Colt 1911 that looked to me like the other Hamilton could quickly grab it and start shooting. But as he stood up to act tough I noticed the top of the wooden block had the name Abigail carved in the top.

I said, "Sorry to be asking so many questions but these days there is so much bad shit out there and we work hard for our money." I walked over to the table and made a show of counting out a pile of fresh fifty dollar bills. Both Hamilton brothers flanked me and counted along the sides of me. What they did not notice was the other three deputies had moved in behind them. I turned my head on a swivel to look at both brothers, "So, what can I get for this much?"

Rocket said, "Some damn fine speed and grass to start." His brother giggled and then Rocket sealed the deal. "We just got a big shipment early this morning' and you boys are first in line."

And I said the code words for the deputies. "Today is my day." They grabbed the brothers and cuffed them. We had no sooner got them cuffed then another car drove up looking to buy. We packed the brothers back into a bedroom and arrested a fast food burger flipper with hot cash in hand for drugs.

As we were transporting the brothers, Rocket said that he would be out on the street in a few hours and that selling recreational drugs was a victimless crime that did not hurt anyone. I had great pleasure in telling him that receiving stolen property would be a least a twenty month trip to the gray bar hotel. When he asked me to explain, I told him about the box with Abigale engraved on the top being reported as stolen from his own sister-in-law's house. And that since it was in his trailer it would be considered as being in his possession. The look of shock on his face was something I wished I could share with his ex-wife.

One of the other deputies added that the insurance fraud would probably add yet another three to five years away. They were eerily quiet until he got them to jail receiving. Both brothers got belligerent and Rocket tried to head-butt me. Then Rocket snapped off a roundhouse kick that caught me high on the thigh, sending me into a wall. Rocket ended up on the bottom of a pile of deputies. The battery against me earned him an extra six months on top of a seven year trip to the state pen. His brother received twelve years. But both were dead within a year. Larry 'Rocket' Hamilton died when his cellmate slit his throat for calling him a punk ass bitch and the brother overdosed a few weeks later.

I traced down his ex-wife who was waitressing at a Waffle House to let her know about the demise of her former husband. She had asked me to keep her updated when I returned the box with her mother's ashes that was released from evidence. With exhausted eyes and pinched lips she told me that was the first good news she had heard in a long time. As I was leaving she said, "You know, they would have probably killed me if you did not chase that damned black 'vette that day. My former mother-in-law let me know that my darling hubby owed five large and would have had no qualms about wrapping me up in trash bags and burying God knows where before filing for life insurance.

"Who did he owe the money to?"

She took a deep breath and weighed the options available to her at that time. I guess she figured the odds were very long on my success and said, "Some accountant looking guy with a Hispanic name." That description fit a good percentage of the residents of Texas so I let that lead slip into the void.

Now years later I wonder if that accountant guy with the Hispanic name was the man we found dead in a car at a rest stop. What goes around, comes around. And often at the worst possible time.

Chapter 10

The next morning I found a car that was parked by the side of the road with a flat left rear tire. I was late heading to work when I spotted her. There was a blond woman in a billowing blue dress studying the flat tire when I pulled up. Her golden hair seemed to float on wafts of air. She held her skirt down to keep the wind from lifting her skirt in a mostly successful effort. That air also brought me a scent of vanilla and flowers to me. She smiled broadly at me as I got out of my patrol unit. I had been on my way to get something for lunch after not eating with the old man. I asked, "Do you have a spare tire?"

"It's a rental car so I'm not sure." Her voice was syrupy deep southern and her eyes had a twinkle. "A lot of cars do not come with spares anymore to save weight and increase mileage." I pulled two very heavy suitcases out of the trunk and found a spare tire. I grabbed the heavy duty jack and lug wrench out of my patrol unit and soon had the tire changed. As I put the flat and her luggage back in the trunk, she smiled at me warmly. There was a beauty mark side just above the left side of her ruby lips and arctic white teeth. "Thank you so much."

"Where are you heading?" I was wrestling with the lugs nuts on the flat tire and enjoying her company. Her perfume had my attention and her accent was very easy on my ears.

She glanced at her watch, "Well, I am supposed to be at Our Lady of Guadalupe in ten minutes. Wedding rehearsal." It was obvious that this was a woman who did not like being late.

I found myself grinning at her. There was an infectious joy about her. "It is only two miles up the road on the right. You'll make it with time to spare."

She climbed into the car and turned to face me. "Right now I think I'd rather stay here with you." She seemed nervous and gave me an awkward smile. I watched as she drove off wondering what the Hell she meant. Her perfume lingered in the breeze.

—

The Sheriff and other county departments had an archive and at one time had been a small private prison off the interstate. For a time the top corporate embezzlers, swindlers, and crooks lived a fairly austere life within the minimally secure fencing. The corporation that ran the prison went bankrupt after its chief financial officer absconded with the majority of their funds and the corporation owed the country a great deal of money. So the county board foreclosed. The county even made extra money leasing space to other counties and municipalities but not as a prison. Well reinforced walls, fences topped with razor wire, and lots of areas that can be locked make for a great storage facility. Hence the McDavey Country Archive.

The head archivist was a skeletal man with a shaved head named Benson Freeman. Freeman was born to be a fifth generation sharecropper before leaving McDavey Country to join the Navy. Then he worked for the Library of Congress for thirty five years before returning to the family home to care for his elderly parents. I guessed he was pushing seventy but he had the posture and physique of a much younger man. He had been retired for a while but he was too easily bored. So he looked around for a job at an age where most people were already on the shelf. Somehow he ended up at the country archive. It was obvious he enjoyed the work. He peered at me through his thick glasses and it felt like I was on the wrong end of a microscope. "The Blue Dogs?

When I was kid they sold pot and pills. That was way more than twenty seven years ago." Freeman typed a few keys on a computer and gave me an answer on what we had on the Blue Dogs. "Well, fifteen newspaper articles. Six trial transcripts and forty three evidence boxes. Did you know the name of the Blue Dog requesting a new trial?" He would have received requests for records for the attorneys involved with the case.

"No, but I can guess." He now had a tired, world worried air about him. Freeman smiled and said, "William 'Shorty' Feather has become quite a jailhouse lawyer and occasionally requests copies from here. It would not surprise me that he took a legal shot in the dark and found a target." I shook my head to let him know I had zero details on the case and then he said the name Wilson Birdsong. He watched me nod my head. "I went to school with his daddy. Grandma Birdsong wanted Wilson Senior away from the reservation where she felt there were bad influences and shipped him off to her brother Roy. Roy was a wizard with farm equipment and had Wilson working for him after school. Wilson the Elder picked up his uncle's touch with machinery. Plus he was the sharp one at school. When I was in the Navy I heard Roy had been killed, trapped between a stone fence and a tractor.   Then years later I saw Wilson

Junior in the news. He is, or was, the splitting image of

his old man. I followed the trail and his lawyer screaming

that drugs were one of the few options young men had on the

reservation for a middle class income."   Freeman was

probably a better resource than the archive he tended. His

local knowledge was invaluable and buttressed my own. He

too had heard that Wilson was a quad but doubted that would

keep him from trying to run a drug lab from several hundred

miles away. "Wilson was always a little too ambitious."

He made copies of everything available I asked for

while apologizing that the records were some of the last on

the list to be digitized.   He then went to work on my

second request. And this time the records had been

digitized but he still had the hard copies available.

"Rachel Lopes or Florez.   I spelled both last names and he

came up empty for any records.   However there was a case

file for Richard Lopes.   Freeman checked it out to me and I

read through a half inch case file twice.   A week before

Rachel and he disappeared, Richard was picked up for

questioning about a murder in Waco.   He was not a suspect

but he was a known former associate of Flaco Herdez, who

was a long time bad guy for hire along the border.   The

Waco PD had sent a couple of dozen photos of a hotel room where Herdez had executed a trio of low level drug dealers for not making their quota. Herdez had been identified by a hotel clerk and security camera footage when he rented the room. Later he was caught on another camera using a credit card belonging to the parents of one of the executed dealers. During the interview Richard admitted knowing Herdez many years before but insisted that he had no contact with the man in many years. He stated that Herdez was a 'bad dude' and that he tried to stay as far away from him as possible. The interviewer was my grandfather and without a copy of the recording it was hard to guess what his tone of voice was from the transcript but his choice of words told me neither of the two men in the interview men were happy.

The last sheet of the folder was Herdez's rap sheet. He had started a life of crime at an early age with shoplifting, selling grass, and petty theft in elementary school. His crimes escalated as he hit adolescence and he went to prison for a term of two to five for armed robbery when he was nineteen. He made a return trip ten years later for manslaughter but the conviction was vacated. There was no mention in the file for the vacated sentence.

I then dug into Herdez's files and read the transcript of a prior arrest for pistol whipping a drug courier. I had a picture of a punk kid in my mind but I did not know how old he was when the interview took place. I went back to the top of the rap sheet looking for a birth date and that is when I noted Verde's full name was Abel Domingo Herdez Flores. Was there a connection to Rachel? Father, brother, Cousin?

I have never been a big fan of coincidences. And I had a hunch that Abel Domingo Verde Herdez was Rachel's father and the man from whom Richard took her away from.

Maybe there were other records on his family members, especially Rachel. If she had a juvenile record it was probably sealed long ago, lost, or long ago recycled.

We made copies of all the records Owen had requested and I put them in my vehicle, fully intending to head straight back to the office. I found myself driving by Our Lady of Guadalupe. The rental car was parked there and the blond woman was talking on her cell phone as she leaned up against the driver's door. The dry breeze fluttered her skirt and provided a glimpse of some very long legs. I drove up so that my driver's window was opposite hers. "Everything okay?"

She smiled that dazzling smile. "Yes but I am on east coast time and was a little bit early." She glanced at her watch and said, "My fiancé said he and his family are running late." She made a shrugging motion.

"Who are you marrying?"

"Scott Fisher," she said and then proudly raised a rather small solitaire ring. "We met at a conference in Baltimore." The ring was smaller than I would have expected. Scott had gone through a string of very expensive cars, boats, and other toys. In comparison, the ring looked cheap to my memory of the other purchases. Something was not wringing true and I wondered what Scott was scheming.

"Congratulations," I said hoping my face would not betray my true emotions. Scott Fisher was frankly an idiot. I wanted to tell her that but I kept my mouth shut. His parents were both corporate lawyers and subsidized their poor parenting by buying Scott anything he needed or thought he needed, He was supposed to take over dad's law firm but could not pass an undergraduate English class or a bar with a good happy hour. Somehow he got a job with the state agriculture department that involved a lot of travel, minimal time behind a desk, and a state provided luxury SUV that may have been arranged by his very well connected family. He had a problem with driving under the influence, lot lizards from the local truck stop, and picking fights at bars with guys two or three times his size at a time when Fisher was well past the legal limit for blood alcohol content. This woman was too good for Scott Fisher and I was seriously debating telling her to get as far away from him as possible.

For a moment there was a flash of uncertainty on her face. She must of sense I was less than impressed with her intended choice for a husband. "I'm Jane Morris." She stuck out her hand for me to shake. Her grip was firm but her skin was cold.

"Will McDavey," I said. "When does your family show up for the wedding?"

"Tomorrow and Saturday is the big day. Did Scotty invite you?" She seemed so excited and so happy but seemed totally oblivious to the fact that she was about to marry a jerk. But was it my place to tell her the truth about her intended.

I shook my head. "We're not exactly buddies." I dealt with enough assholes at work to be on good terms with them on my limited time off. So there was a lack of being disturbed by a lack of a wedding invitation address to me. And if 'Scotty' had invited me I would probably have ignored it.

"Would you come for me? If I gave you an invitation?" She smiled again and said, "Please?" Something inside me wanted to help her.

Her perfume caught my nostrils and it felt like I was being enchanted. She had a beguiling charm that was working on me. "Well, since you said 'please'. I will try but I may get called into work. We're shorthanded. If I am not there it is because I have to work." She handed me an engraved invitation and I handed her a business card. "Any problems, please call." I drove off reluctantly.

Over the radio came a request for backup and I quickly responded. Deputy Sixto Ruiz had pulled over a twenty four foot moving van that had rolled through a stop sign. The driver had pulled over and then bolted. As Ruiz checked the cab of the truck he could hear a person or persons unknown yelling from the shuttered back of the vehicle. The truck itself was ancient as was the padlock holding the rolling door shut.

I asked, "Human smugglers?"

Six nodded, "Yes, I think, but they are not speaking Spanish." After pulling a set of bolt cutters from my patrol unit, I walked to the back to the vehicle and asked Six if he was ready. "As ready as I'm going to be," He said with a smile. We had no idea of who was in the truck and their level of belligerence. The hasp of the lock cleanly broke under the pressure of the bolt cutter jaws and I pocketed the lock. I flipped the latch that kept the rolling door shut, took a deep breath, and raised the door.

The stench hit me first. Thirty one people had been locked in the back of the truck for days. There were two five gallon buckets from the Home Depot for toilets and a flat of bottled water that was all empty for the poor folks locked in the container. I had no way to guess how long they had been locked inside. Haunted eyes looked back at me with looks of regret, resignation, and fear. I was lucky that two other patrol units arrived at the time along with an ambulance. The people inside were too scared, hungry, and tired to try and escape. Eighteen women, ten men, and three infants had travelled the back roads from El Paso with two flats of water and a five gallon plastic bucket for a toilet

A young man covered in filth with sunken cheeks began to speak rapidly with his hands raised over his head, pleading for his life. It took me a minute to realize he was speaking Mandarin. He spoke very quickly and I could not understand him, not that my Chinese was anywhere near being proficient.

I said, "Méiguānxì" It is okay. I had learned some simple phrases years ago for situations like this. I turned to Six, "Call the Border Patrol for help. Call Child Protective Services for the infants, and get someone to grab some fruit and water from the grocery store. And get someone to make sure the women are not part of some sex trafficking ring. But first some water and food." I handed him sixty dollars from my wallet for the groceries. "Then we need a translator or two."

"I speak English," A middle aged man said as he peeked out of the truck. He appeared from inside the van and looked resigned to a bad fate. His face was full of defeat, shame, and exhaustion. His clothes were beyond wrinkled and his horned rimmed glasses were askew.

I asked, "Is anyone sick or injured?"

"Exhausted, dehydrated, and … frustrated." He watched the paramedic approach with suspicious eyes. One of my deputies had grabbed some bottles of water from his patrol unit and was handing them to the folks in the truck. One of the babies started to cry with their mother softly shushing it. "May I get out? To stretch?" I and a paramedic helped him down. The man was wobbly and seemed as if he was going to collapse. He nodded to me, "Thank you for ordering the food and water."

Over the next hour we found out the people in the van were from an extended family who had paid smugglers a large fee and were still on the hook for more. Relatives back in China would be harassed or worse if they smuggled laborers did not make regular payments. Being caught and shipped home was no excuse for missing payments. The man said his name was Ma and he admitted that he had been sent back once already and owed sixty grand before interest. He said with a sad smile, "Not my first rodeo." He told me he had worked in Dallas for a decade before returning to China for his mother's funeral two years before. He had to save up money to get smuggled back into Texas.

The twenty four foot van was from Tyler and had been sold a month before. The truck had not been re-registered but the former owner had records on the sale. The buyer of record was a produce company in San Angelo that did not answer the phone. I was pretty sure the driver had gone to ground but would be impossible to find. I was able to borrow a school bus to transport the Chinese to the old armory that doubled as a shelter. I was tempted to use the bus we used to transport prisoners from jail to court and back but I did not want to panic the passengers with a dull gray bus with bars on the windows and rings for shackles set into the floor. Ma and the folks gratefully ate the fruit and drank the water we got for them and all seemed to be reviving.

A Border Patrol official called to say they were unable to take over the passengers for the truck for at least an hour, or so. Six and two others agreed to stay with them. I reluctantly walked to my Yukon, kicking up the dry dust with my feet. My deputies were more than capable of handling the situation and I left them to their task.

Back in my office, I had a series of emails and phone calls to answer and soon it was past six o'clock. The arrangements to get the copies Benson Freeman had made for Owen to be shuttled to Owen's office. I made a quick tour around the station and was happy that all was in its place. Sixto had returned and let me know the CBP had taken the Chinese off his hands. My last stop was the lockup. For some reason I decided that I had not been to our jail for a while and decided to drop by to see what was going on there. One of my deputies was locking up a pair of young female shoplifters who had been caught red handed. Both were crying and boo-hooing. Both had prior arrests for shoplifting in Dallas, Plano, and Arlington. And both were demanding their parents and lawyers. They had tried to swipe some cheap costume jewelry from a local boutique. One was named Lexus and the other Amanda but I could not tell them apart as they both wore too much eye makeup and the same cherubic family face of the Fisher family. Lexus wore a revealing blouse much too old for her and Amanda was braless under a t-shirt with 'high beams on'. Their complaints got under my skin. I said to them, "Sorry but you are here overnight. The judge takes the bench for arraignments tomorrow at nine. I can call your parents and tell them where you are."

Lexus spat, "Fuck you, asshole!" She wore expensive clothes that were made for an older young woman and what she wore made her look cheap. Her makeup was plastered on her face thickly. She looked like someone looking for something to rebel against and not having a whole lot of success. Under the 'war paint' I could see a frightened and angry kid. After a half-hearted effort to impress the deputy and myself with her boobs she began to pout. "Go ahead - call my parents!"

The other said, "Like they give a flip." Her makeup was a little neater but her jeans had more holes than material and her top seemed to have been ironed by a lawnmower. She pulled off the angry youth look a little better than her companion but it still came off poorly.

"You probably have enough cash in your purses to make bail, if the judge sets it on the low end," The deputy said. "Which makes me wonder why y'all just didn't pay for the merchandise instead of going for the five finger discount."

The two young women just looked back at us. They were now as bored as they could be and seemed to be willing to keep quiet and just wait for their court appearance. Or maybe they knew they had already been read their rights and their explanation of the theft would be used against them in court.

I forced a smile, "Must be busy with the big wedding on Saturday." Both looked confused for a second and then told me to screw myself. "Or not," I said. "Someone told me Scott was getting married this weekend."

I think it was Lexus who said, "Why buy a cow when you can get one to blow you anytime you want? Brittany Lewis has her lips wrapped around his dick at least twice a day, or that scrawny worm that he calls his dick." The other young woman screamed with laughter. Away from the young women I told the deputy to wait half an hour and call the parents.

The deputy shrugged, "I fear the apples have not fallen far from a rotten tree. Did you see the mom's name on the rap sheet?" He handed over the papers on one of the girls and there was the name of Jennifer Fisher-Mocher. Scott Fisher's sister. Jennifer the previous year had gotten into a fist fight with a waitress who had cut her booze off and without realizing the waitress was a Nidan in Aikido. Mrs. Fisher-Mocher attempted to slap the waitress and ended up with his arm pinned behind her back with her face planted on the floor. Jennifer then spat on the arresting deputies before she voided both her stomach and bladder in the backseat of a cruiser while telling anyone in earshot how she was 'going to sue the shit out of everyone'. In court she cried that the entire world was against her and the judge greatly reduced her sentence. On the way out she called the arresting deputy a cock sucker while a television station was recording an interview with him. My deputies were not fans of Jennifer Fisher-Mocher.

"Ouch." I forced a smile as I handed the papers back and said, "Well, at least we will be graced with a visit from Westmoreland Heart, a Legal Corporation tomorrow. So double check your report before you file it tonight. No typos or anything to give him leverage in court. Anything odd about the arrest that I should know about?"

"No, sir." The deputy said quickly. "The shop owner saw the girls swiping costume jewelry into a Victoria's Secret bag and had her assistant block the door before calling us. I arrived, asked the girls, er, young ladies if they had stuff they had forgotten to pay for and they said 'no'. I asked the see into the bag, they called me a pervert just wanting to see their undies, and the taller one kicked me in the shin. I cuffed them both and then peeked into the bag. The shop owner identified the items and went to get me a copy of the security video." He then tapped his body camera and smiled. "I've uploaded my body cam footage already." He was ready for anything the Fisher family or lawyer Heart could toss at him. Sometimes we got lucky and had all of our ducks in the proverbial row.

I said, "Document everything including the bruise on your shin, if you have one. I'll ask the DA's office to make sure to add assault on a law enforcement officer to the charge sheet. I am taking the night off for once." I went back to my office and made the call to the DA's voice mail. My private cell phone rang and I answered.

"Hi. This is Jane Morris. You helped me with a flat tire earlier today." She sounded cheerful and happy over the phone. My mind remembered the scent of her perfume.

I said, "I remember. How are you doing?"

She signed, "Find. My future in-laws arrived late and in a bad mood. But the church is very beautiful and I see why Scott's parents want us to get married there. But enough about that. I want to thank you for changing that flat tire. Can I pay you back by buying you dinner, if you haven't eaten already?" She sounded a little coy. "I hope you do not have plans already."

"No, I was just leaving my office and was going to grab something." My stomach seemed to say to me 'Oh, now you remember me?' and I decided it was time for some food.

"Is the Mexican place by the courthouse any good?"

"Toro Grande? Some of the best food in the county. Give me fifteen minutes to change out of uniform and I will meet you there." Did she know her fiancé was getting regularly serviced by Brittany Lewis? I asked myself 'why did I care?' Because she was engaged to a sphincter of great dimension and I wanted to warn her or hurt him? But sometimes you only realize just how lonely you are at just the wrong time.

"See you then," she said before disconnecting. I wondered why she really was not dining with her fiancé and or his family. Where was Scott Fisher? Was Scott off with Brittany? I hurried to the locker room, pulled off my uniform, took a quick shower, and dressed quickly. I wore Wranglers, a snap button shirt, and old but well-polished boots. Before I left I called the county DA's office and left a message on the head prosecutor's voicemail asking for a call back.

A voice from the other side of the locker room spoke up, "You play with fire, McDavey, and you'll get your fingers burned." Aaron Watson was the country constable and had use of the locker room due to the proximity to the courthouse. He had played baseball professionally as a sinker and curveball pitcher for a handful of teams until he retired a dozen years before. He was putting on a fresh uniform shirt as he came around the corner. "She's got a meeting tonight with the State Attorney General's people. I will admit she was a lot easier to deal with when she was banging you on a regular basis and that bastard husband of hers was off having his mid-life crisis. She has been a pain in the ass since you two split up. Hell, she even let that evil little twerp move back into her house. She has had me running ragged serving paper all over Hell and back.

"How are you doing? I have not seen you for a while"

He laughed. "I told you she has been running me ragged. With some many farmers and ranchers going belly up due to the drought I am handing out bankruptcy and tax notices like crazy." He paused and looked at me carefully. "I've been hearing shit about you. I want you to know I do not believe it. Fuckin' Freebies asking me if I had seen you walking around with big black suitcases and implying they would help me if I helped them. I did not take them up on their offer. But I know others will so you'd better watch your back."

I thanked him and he told me to enjoy my night off work. I hurried out a side door, cut across the courthouse square, and crossed the street. Julie Morris arrived from the other direction which meant she was probably staying at the bed and breakfast run by the Townsend family. Morris was wearing a dark red sundress with spaghetti straps, strappy heels, and her hair piled high on her head to reveal an elegant neck. "You look marvelous," I said, surprising myself when I heard myself speak those words.

She grinned, "I was quite the mess earlier. Shall we go in?" We were seated in a booth in a back corner in the modestly busy restaurant. She quickly ordered a pair of margaritas before asking if I had to go back on duty.

"No, I am off for the evening and out of uniform. A margarita would be a wonderful thing," I said and the waitress quickly sashayed away. "Thanks for the invitation for dinner."

"Well, thank you for coming to my rescue today." Our drinks arrived and we both took long, appreciative sips. "I bet you're wondering where Scott is?" I nodded but kept my mouth shut. "We had a fight. The fight was about you."

"Me?" I was pretty sure I was not anywhere near being on his top ten friend list but did not think he would go off the deep end over me. Over changing a car tire? I assumed that he despised me as much as I despised him but getting upset over someone changing a flat tire was ridiculous. My gut hunch told me there was something deeper

going on here. And it seemed like a good time to keep my
answers short and my ears open.

"Yes, it appears that you are a sore spot with him. I
told him about the flat tire and you helped me. He was very
upset that I had not called him and I reminded him that I
had called him and got his voicemail. He went ballistic.
And then his best friend took him off for a bachelor
party," She said, "You're the only other person I know
around here and I hate eating alone." The waitress
appeared again, we ordered, and then when left alone Morris
said, "I must sound like I am looney tune or something."

"No. Perfectly understandable." I wondered if I
should inform her to get a medical checkup on her future
hubby to make sure Brittany Lewis had not provided an
unwanted venereal wedding present. Then I would have to
tell her why I suspected he needed to be checked and we
would both be down the rabbit hole. It was time to bite my
lip.

"I'm staying at a B&B but the owners are going to a
concert in Fort Worth and are staying at a hotel down
there. They said they would be back after lunch tomorrow."
She said the owners were old friends of the Fisher family

and were glad to see her but were not giving up their tickets for the concert.

I nodded. "Rachmaninoff and Musskorgy." My mother had been a fan of classical music and tried to expose me to more than Southern Rock, Hank Williams, and Texas blues.

A look of amazement flushed across her face. "I am impressed that you know that."

I did not tell her that one of the department secretaries was also a bartender at the theatre and had hung posters in the breakroom. "I felt so alone and with Scott gone and my hosts gone. But then I remembered you." She paused to take another sip and to change the subject slightly. "So, Scott told me that he had a problem with drinking and driving in his past but that it was well behind him. And he told me that his dad and your grandfather had some sort of fight. So your family and his family are not exactly warm and cuddly with each other. So what was that fight about?"

She paused and I could tell she was leading me as a witness very skillfully. "Not much of a fight. My grandfather was the sheriff many years ago and found Ben Fisher had crashed his car into a fire hydrant. Scott's dad was young and on a bender. Imagine hundreds of gallons of water shooting into the air and your future father in the law trying to recreate Gene Kelly's *Singing in the Rain* routine. Ben tried to sucker punch my grandfather to get away and got his head broken in response." Our food arrived and we ate in silence for a while. "My grandpa told me that sometimes being a deputy is often like being a babysitter in a daycare. Some kids are good, some are cranky, some test the limits all the time, and others have a bad streak. Scott and his dad were or are limit testers. And one of your fiancé's nieces were arrested today for shoplifting and will be in the lock up overnight."

Morris laughed. "You're kidding, right?" The look on her face was equal parts shock and humor. She started to laugh. Then she realized that I was being serious.

I sighed. "Sadly no." We were quiet for several moments as the awkwardness built between us.

"Are you married? I saw no ring on your finger and I just assumed your status." Her question threw me off track. She had a rather seductive smile on her face. The woman was attractive and interested in me. Or was she being polite? And I could hear an echo of the old man's voice adding 'She has already demonstrated a poor choice in men with Scott Fischer so why not you too'.

I shook my head. "I came close once."

"How close?" There was something about her that made me want to share me with her.

"When it came time to set a date she kept postponing. Neither of us wanted a big wedding. I suggested we get married on a trip to Mexico or Jamaica or Hawaii. She balked.   We were both FBI Agents and I was assigned an undercover case and had to disappear for a while. I warned her I could be out of reach for a while and she shrugged it off, said she understood. When I got back five weeks later, the engagement ring was on the kitchen table with a note that said 'sorry but no'. She had transferred to an assignment at an embassy in Japan."

"Do you ever hear from her or about her?" There was a level of concern in her voice that seemed genuine.

"No, I left the FBI a few months later which cut me off from most of the gossip grapevine. But I did hear third hand that she is happily married with a set of twins. And I honestly wish her the best."

She gave me an engaging smile and I felt like a cheap piece of metal around a magnet. "I was engaged to another guy when I was very young, my parents and his parents objected. We were only six but we both liked peanut butter and jelly sandwiches, Batman, and especially kittens. I ran into him a few years ago at an airport with his wife and seven kids. All boys and they all looked like dad. I felt like I had dodged a bullet. Oh, I probably should not say that to you," She said. "I had a long dry spell after him."

"No problem. So why are you getting married here?"

"His family is pretty large and they all wanted it here. My family is small and mobile – just mom and my brother. We are, or were, thinking of settling here after I finish my residency next year. I want to be a general practitioner." She took a sip of her drink, "We'll have a small party for my friends and co-workers back home sometime later."

"County general needs all the professional staff they can get," I said. "My grandfather's wife is on the board there. She used to be a surgeon in Boston."

"Willow Montgomery?"

I smiled and nodded. "Yes, that's her."

"I talked to her last week on the phone, Scott's mom set it up." I told her Willow was a good friend to have on her side and asked her other innocuous questions about the wedding (mostly planned by the mother of the groom), the honeymoon (a surprise that was set up by the groom and funded by the mother of the groom but a complete mystery to her however she thought it might be somewhere like Aruba or Cozumel judging by the packing list), and other chit-chat. She seemed a little too interested in my life and I had to keep redirecting the conversation but she always managed to turn the topic back to me. "Can I ask you a question? Is following in your grandfather's footsteps to become a sheriff a Texas thing, a family thing, or what?"

"A pure accident. Long story short is I came home from my time with the FBI pretty banged up and two thugs had tried to ambush the old man. His department was shorthanded and I pitched in as best I could. The doctors said the old man had to retire, his new wife wanted him off the job, and he surprised everyone by actually retiring. The new sheriff was incompetent. He was asked to leave after doing too many favors for too many people. The county board asked me to run for election a bit over a year ago. I won, somehow." It did not mention that nobody else ran for the job, or that other potential candidates told me that they saw the job as hopeless, and that is almost impossible to lose an uncontested election.

"Banged up? What do you mean?" There was something so earnest, so friendly about here that she was beguiling. It would be so easy to be with her.

I pointed to my sternum. "When they hand you your body armor and tell you that it will stop most bullets they do not tell you that a nine millimeter slug is travelling a few hundred miles an hour when it slams into your body. Ribs break, muscles bruise, and so forth." I pushed my dinner plate away, "Well, I was shot, returned fire, and killed the guy who shot me. The only trouble is that the dead man ended up being law enforcement. Long story short was there was a lot of politics, the review board cleared me but dead man's friends wanted a pound of flesh and it was evident my career at the FBI was really over. They sent me to a review board and had enough political clout to put me deep in the shit. They lost and I was medically retired as a way to avoid embarrassment and future confrontations."

And they had thought it was a way to keep me out of their hair forever.

She had finished her meal and the waitress dropped off the bill. Morris paid, insisting over my objections that I should pay, and asked what was there to do in Paragon for fun.

"Do you dance?" She looked surprised but agreed to go with me. We headed down the street to 'KO Corral' where a local band was just taking the stage. She looked a little nervous and said she did not know any country dances. "Relax." After coaching her through a pair of two-step songs before she excused herself to use the restroom. Too much booze she had joked. I actually felt relaxed for the first time in a long time and realized the funny feeling on my face was a smile. When she returned the band was starting a waltz. I took Morris in my arms and counted out one-two-three and after a few moments she relaxed, smiled, and looked genuinely happy. We moved across the surprisingly full dance floor in a rhythmic swirl. The smile on her face was mesmerizing.

She seemed really happy and felt really good in my arms. She gave me a very seductive smile. "This is nice. Do you usually dance after work?"

"That is practically all we do around her. It's like a musical and frankly it can cause traffic pattern problems on the streets," I said. "But, no. It's been a while since I have gone dancing."

She said, "So what do you normally do after work?"

"Soak in my hot tub."

She smiled at me, "That sounds good to me. Let's go!"

At that moment both my cell phones rang. I answered the work phone. Janet said, "Some a-holes from the Federal DA's office jumped over the locked gate at Lily's place. Sparkle and Cuddles were there and chased them off the land. One of the Feds got an M4 rifle out of their vehicle and took shots at the two bulls. Lilly and Vincent arrested them and then the FBI sent a second team." There was a pause, "Lilly wants the balls off the guy with the rifle and I am tempted to let her borrow my Buck knife. You might want to talk to Lily. She's at her place with the vet. And there are about fifteen FBI idiots there too."

My private phone had a text message that simply said, "Do u have my sparkly earrings?" But at the same time a call came through that I decided to ignore.

I looked at Morris and said that I would have to give her a raincheck. On the way back to the office to get my patrol unit, I looked at my personal cell phone and saw the simultaneous call was from a Fort Worth number I did not know and there was no voicemail left by the caller. In hindsight, I should have called back and it would have saved a lot of grief.

Sparkle and Cuddles were a pair of former rodeo bulls that were roughly the size of medium size pickup trucks and each had notoriously bad humors. In the fading daylight they looked angry and enormous. I pulled up and found the two bulls pawing at the ground eyeing a small contingent of people in windbreakers with the FBI stenciled on the back. None had been with Ayce at the Soto house and both looked as upset as the bulls. Nylon windbreakers in the Texas heat are like wearing a sauna. One of the local vets was there trying to explain to one of the FBI agents that trying to shoot a bull with a .223 round was not only to be ineffective but she would testify it was animal abuse. Cuddles look like he had a scratch on his shoulder and the vet said it looked like the round had grazed the animal. Cuddles were a lot calmer than I expected. Lilly was behind the FBI agents sitting on the ground with her hands cuffed behind her. Deputy Vincent Peralta was arguing with one of the windbreakers wearing FBI agents about something but went silent as I walked up to the group. Lilly spotted me and the frown on her face flowed into a vicious smile.

An officious little man shot the cuffs of his FBI windbreaker and sneered at me, "Are you Sheriff McDavey?"

"I am."

"We have a warrant to search the house," he said. "But we cannot get past the bulls and your deputy refuses to … put them away."

"Can I see the warrant?"

"It is on the way."

"Not good enough. No warrant present means there may not be a warrant and you are just trying to bluster your way in for an illegal search. By the way, you will take the cuffs off of my deputy immediately or I will notify your professional responsibility office about this situation and they will have their noses so far up your ass you will never need to ever worry about having a colonoscopy. Do you understand me?" One of the FBI agents immediately pulled out his handcuff keys without having the officious man prompt him. "And who took the shots at the animals?"

The little man puffed out his chest and said proudly, "I did."

"I will be reporting you to Professional Responsibility for poor judgement and downrange bullet management. There is a daycare center a hundred yards away from here." I handed him one of my business cars, "Have your SAIC call me before COB today or I will skip regional PR and call DC. You copy me, agent?"

There was a glow of anger in his eyes and I could tell he was worried about having me report him to Professional Responsibility and his Special Agent in Charge by the close of business. He knew he had screwed up but he was not sure how badly. He had tried to bluff his way with no search warrant and mismanaged the situation. And he knew that I knew he was wrong to the point he had no defense.

I walked over to Lilly and motioned for her to stay seated. I looked at her mouthing words 'keep your mouth

shut' as I looked at her before saying aloud, "Is it okay
if I put your pets into your barn?" She nodded and I
looked back at the agent nearby. "Okay to put her bulls
away?"

He nodded, "Sure." I started walking back to my Yukon.
"Where the Hell are you going, sheriff?" I opened the back
of my patrol unit and returned with a metal bucket. "Why do
you have a bucket?" The agent suddenly looked to be about
twelve years old and was obviously not used to farm
animals. His eyes went from my face to the bucket and back
several times.

Lilly laughed. "City boy." I shushed her but the
smirk on her face remained. She knew what I was going to do
and gave me a wink.

I climbed the fence and the two bulls eyed me
suspiciously. At any moment either one, the other, or both
of the half ton animals could charge and turn me into
ground round. But I held the bucket so that they could see
it and I made sure it had their attention. The bucket was
kept in front of me as I walked up to the two bulls who
looked much, much larger up close. I stopped about twenty
feet away and then slowly put the bucket down. The two

bulls eyed me and one of them took a step towards the bucket. I picked up the bucket and walked slowly across the pasture to a closed gate. I opened the gate, leaving it open and crossed into another field while making sure I kept the bucket in the view of the two bulls. The doors to Lilly's stock pen were open and I walked in with the two bulls behind me. We entered a pen and the bulls were still eyeing the bucket hoping for a treat. I made a quick but wide turn and was back at the pen gate before the bulls could react. It took me a moment to close the gate and secure it. There was some hay nearby and I dropped some in the pen so the two bulls could have a snack.

When I got back to the front pasture, Lilly had a piece of paper in her hand that she was reading. The search warrant had arrived and they had given it to her. Soon the FBI Agents were swarming her house. She looked at me, "Thank you for the suggestion of putting my bulls in the front pasture."

"Did it work?"

She sighed, "I think we bought her enough time. I am pretty sure she got away." Lilly had someone staying with her who was not supposed to be around and she had told me before I was elected sheriff. The person in question was between a rock and a hard spot. I had agreed to keep Lilly's confidence as best I could.

It took the FBI until nearly midnight to finish searching the house. The vet checked the two bulls and pronounced them healthy. As the FBI drove away, Lilly tried to thank me. I shook my head and said, "Don't thank me yet. And I may need to borrow your bulls for my place."

Chapter 11

I had just started the engine in my patrol Yukon in an attempt to leave Lily's place when the radio squawked, "All units. Code three to fifty-one-oh-one Commerce. Officer down." Commerce was two miles away and I was the third unit to respond. The paramedics arrived just after me. A small child had darted out from between parked cars and had smacked into a car stopped at a traffic light. Luckily it was a glancing blow but the kinetic energy was enough to bounce the tot into the side of an old Oldsmobile parked at the curb. The kid was whimpering and held his right arm in a way that suggested his collar bone was broken. His mother cradled him, cooing reassurances. Deputy Sheriff Lyle Cousins held a bloody bandage to his own forehead. In the back of his patrol unit was a serious upset man who kept screaming about kicking everyone's ass.

Nearby Rasheed Ali was leaning over his car. The kid had put a dent in the side of the car but there was no significant damage. But Ali looked devastated. "I only saw him in the corner of my eye as he darted out from between the cars. It sounded like he slammed the car pretty good."

"How fast were you going?" I was watching his eyes and he showed no signs of intoxication. He said he had been stopped at the light, heard a man yelling, and then the kid flew out from between parked cars before smacking into his car. That seemed to match the evidence and a pair of witnesses backed up his story. Ali was a quiet man who ran an accounting and bookkeeping service. I had met him a few times at community functions but did not know him well.

The paramedics had the kid on a stretcher and were preparing him for transport to the hospital. The mother was a mess. She gave me a sorrowful look, "I just put him down for a second and he dashed between the cars into traffic. Thank God the car was stopped at the traffic light." I was glad to hear that the mother acknowledged that the car the kid ran into was not in motion. The potential for a nasty he-said-she-said courtroom battle was approaching zero.

"He'll be fine," I said. The kid had some abrasions, a bloody nose, and an arm in an air cast. Kids were very resilient and I had seen worse injuries at little league baseball games.

"I don't have insurance." She closed her eyes and tears poured down her cheeks. Her body was emaciated and her clothes had seen better days. My first guess was that she was a recovering meth head, or at least trying to recover. The kid looked healthy enough with the broken wing withstanding.

I asked if the man in the back of Cousin's vehicle was her husband and she said he was her ex-boyfriend. He had confronted her on the sidewalk while she was carrying the kid to her car. Her son did not like ex, squirmed to get down, and then darted between the cars. She was evasive about his being abusive to her or the child and I guessed a check of the files would probably pull up half a dozen domestic disturbance complaints. She again said she had no money for medical treatment.

"The County hospital treats everyone regardless." I handed her one of my business cards and told her to have them call me if they had questions. The county was hurting for money but a hurt kid's treatment would cost less than the rounding error on the account ledger.

"How am I going to pay for it? And the dent in the car?" She climbed into the paramedics van after her kid.

As the ambulance drove away, Jimmy Walker said he wanted to speak to me privately. He had been part of a small crowd watching the proceedings. Walker had been with the Texas Department of Public Safety for many years and had retired the previous spring.

"What's up?" I asked. We had walked over to a shuttered store front for privacy.

"I know the mom. I arrested her a few years ago for solicitation. Her last name is Robinson. Her pimp was Shiny G." Edison 'Shiny' Garfunkel was a well-known pimp specializing in underage runaways of any gender who had been found a few months before with a carving knife inserted under his sternum. He mainly worked Dallas but recruited the young and dumb fairly widely. "Run her priors and tell Fort Worth Homicide that one of Shiny's girls has appeared. I know they have paper out on her for witnessing an armed robbery. They may want to talk to her." He nodded and he took a deep breath. "There is more to this tale, sadly. She's my niece." He looked me squarely in the eyes.

I felt like I had been hit in the gut with a well swung sledge hammer. "What do you want to do?"

"I will call my sister and her husband. They will probably want a visit with her. She disappeared about three, four years ago. Without a word." There was pain in his eyes. "I did not recognize her until I heard her voice. Never knew she had a kid. Can you get someone to the ER to watch her? Maybe offer to put her up in holding?"

"I am sorry Jimmy. We'll treat her like family. And if you need anything else, get on the phone to me." I walked back to my Yukon. Morris was standing by the Yukon looking unsettled.

"Are they going to be okay?" She was genuinely concerned.

"Yes," I lied. Physically they would be fine. But his mom was a potential ticking time bomb and I should be on the phone to Child Protective Services to express a concern about his welfare. I looked over at Morris, "I need another drink. Thank goodness I am technically off duty."

Lyle said he would take the man who assaulted him to the lockup and do the paperwork. I told him to call for another unit to do the transport and get to the hospital to check on the mom after telling him what Walker had told me about his niece. I also ordered him to get checked out by the doctors too. He said he was fine and would swing by the ER after putting the arrest in the computer. He had been eating a salad at a nearby restaurant when he heard the scream as the kid ran into traffic and found the screaming man. Threatening the mother. Cousins told the man to calm down when the man took a swing. The man had on a large ring which cut Cousins as it glanced off his forehead. Cousins Tasered the man and then put him in handcuffs. A second office arrived and took statements. I arrived right after that. I thanked Cousins and told him to take care of himself.

Ali was sitting in his car with his face in his hands. I peeked in at him, "How are you?"

"Not okay. I keep imagining that I ran over that poor child." There were tears in his eyes. I told him sometimes it is better to be lucky than be good. He refused my offer to follow him home before he slowly drove off down the road.

And then I turned to Morris and wondered how the Hell she followed me.

—

The Rest Haven Grill was an old funeral home turned bar and grill with the emphasis not on the grill. There had not been a lot of redecorating done when it went from being a funeral home to a restaurant. It was only a few minute drive away and we were both quiet during the trip. The bartender was a rheumy eyed woman named Janice who quickly put a pair of ice cold Pacifico beers in front of us. "The biggest problem with my job is that you end up like a lifeguard at a crowded beach where too many potential drowning victims are playing in the surf among sharks, stingrays, and jelly fish. That kid is going to have a rough life. His mom has had a rough life. And in fifteen or twenty years it will all cycle over again."

"And you feel responsible for all of them?" She took a long pull on her beer. "I wanted to be a doctor because a friend of mine had cerebral palsy. I thought I could fix her. I needed to fix her. One day it was too much for her and she overdosed on some pills. And some part of me still feels responsible." She finished her beer and said, "You mentioned something about a hot tub?"

We drove in my patrol SUV to my place in silence. After I parked, she climbed out and walked over to the hot tub. I pried off the lid and turned on the jets. She unbuttoned her dress, slid the spaghetti straps off her shoulders, and dropped the wispy fabric to the ground. Off came her shoes. She then hooked her thumbs inside her panties and slid them down. She climbed into the hot tub, grinning at me, "You're not going to keep me waiting, are you?"

"No, ma'am." I peeled off and joined her in the hot, bubbling water.

"Am I shocking you?"

"Not at all. I am enjoying it."

She entangled me with her arms and pulled me close. Her lips found mine and her hands slid to my rear. She pulled our hips together. "I want to be here now with you. This is not revenge against my former future husband. Do you understand that I want to be here with you? Say 'yes, ma'am'."

"Yes, ma'am."

"I love a polite man," She said as she pushed my mouth to her breasts. We went at it for quite a while before heading off to the shower and my bed where things picked up again. Somewhere be both slid off to sleep and in the

middle of the night we woke up entangled and started again.
My alarm clock went off and she muttered something before
getting up to head off to the bathroom. She started the
shower and asked if I was going to join her. We showered
together.

—

When I was getting fed up with my career with the FBI,
I got a call one morning from Willow. "They shot him," She
said. The old man was driving home late one night after
driving back from a court appearance in Arlington. A car
pulled out in front of him on a narrow road, blocking his
path. Another car pulled up behind to block any retreat.
The driver of the first car got out and fired a fully
automatic rifle leaving a series of holes from just in
front of the front bumper into the passenger compartment of
my grandfather's 1967 Pontiac Firebird. Luckily the gunman
was not a skilled marksman and the rapid fire caused the
barrel of the gun to rise uncontrollably. When the barrel
rose he sprayed the driver of the second vehicle fatally.
By pure chance a deputy returning to the station happened
upon the ambush and was able to put two rounds into the
gunman as he tried to reload.

The old man took rounds through the area under his left armpit, the meat of his left shoulder, and at the scalp line. The activity caused him to have a heart attack. He stumbled out of the car and collapsed into a puddle of his own blood. By the time he got to the hospital he was in bad shape, unresponsive and confused. He was rushed into surgery, the doctors worried about the wound to his skull and it took a while to determine he had suffered a heart attack. He was in bad shape and he was not expected to survive when Willow called me. The doctors did not know him too well.

It took me almost two days to get a flight home due to holiday travel traffic. Willow and I had a somber Christmas by the old man's bedside. He had suffered a bad concussion when the bullet pranged off his thick skull and the doctors kept him heavily sedated. Willow looked at me, "How are you doing?"

"I'm going to quit my job," I admitted. They had finally ground me down. My ribs hurt. And I felt like a failure.

"Why? I thought you were doing so well?"

I explained to her that I was permanently on the Bureau's shit list and blamed for ruining an operation back in my early days. Getting all the crappy assignments was getting old and it dawned on me that I was going nowhere. Willow listened intently and told me when I finished that it sounded to her like I was making the right decision. Then she added, "He will need your help. He may not come back from this one." She nodded in the direction of the old man and it hit me that I owed him. He took me in without question when my parents died and now he really did need my help. But would he accept it? "My help? He does not accept help easily, especially from me."

She shook her head. "The last few years have been very hard for him. For us. He was thinking about not running for re-election. The stress of all the new laws and regulations plus he is not exactly picking up all the computerized systems. He has more than enough years on the job for his pension. And technically we are still newlyweds and he owes me a honeymoon."

I felt conflicted as it was impossible to imagine the old man not living a life where he no longer donned the uniform and belted on a gun belt every morning. Would be miserable and mopey without the job that had molded and

defined him for so long? We sat in silence, hardly leaving
the room for two days until the doctors reduced his
sedation and he slowly came around. I wondered if he would
regret not dying or how the heart attack combined with the
gunshots would hamper him. He took one look at me and said,
"Why the fuck are you here?"

"I am happy to see you too, grandpa," I said. And
honestly I meant it. For the next few days he slowly
regained some strength and the doctors released him. He
took my news about leaving the FBI quietly. "I have no idea
what to do next."

He let a little smile grow on his lips. "For some
Goddamn reason you thought the FBI was the pinnacle of law
enforcement. And now you know that is bullshit. Well, until
you figure it out, the sheriff's department is shorthanded
and with me out they could use an extra body even if it is
just directing traffic. With me in here they need all the
help they can get." Six days later I was in a deputy's
uniform.

I had no idea why the memory of the old man popped
into my mind as I dropped Julie Morris off at the B&B early
the next morning but it did. Possibly it was because I

began to see a life after being sheriff with her. She gave me a warm kiss and then told me to call her later. She said she had to talk to Scott first thing in the morning and would let me know how it went. Her plan was to tell him to shove his ring up his ass and never contact her again.

I drove to work and noticed I had a voicemail when I arrived in the parking lot. 'Sheriff, you do not know me but we have a common interest or two. I will contact you later but I wanted to warn you that you have some very nasty folks who do not mean to do you well, if you know the old Texas joke. I will catch up to you in a day or so.' The voice was male and with a hacking cough as if he was a long time smoker or needed to move a battleship out of his lungs.

Janet Polk was furious when I got to the office. Just as she was getting up for work there was a pounding at the front door of her house. Ayce Huggins held up her FBI credentials and a search warrant. They took her laptop, her work cellphone, her husband's cell phone, her husband's tower computer, and the game console her kids used. "Fucking Carl Owen and fucking missing suitcases." My husband and kids were so upset that they did not go to school today.

I went to my office and called Carl Owen's number. His secretary said he was not expected today but she would give him any messages when he called in later in the morning. I asked her to have DDA Owen call me as soon as possible. My frustration built and I disconnected the call.

Mentzer had left me an email that said the Blue Dogs were definitely history and were not back in business. And if any was posing as a Blue Dog the parties he had talked to would have quashed it.

My private cell rang and it was the man with the cough. "Sheriff, there will be a package for you at the front desk with a return address of OKC. Please review the contents and I will call back later." He hung up before I could get a word in edgewise.

My personal cell phone rang again. Beverly Wang said the FBI was at the gate to the naturist resort demanding entry. I told her to let them know that I was on the way and not to let them enter before I could get there. Fifteen minutes later I found Ayce Huggins on the outside of the gate demanding entry and Beverly Wang on the inside telling her to wait. Beverly insisted that she had no right to allow Ayce on that part of the property. Ayce handed me the warrant. I read it and handed it back. I then used the garage door opener for the gate after reassuring Beverly all was okay. Just as the gate opened, Lizard drove up in a jacked up four wheel drive pickup. Lizard took the warrant and then gave Ayce a dirty look, "I'm his lawyer, and for the next hour or so, your bosom buddy. I want a complete inventory of everything you take. Got it?"

Ayce snarled, "Got it." They followed me over the bump in the berm to get onto my part of the property. At the house, I unlocked the front door and stood aside. I went back to my Yukon to radio in that I would be delayed and unavailable for a long time. By the time I was back into the house, it looked like it had been ripped apart.

Ayce and two other agents went through my filing cabinet in my office that held all my bills. They took my laptop out of my office and booted it. Just past the power on self-test the booting process stopped and asked for a password. Ayce said, "I want the password."

"No," said Lizard. "My client cannot be compelled to surrender his passwords. Fourth and Fifth Amendments, sweetie." Lizard had a small video camera running and made sure to capture all she would with it. Ayce said they would take the laptop and have one of their experts crack it. I knew it would take them a long time to crack it but they would probably get in after a solid month of work. And the worst thing on the laptop were some memes and a video of Mr. Rogers flipping off a TV camera.

One of the agents peered at the screen of my laptop, "What operating system is this?" He tapped a few keys and seemed very confused.

I said, "A UNIX variant. And the file system is encrypted." Someone very smart could get all the info off my system but there was nothing sensitive on it and that very smart person would spend a lot of time making sure I had not done something clever on that laptop that was hidden. My private emails were all on a cloud server and also encrypted. I knew Ayce would focus on the laptop almost exclusively and waste time.

"We want the encryption key," Ayce said. This time a little more forcefully.

"Nope, not going to happen, Honey," Lizard said. She looked at me and gave me a look that said I was not going to give anyone the password. It looked like Lizard was ready to batter me to keep me from giving up the password.

The third FBI agent was cursing in my bedroom and by the time I made it into that room he was putting something under my bedside lamp as was startled when I appeared. I lifted the lamp and found a small black disk-like thing about the size of a penny. I said, "What is this?"

The FBI agent sputtered, "Nothing!"

"It is a listening device," Ayce said. "But not one of ours." She had followed me when I went searching for the third agent. She put out her hand to the other agent in the room and he gave her a similar disk to the one under the lamp. She explained that the third agent was putting the device back where he had found it.

Lizard shot Ayce and then gave me dirty looks. "Someone bugged your bedroom?"

Ayce nodded and said it was not her. Then ignoring the bug she said, "Are you ready to help us get the money back?"

"Out of my house," I said. Lizard grabbed me by the arm and escorted me outside. "I want them out now."

"Not with that search warrant in that bitch's hand. Go back to work. Let me handle this," She said. "They are trying to get a reaction from you. Nothing you can do here is going to do you any good. Do not make yourself a hole I have to pull your ass out of later. Please." She ordered me to leave. "Remember you are paying me a whole buck to represent you and I want you to get your money's worth." We both laughed.

I went back to work. I had no idea where the money was. But if I had it, I wanted to shove the money up the rear ends of Carl Owen and Ayce Huggins. I wished the bills were perfectly crisp, with extra sharp edges, and would leave paper cuts.

There was a package on my desk sent from someone in Oklahoma City better known as OKC. Inside the package was a Manilla envelope filled with pictures of a man drinking a soda in a fast food restaurant? It looked like he was in the Whataburger one county south and the man in the photos took me a second to recognize. All the photos had been taken through a window and the resolution was not great. It was the dead body from the rest stop. And in the last of the dozen or so photos of the man was the man walking out the door with Ayce.

So Ayce did know who the DB was. And knew him fairly well. The photos were date and time stamped the morning of the day we had found the man in the car. They had met for breakfast. So why did Ayce not tell me about that fact?

I thought about her in my house tearing it apart. And who would bug my bedroom? The only folks who could get into my house were people I trusted. Was that agent planting that bug and just pretending to find it? Or was it from the woman from the night before! I sat at my desk trying to remember if I left her alone in my room and realized that she had plenty of opportunity to plant the listening devices. My private cell rang and I saw the phone number was Lizard's. "You need to come back fast. One of the idiots took a grinder to the hinges on the old gun safe in the workshop and set everything on fire."

I drove with lights and sirens on to my house and arrived just as the fire department had given up their efforts. The fire had started in the workshop and the dry conditions had made everything else around like tinder. There was an old safe in the corner of the room that ironically was empty (I had a gun safe in my bedroom) save for some old family photos and a family bible from the 1840s. One of the FBI agents noticed the exposed hinges and, since he could not lift or pry up the several hundred pound safe for transportation, had tried to grind out the hinge pins with a grinder. But the sparks from the steel flew into the air and Lizard told me she was screaming at him to stop when she noticed the smoke. The dry wood in the structure had turned to kindling and the sparks from the grinder had set a rug to blaze. Then she noticed there was more smoke. The house was fully engulfed by the time she stamped out the rug. Then the blaze spread. The barn that my mother's grandfather had built himself after returning from the horrors of battle on Okinawa collapsed, spewing a stream of sparks into the sky just as I arrived. The house was mainly embers and ash while the barn looked like a campfire from long ago. I was standing there looking at the mess when I felt Lizard hugging me. She muttered, "I am so sorry."

The paramedics were preparing to transfer one of the FBI agents to the hospital for burns on his hands and one of his legs. I had seen too many idiots with similar burns who had been pouring gasoline on a campfire not to recognize the pattern. As the paramedics drove away, I noticed that they had cut away part of his pants and had left it on the ground. I picked up those pieces and carefully put them in an evidence bag before locking it in my patrol unit. And yes, they reeked of something chemical under the smell of smoke.

I was in too much shock to say anything as I watched the embers glow. Everything I owned that was not burned up was what I was wearing. There was movement off to my right and it was Ayce getting into a heavily tinted Chevy Suburban. Ayce winked at me before she slammed the door shut.

Lizard shook her head. "You can stay with me, if you want. The good news is that everything they packed up burned too. They had set it by the front door. They were very interested in your bank statements and I heartily told them I would instruct you to change banks today." She paused, "You are insured, right?"

"Yes, the house, work shop, and the barn." But everything I had accumulated in my life was now ash. The few things I had from my mom's family were ash. I would really only miss the photos and the old Gretsch guitar but the pain would be deep.

"I hate to admit it but I was always envious that you got grandpa's old place. But this hurts. I am so fucking sorry, Willy." A tear rolled down her cheek and she wiped it away with the back of her hand.

"I am not sure it was an accident. The pants they cut off that one agent look like he spilled some sort of oil on them and that is how he got burned. They think I stole that money and want to see if I will go get it for living expenses. Where was Ayce and the guy who got burned when you were yelling at the asshole with the grinder?"

"How did you know the guy with the grinder was not the one transported?" She looked shocked. She realized the agent with the grinder was not the one who was burned. "I do not know where they were."

"A simple spark should not have brought the place down. I would not put it past her to set a fire in another room while you were dealing with the grinder guy." I knew the place was dry because most everything in Texas was thanks to the drought. But the loss was too complete to not be aided by some sort of accelerant. I guessed she either raided my liquor cabinet or the Tiki torch oil from under my kitchen sink for the accelerant. The average household has many accelerants just lying around and Ayce could have used almost anything. I told Lizard of my doubts and she said that an investigator would be on it as soon as she could.

Lizard forced a smile. "The good thing is that they do not know what a mean little fucker I am," She said.

"Do not go too wild," I replied.

"No, they brought this on themselves. You did not start it but we are going to finish it. She will reap the crop she sewed here."

A few days later Laurel Hardy confirmed it was citronella oil for Tiki torches soaked into the remains of the man's pants. The fire marshal said the burn pattern was not from the sparks but from an accelerant in the mud room area by the woodshop. And I had Tiki torches and their oil in the workshop.

Chapter 13

One of my instructors at the FBI Academy in Virginia noticed that I rode an old shovelhead Harley-Davidson motorcycle. I could not afford anything else. She eyed the bike one morning in the parking lot and then me. "Are you good with bikes, er, motorcycles?" I really had no idea who Joyce Schultz was or her full reputation but I could tell she was thinking very hard about something. She asked me about how I obtained the old Harley and dummy here went into detail on rebuilding a seized motor, upgrading the transmission, and straightening the frame. The bantam sized woman wore her gray hair in a bun and wore cat's eye glasses. She spoke in a crisp Boston Brahmin accent, "You're McDavey, aren't you?"

"Yes, ma'am." She eyed me carefully and then said she needed to talk to my other instructors. At the end of classes one of the chief instructors caught me as I was leaving my last class. He took me to the administrative area where a conference table occupied a large windowless room. Schultz sat at the head of the table with my academic transcripts spread out on the table. She said she had an assignment for me. And then she asked if I knew the word 'voluntold'. When I said that I did not she informed me it was a contraction of being told to volunteer for an assignment. They had a job they needed to be done and I was their sole candidate for the position. I would take leave from my classes immediately and await further instructions.

A week later I found myself opening a new motorcycle repair shop in central Florida. There was another shop not too far up the road that was suspected to be a distribution point for drugs, guns, and women. I had been told the owner was a nasty piece of work and to expect anything. The original plan was to provoke the other shop into interfering with our new startup shop. But one of the first persons through the door was a man the rough size and shape of a dump truck who said his name was Buck Waterstone, the owner/operator of the other shop. I expected a confrontation but received a big surprise. He said his mechanic was going on an extended vacation for health reasons and wanted to know if he could send his customers to me. I asked how he was going to make money without a mechanic. Waterstone explained that most of his customers did their own repairs but he bought parts and

Waterstone sold them with a small markup that was enough to keep him in beer. His mechanic had mainly been doing major overhauls, usually at the end of riding season. He told me in a rambling story that he was living off a medical disability, his savings, and a wife who had a trust fund of an enormous size. The shop was a way to get him out of the house, buy his own parts on the cheap, and was a tax write off. The business was mainly a hobby to keep him out from under the feet of Mrs. Waterstone during the day. He was not what I expected and did not seem like a ruthless crime boss. But I thought what would a crime boss look like if they were scoping out the competition? He left me a business card and hand wrote his private cell phone number with 'call any time' scrawled underneath before he left.

Schultz was ecstatic when I gave her the news. She then informed me to wait for Rafferty and Simmons and to formally take over the undercover operation. I was up to that point just setting up the foundation and the team of Rafferty & Simmons would do the real work, or so I was informed. My job was to be a grease monkey and observer – nothing else. I was also informed that Rafferty & Simmons were the golden hair children of the Deputy Director and had worked miracles in the past and it would be a great honor for me to be allowed into their presence. A few days later an odd couple of characters wandered into the shop just before closing. I was doing a valve job for a customer referred by Buck Waterstone. Ralph Rafferty wore cheap three piece suits despite the extreme heat of the Florida weather and white patent leather shoes that were ash covered from chain smoking cheap cigars. Eric Simmons looked like an ex-special forces caricature with buzzed hair, polo shirts tailored to show off his biceps, and a default mode command voice. The first thing they did was try to rip me a new butt hole for meeting with Waterstone. "You never meet with a target without backup."

"I had no choice. He walked in here of his own volition." I did not ask why the Hell it took them nearly two weeks to show up when I had been pushed out of the academy early to get things set up and working.

"'Volition'? No dip shit Florida DA is going to want a case with you using a word like that. Now Waterstone's lawyer can claim entrapment. You have totally fucked up the case." Rafferty paced like an angry animal for a few moments and then tried to intimidate me. Simmons was suddenly standing an inch from my nose like a Marine Drill Instructor. With my family background that did not work.

"So after fucking up my operation, what the fuck do you have to say for yourself, asshole."

I forced a smile and said, "There was no enticement so no entrapment. He even is referring his customers to me. By the way he is having a pizza night in his shop and he said to invite anyone who might be interested. Should I RSVP for you two too?"

"How the fuck do you agree to eat with a slime ball?" He went from rage to full fury. He ranted about Waterstone for quite a while but eventually both Simmons and Rafferty ran out of venom and invectives.

"My orders from Schultz were to set up the shop, blend into the environment, keep my eyes open, learn as much as I can, and wait for you two. I have set up the shop, am part of the local environment, have learned a great deal about Waterstone's operations, and now you two are here." I was very tempted to add the word 'finally' at the point but did not. "Please tell me how I have contradicted my orders." I kept my voice low, the rhythm slow, and my face calm.

Rafferty took over and said, "So what have you learned?"

"As I detailed in the case file, Waterstone is pretty much as he described himself. He has a rich wife, a disability pension from the Post Office after a traffic accident, a hobby business, and comes across as a nice guy. I have been to his shop twice and witnessed nothing suspicious. The back of the shop is crammed full of old parts and if he has drugs, guns, or hookers they are not there." The back of the shop looked like a hoarder had been there for a very long time. I then gave them the name of the bank Waterstone used (mail envelopes in the trash), the name with the number of his lawyer (note taped to his computer screen), and other incidental bits of observed data such as the alarm code for the security system (shoulder surfed).

"Could he be laundering money?" Simmon's voice was now almost a whisper.

"Maybe but it is not obvious. A simple look at the books via the graces of the local franchise tax bureau should not show more than a few grand a month income from what I have seen. The customer transactions I saw were done with a credit card, not cash," I said. "So what makes Waterstone a person of interest?"

"Someone of great importance said he was dirty. That is enough for you to know." Simmons gave me the evil eye and told me that he sincerely hoped that I had 'not screwed the pooch' on the operation and then added a promise to rectally insert his foot into me if I had.

Rafferty came with me to the pizza night at Waterstone's shop. Once a month the shop had pizza, beer, soft drinks, and brownies at closing time for customers. Then the group would migrate to a bar down the street. There were fifty or sixty people when we showed up and several others arrived soon after. The place was crowded and most people gathered outside the shop on a sidewalk area equipped with wooden picnic tables. There was not much standing room inside and there was too much clutter in the back for more than a pair of people with the piles of junk. I introduced Rafferty to Waterstone as a silent partner who financed most of the shop where I worked. Rafferty looked like he was afraid of catching some communicable disease as the two shook hands while Waterstone appeared to be a big, jolly man. I asked Waterstone if I could show the silent partner around his shop and was told that it was no problem. The shop's sales floor was spotless and Rafferty liked that neatness. But he was slack jawed as I showed him the tightly packed spare parts and equipment in the back of the shop. There was no way to pull out a muffler from the stack of parts without dislodging seats, foot pegs, handlebars, or saddles bags piled around them. Waterstone was a bad manager of his inventory and could easily make a small fortune selling off his excess. There were several older bikes that needed relatively insignificant repairs to be made road worthy again. Waterstone was not a good businessman and not exactly detail orientated. I could not see how such a lackadaisical man could also be running drugs. On the way back to our shop, Rafferty said, "That man has Obsessive Compulsive problems with hoarding parts and old bikes."

I asked, "Do you still think he is dirty?"

"As a muddy skunk." He said Waterstone had a long record of doing bad things and my job was to get evidence against him not try to judge the man. But other than being bad at business I saw nothing that I could proceed upon at that time. When I asked for what to watch for all I was told was that I would know it when I saw it.

A few days later a judge approved phone taps, video surveillance, and record grabs. I was ordered to keep on doing what I had been doing while more senior special agents did what Simmons called 'the real work'. My job was to maintain the front. There were a dozen agents assigned to the case locally and many more back at the region office working to put Waterstone away. Every morning we would have a team meeting to bring everyone up to speed on the previous day's activities. Each meeting made me more frustrated as the rest of the team saw the lack of evidence as proof they were missing something.

I knew I was still technically in the FBI Academy and still 'green'. But it seemed to me that Waterstone was exactly what he appeared to be. I asked to see his history files and was gently rebuffed. 'Not your monkey, not your circus'.

From the bank records on Waterstone, it looked like the shop almost or barely broke even for the past several years. Phone taps revealed nothing except that he liked extra pepperoni on his pizzas or extra mayo on cheeseburgers that were ordered for lunch. Rafferty and Simmons ordered me to stay as far away from Waterstone as possible. But the big man would call every few days with news that he was sending work my way and would drop by once a week at lunch time with a couple of pizza boxes in hand.

What I took for being the actions of a good nature of a nice man was seen by my two fake silent partners as proof of a manifestation of evil. "You must have tipped him off and he smells a rat," They would say even as they ate his pizza after Waterstone departed.

I was ordered to break into the computers of Mr. and Mrs. Waterstone and found nothing odd. His old Windows machine showed nothing odd other than a few pictures of a barely dressed that turned out to be Mrs. Waterstone. Her Apple showed her impressive financial portfolio. The wife had many widely dispersed business interests and, if anything was wrong, may have been too generous to some folks who had not repaid her largess. The one thing the team remarked on was that Burt did have an odd collection of GIFs on his laptop at home with pretty girls sitting on chrome choppers. A closer look revealed the women were all professional models and Burt had owned the bikes in the past.

The phone taps and video surveillance captured nothing interesting. The financial types did notice that one of the bank accounts paid five grand of the first of each month to a medical facility in Costa Rica. The payment was set up years ago to be done automatically from a trust account. I took a little digging to find out the reason. The big man had an adopted daughter from a previous marriage with limited mental and physical capacity that he covered her bills. Simmons read a copy of her medical charts looking for proof the Waterstone had injured the woman until he found that these problems were from infancy, before he had married the mother.

Then one day when Simmons and Rafferty were bemoaning how sharp Waterstone was to avoid them finding out what he was doing, a tall woman dressed in an elegant suit walked into the shop. She had the sharp, chiseled features of a model and dressed exceptionally well. The diamond in her wedding band could be mistaken for a crystal door knob. "I'm Mrs. Waterstone. I believe you know my husband and I have a business proposition for you."

Rafferty and Simmons looked like hungry dogs let loose in a butchers shop. Rafferty said, "What is it?" He was salivating like a hungry wolf and later said he thought she was there to offer to turn witness against her husband.

She sighed heavily. "My husband has some health issues. His doctors want him to greatly simplify his life. The motorcycle shop is more of a hobby than a profitable business and we do not need it to live. I would like to be done with it. Land, building, and all inventory – lock, stock, and barrel. Would you consider buying him out?"

I nodded, "We would consider it. Do you have a price in mind?" She did and named a price that was roughly ten percent of the worth of the business. I told her the price was very low and Rafferty elbowed me to shut up.

Then she said, "There is a condition on that low price. Buck needs to come down here a few days a week to hang out. At least for a while. He needs the male comradeship."

"To be honest ma'am, I genuinely like Buck. We'll have to talk it over to see how our budget is doing but the offer is more than fair and I would like to have your husband around to talk to when things are slow," I said. Both my silent partners blanched when I said that. She handed me a business card and asked me to call when we had a decision either way. I watched her walk out to her car and drive away before turning to face Rafferty and Simmons. "Well?"

"We need to buy his shop!" Simmons was nearly purple with excitement. He was smiling for the first time since I had met him and that creeped me out big time. He was not a naturally happy man and smiling looked painful for him.

Rafferty said, "This means we can crawl through his shop at will." I sincerely doubted he had been this happy since he was a kid at Christmas time.

I held up my hands as if surrendering. "Let me go over and audit the parts. The price is too low and a reasonable buyer would want to check out the stock on hand. Due diligence." I tried to explain rusty inventory, damaged good, and regular good business practices but I was told that did not matter. But they did want me to inspect the building.

"Good! Go inventory! It will let you plant bugs while you are there," Rafferty was giggling. "He has to have something hidden over there that he wants to pin on us." I excused myself saying I had to go to the restroom rather than telling him he was paranoid. When I returned, Rafferty muttered something about Schultz being happy when she heard the news. He told me to get lost as they had to strategize. "You're not truly a FBI Agent and there are some things we need to keep from you."

243

Not a FBI Agent? Joyce Schultz had said I would be treated as a full agent. I was going to be official when my class graduated in a few days. I had done everything to qualify to save five weeks of classwork and the graduation ceremony itself! She said that it was all a mere formality and technically I would be an agent the day my class graduated. I opened my mouth to question them but Rafferty told me to go away. I asked, "What the heck do you think you have on the man?"

Simmons said, "He makes money transfers to Costa Rica or Panama on a regular basis. Right?"

"He has a special needs daughter from a previous marriage and he pays for her medical care down there," I said. That had been checked on and documented as true. Rafferty told me I was making things up. But when I told him I got that information from the current wife from our own research, he grew furious.

"Many years ago he smuggled prescription drugs and got caught. He bribed his way out of a jail in Nicaragua. One a druggie, always a druggie! He is just playing at being honest." Rafferty scoffed at me insisting the Waterstone may have been dirty years ago but now he was apparently

clean. Rafferty told me to get my head out of my ass.
Simmons said it was a mistake to have me on the operation.
I walked out wondering how things had gotten so crazy.

There was only one local bar for refuge and I
nursed a cold beer by myself until Mrs. Waterstone
appeared. She wore jeans, a Jimmy Buffett t-shirt, and old
Converse sneakers. While the clothing had been downgraded
from her expensive suit she still looked amazing. She
nodded to the bartender as she sat next to me and soon
received a Bahama Mama. She smiled, "I have a confession."

"I'm no priest."

She chuckled. "You've been living like one. And your
partners are assholes. Rapperty, Rafferty? He has the
looks of a man who would drop a date rape drug into a
woman's drink at a church social and Simmons looks like he
couldn't get it up with a fist full of Viagra."   I had to
laugh and she seemed to be enjoying my company. "Buck's in
the hospital. Years ago he did something dumb to help a
buddy and got caught up in a situation in Central America
when the buddy decided to get rich quick with drugs. He
helped the buddy get away from some cops by crossing a
swamp and ended up with some very nasty amoebas in his

liver. He also caught Malaria and jungle rot. They lost the drugs in the swamp and got caught anyway. The buddy was the son of a Congresswoman from California and got off scot free. Buck had to pay La Mordita to get out of jail. So no US criminal record but the health problems persist. Usually they can be managed but not when all hit at the same time. Tears welled in her eyes. "So today they did a blood test and then another blood test. Too many white blood cells. The doctor said he was fighting off something and they did more tests. Bowel cancer."

"How bad?"

She shook her head. "Buck said the good news is that he won't have to figure out what to buy everyone for Christmas." A tear rolled down her cheek and she gulped down her drink.

"May I go see him?"

She nodded. "Yes. I put your name on a very restricted list of visitors. He is at Country General in a private room. I'm going home to call friends and family. I did not want to leave him alone but he said he wanted to nap and did not talk to anyone on the phone. Could you go sit with him? I need to get my work squared away and cancel some meetings before I have an old fashioned good cry. I would feel better if I knew someone was there with him. Someone he liked."

"I would be honored." My heart was in my throat and tears were welling up in my own eyes.

"It should only be ninety minutes or two hours, or so." She gave me a hug and we both wiped away tears.

"No problem." On the way to the hospital I called both Simmons and Rafferty but had to leave messages on their voicemails. I found Buck watching a replay of an old basketball game from his hospital bed. I sat down quietly and we both watched Wilt Chamberlain and the Los Angeles Lakers manhandle the Celtics. When the game was over he turned off the television. I said, "I did not know you were a basketball fan."

Red Auerbach and the old Celtics were his favorites as a kid and he wanted to grow up and wear the green and the white. He grew up in South Boston when the Winter Hill Gang and Whitey Bulger were running things. His stories came fast and strong as Buck enjoyed telling me about his life. It was obvious he was a little fuzzy from the medications and he was feeling no pain. A nurse came in to check his vitals and that made Buck stop for only a moment. He resumed as soon as she left he started to resume the story he was telling but stopped in mid-sentence. A wave of pain rippled through his core and I hit the call button for the nurse. The clock on the wall said it was five after eight in the evening. The nurse checked his vitals and called for the doctor. I held Buck's hand as they wheeled him on a gurney to the operating room. He squeezed my hand one last time and then they took him through a huge door. I felt like I had been kicked in the stomach. Mrs. Waterstone arrived not a minute later and we held on to each other and cried.

A doctor found us an hour and a bit later in the cafeteria and slowly told us about the aneurysm that had burst in Buck Waterstone's aorta. The medical staff had tried all they could but to no avail. Aortic aneurysms are hard to fix and Buck was not strong enough to last through the procedure. Buck Waterstone had pretty much worn out as much of his body as possible and finally the weak link failed. The doctor told us to go get some rest and Mrs. Waterstone bravely thanked the doctor. I followed her home and then went back to the shop where I slept in the back room. This was the first time I resented sleeping in the shop while all the others were staying in hotels. I left more voicemail messages for Rafferty and Simmons before I went to bed pleading with them to call me as Buck Waterstone was deceased. I was still sleeping at dawn when Rafferty kicked my cot in the back of the shop to wake me up. "Get dressed. We finally got Waterstone. A judge is waiting to see us so we can get an arrest warrant."

"What charge?" I was shocked and then started to tell them Waterstone was dead. But I was instantly cut off and told to shut the fuck up or else.

"Did you get my voicemails from last night?"

There was an index finger in my face before. "Shut the fuck up, McDavey! I do not want to hear anything out of your yap unless you are directly asked a question. Conspiracy to commit murder is the charge, for your information," Rafferty look pleased with himself. I climbed into my clothes and Rafferty told me I looked like shit. "All I want from you is nothing, nada, zip, zero! Do not open your yap unless you are asked a question and then answer with the absolute minimum amount of 'verbiage'. You got that, asshhole?" I followed Rafferty in my vehicle to the manicured mansion of a Federal judge. There were a dozen FBI Special Agents already waiting and Joyce Schultz was their queen bee. We were seated in a formal dining room while a warty looking judge sipped her coffee. Rafferty handed Schultz some paperwork and said, "This is it. Let's get started."

The judge looked at Schultz, "And why am I out of bed so early on a Sunday?"

Schultz started the proceedings. "One Byron 'Buck' Waterstone has been under surveillance for some time. Last night at eleven fifty two he called a known organized crime figure to arrange the murder of Agent McDavey." She pointed at me to signify that I was McDavey. "McDavey opened up a rival motorcycle shop near Waterstone's compound and Waterstone did not like the competition. We have a copy of the audio and a transcript of the conversation. Voice print analysis proves it is Buck Waterstone making the call."

I heard my own voice before I realized I was speaking, "Eleven fifty two? Last night?"

Everyone else in the room but the judge was obviously frustrated by my interruption. Schultz glared at me, "If I may continue?"

"Impossible," I said. Furious faces turned to look at me. Now even the judge was mad at me. Simmons was clenching his fists and looked like he was going to wade into me to give me a beating.

Simmons barked, "I thought I told you to shut the fuck up unless it was important."

"It is important. It is impossible that Buck Waterstone made that call at that time last night."

The judge asked, "Why impossible?"

"Because Buck Waterstone died on an operating table at County General from a burst aortic aneurysm a couple of hours before that. I was at the hospital when they took him into the operating room and I was waiting with his wife when the doctor informed her of the death about nine last night. So unless there was a séance going on, Buck Waterstone was not on the call."

Rafferty look pale and Simmons said he was going to 'royally fuck me up' when it was discovered that I was lying. I looked over at Schultz and told her Waterstone was dead and there was something else going on to try and frame the dead man. She looked frustrated and angry as she said we had to go see the body.

An hour later a half dozen of us were in the hospital morgue with the remains of Buck Waterstone. And in the morgue was also the remains of my career as an FBI Agent, but that took a few years for it to be declared officially dead. Schultz asked the medical examiner dozens of questions while Rafferty paced like a caged lion. There was no autopsy scheduled as the cause of death was already known. The time of death was carefully scrutinized and it was obvious that Buck could not be heard on a call at eleven. After we finished, Schultz handed me an envelope from her briefcase. She said without enthusiasm, "Here is your diploma and credentials. Welcome to the Federal Bureau of Investigation." There was an iciness in her voice that made it quite evident that I was not wanted by her in her club.

"What about the audio of Buck wanting me dead?"

She looked at me, "I am sure there are a lot of your fellow agents who would prefer you in that state, don't you think?" She nodded with her head and soon we were the only two in the morgue who were living.

"It's false, made up, bad evidence. It was being used to get a warrant," I said.

"You are correct. Sometimes we have to cut corners, set the facts just so, and rig things so the bad guys do not win all the time," She said. "We wanted Waterstone as leverage against an old associate of his. We didn't give two shits about Buck as we wanted a bigger prize. He was a stepping stone. And now we lost our last chance at getting him. And when this is all written up, edited, filed, and then presented to the big bosses in Washington, D.C. the blame for the failure will be spread around. You, because you will be seen as a young and inexperienced, will get a pass. Rafferty and Simmons will catch hell for not supervising you closely enough. Rafferty will probably have to retire and Simmons may be able to claw some position in some shit town. And I will take most of the blame for not getting the bigger target, not supervising the entire operation, and for suggesting using someone still in the academy. I will probably get to teach for another year or so, or until they decide to retire me. But my career is essentially over."

"But why would they risk so much over one man? The more I dug into Waterstone and his shop the clearer it became that he might have been a bad businessman but he was not doing anything illegal."

She took a deep breath, "Yes, the tape was probably kludged together by Rafferty and Simmons. Yes, the tape would not have stood up in court. But we never wanted to go to court. We have a legal system not a justice system. Justice would not have us grind on a Buck Waterstone to get to a drug and prostitution kingpin. We wanted him to rat on an old friend who no happens to hold elective office. The average citizen on the street has no idea that most laws are made by bureaucratic fiat after other bureaucrats make agreements and that law enforcement is way behind, and flat footed in our response. We pick and choose our battles and a lot of those battles are back alley, anything goes brawls. What you have to learn is that you, all by yourself, cannot make a difference." I listened to the staccato percussion of her heels as she left.

Two years later I was performing background checks in Fargo, North Dakota in January when my supervisor took me to a greasy spoon for a low buck dinner. "I was warned about you by Eric Simmons. He said you were a low down, no good son-of-a-bitch and that I should not trust you further than I can toss you. But I've been watching you. You do good work, don't bitch, and I think you are a fine agent. But you are marked by the folks on mahogany row as permanently on their shit list. That is why you get

reassigned every few months to another shitty posting. You

would do a lot better transferring to another agency or

other law enforcement. I wrote a performance review for

you that was glowing. But what went into your files was

anything but glowing. And I received an email this morning

inquiring if you have a passport. I think your next shitty

assignment will be overseas and not someplace pleasant. And

in case you didn't know that newly Assistant Deputy

Director Eric Simmons reviews all field assignments. And

while you are travelling to Timbuctoo or East Bumfudge, you

might want to check out who that new Assistant Deputy

Director is related to and then ponder what your life is

going to be like in a few years when he goes from Assistant

Deputy to Deputy and then to Director. I went to the

academy with Eric and that motherfucker does know how to

hold a grudge." From his pocket he pulled out a fist sized

paper bag and slid it across the table to me. He said,

"These belonged to my uncle. He never trusted a semi-

automatic anything up here in the cold. Best keep them in a

pocket that is quick to get to in case of emergency.

Untraceable and, if asked, I know nothing about 'em. But

something tells me you need an ace in the hole."

Chapter 14

I had court late the next morning and was the second witness called. My clothes smelled of smoke but I did not have any cleaner uniforms nor did I have time to order new uniforms. It was a domestic battery case and I had been the first to the scene. Lori and Larry Pate had been drinking and then slugging each for most of a warm afternoon before neighbors finally called in a complaint. It was not the first warm afternoon they had had a fight and far from the first time the sheriff's departure had dropped by after neighbors complained. Lori met me at their front door of their cheap apartment with a bloody lip and torn clothes. "The bastard's out cold in the kitchen. Please haul his ass off to jail." I remember being surprised she used the word 'please'.

I walked past her and around a pile of old pizza boxes crowned with empty beer cans to reach the bedroom. There was something in the worn shag carpeting that was crunching as I walked. The apartment reeked of various human odors which made me switch to breathing through my mouth. I was surprised when I made it to the kitchen and found the husband sprawled on the floor and looking at me with glassy eyes.

Larry was not out cold but had a welt on the side of his face that was truly impressive and had a broken nose. He told me he was playing dead so she would leave him alone. "You gotta haul her ass off to the nut farm." A moment later she charged into the room and I had to become a boxing referee sending them to separate dingy corners. The only thing they agreed on was that they were both charging the other. I cuffed them both and then transported them to jail. It was now four months later and both had ninety day chips from Alcoholics Anonymous clutched in their hands to show the judge. Both were still pressing charges against each other and were both living in separate shelters. And today was Lori's trial.

The prosecutor took me through my arrest report in great detail when I gave my evidence. Then Armando Jones took over. Armando is the type of lawyer who gives the other 99.999 percent a bad name. As a defense attorney he was slightly better than nothing and somehow got named by the public defender's office to simple cases that even the most casual observer would see were beyond his capacity. He fumbled with his notes and cleared his throat repeatedly with a noise that quickly annoyed everyone who could hear him. He wore a gray pinstripe suit that cost more than most automobiles and his shaved head was burnished to a high sheen. "Sheriff McDavey, why did you proceed to the defendant's address?"

"Radio dispatch operator said to proceed code three -- lights and sirens -- due to a complaint from the neighbors," I said. "Violent domestic disturbance in progress."

"Did you witness any of the violence yourself?"

"No, Sir. Only the after effects."

"Objection," Armando cried. "Your honor, the witness is giving his opinion." I looked over at the prosecutor who was as confused as I had ever seen a lawyer in court. But the prosecutor was smart enough to see the defense lawyer was his own worst enemy.

"Overruled," muttered the judge after a moment of giving Armando a serious visual examination. I had never heard of a judge actually sending a lawyer for a psychiatric evaluation but suddenly felt I might see it happen in the very near future. Armando tried to make substantial legal points but eventually ran out of steam and the judge asked nicely if the cross examination could continue.

"Did you believe the defendant when she said she was struck by her husband?" He was rocking forward on to the balls of his feet and then back to his heels repeatedly, his body wobbling back and forth. And he had his arms folded over his chest as if daring me.

"Yes, Sir, I did." I hoped the prosecutor had all the photos of Lori's injuries ready to show the court.

"Did you believe her husband when he said the defendant struck him?"

"Yes, sir."

He drew the next word out as he spoke to add extra emphasis to it. "Why?"

"Why?" I was not sure what he meant.

"Yes, why." Jones turned to the judge and with a wave of his hands said, "Your honor the witness is not answering the question and is clearly not cooperating."

The judge grinned, "I think the witness is unclear on your question. I know I am." The judge nodded at me, "Please answer the question."

I said, "Why did I believe the defendant and her husband when they said they had been beating the Hell out of each other? Because they looked like they were beating the Hell out of each other." I described the pulled hair, black eyes, blood, puffed lips, abrasions, scratches, and welts that I had witnessed.

Armando Jones grinned at me. "But you did not see them hitting each other?"

"No, my impression is that they were between rounds," I said. The judge chuckled but did not reprimand me. Jones objected to my answer and asked to have it struck from the record. But the judge denied the request. Jones gave me a dirty look and said he had no further questions for me. The prosecution had a few simple questions that I was able to quickly answer. I gladly left the courtroom and went back to work. I had just walked out of the courtroom and turned on my cell phones when the work one chirped.

Dolly Wood had been attacked. She was unlocking her old Jeep after shopping in downtown Paragon when someone grabbed her from behind. She had an arm full of groceries in one hand and her keys in the. The attacker lifted her off the ground and slammed her into the asphalt parking lot. Luckily for her the two dogs were able to get out the unlocked driver's door and attacked. One dog grabbed the attacker by the right wrist and the other grabbed the left thigh. Dolly's screams had been heard by customers in the grocery store and they quickly grabbed the perp. The store manager called 9-1-1. Dispatch sent two units and Janet had called me hoping to catch me as I left court. The store was a block away and I covered the distance quickly on foot. Paramedics were preparing to transport Dolly to the hospital with a broken wrist, collar bone, and possible fractured eye orbit. She was crying but cheerful. When Dolly spotted me she asked if I could find someone to watch her puppies. I told her I would do so. She squeezed my hand with her good hand and smiled. I promised to visit her as soon as I could.

The assailant sat bandaged in the back of a patrol unit scowling. He was a thirty one year old man from Farmersville with several prior arrests for everything from burglary to possession of drugs with intent to sell. He was junky thin, with small, sunken eyes, and stunk to high heaven. I made sure I read him his rights while trying not to gag. Hygiene was not one of his strong points and he had voided his bowels during the scrape with the dogs. I asked him why he attacked the old woman. "I wanted her Jeep. I always wanted a Jeep. Why does an old bitch like that need a Jeep?" His own beater Buick had coughed to a stop down the road and he had to get to Midlothian to pick up his girlfriend. When I told him that Dolly was in bad shape and that attacking a ninety year old woman was a chicken shit thing to do, he shook his head. "I really need to call my lawyer. Dang she didn't look that old."

The dogs had done a number to his arms and one leg so much so that he looked like a shredded scarecrow. He started ranting about 'those fucking mutts better not give him rabies or fleas'. I told him to shut up and told him he would probably have to go through the very painful series of rabies shots as ninety year old women do not exactly bounce back and it might take weeks for her to get the medical records from the veterinarian. His eyes went wide and I loudly slammed the door on his face.

I dropped Dolly's dogs off in the dog run that had been used for our departmental canine unit before our canine retired. I made sure they had water and made a mental note to get them some food. Janet said she would take the pair of dogs home with her at the end of shift.

Sixto Ruiz was at his locker picking up his dirty clothes and looking upset. He told me about how the FBI had searched his place. "They tore the fuck out of my place. They even took apart the hot water heater. Fuckers." He asked if it was true if they had burned my house down and he cursed when I confirmed the story. "Boy, when you get someone pissed off at you, you really get them pissed off at you."

I apologized to him and he shook his head before telling me they were going to live with her parents the next few days and that his wife really wanted him in another job. I told him that I would be sorry to lose him but I would write an amazing letter of recommendation.

I was beyond frustrated and knew I could not work for a while. So I grabbed a cup of coffee and took a short walk.

Laurel Hardy was in her lab entering data for a report when I interrupted her to ask about the car from the creek... "The old Mustang? It was pieced together with parts from three or four cars -- engine, transmission, and chassis. My guess some shade tree mechanic bolted together some wrecks. And tracing those component parts is almost impossible."

"'Almost'?"

She nodded. "The engine was rebuilt by a shop in Fort Worth in May 1981 to burn unleaded gas. You have to change the valves and the valve seats which is not a big deal. The shop riveted a little plaque onto the firewall. They rebuilt the engine, put in a hotter cam, and a bigger carb, the shop is still in business and emailed me the records. The bad news is that the man who paid for the work was named John Smith with no address or phone. The good news is that they recorded the licenses plate. But the car was sold the next year and then stolen off a used car lot two years later." She added it was a case of one step forward toward a goal and two steps back.

"The female from the car. Could you reconstruct her face?" Laurel said it was not her forte but they had some software that may help. "There was a girl from my high school class who disappeared right after graduation and she had a Mustang like that. I know the odds are long but it would keep some nightmares away if I knew that girl was not underwater all those times I drove by for all those years."

"Can you get me pictures of her?"

"Consider it done." I checked my watch and said I had to go to a meeting but I promised to email the photos as soon as I could." After a pair of performance reviews, reviewing some contracts, and reading some notices from the state of Texas on upcoming changes in the law. I took my lunch break on the road so I could drive to the home and find some pictures of Rachel before remembering my home was gone. But the library had the school annuals. There were a handful of pictures of Rachel in the annual along with her senior portrait. I used my cell phone to take copies of Rachel's pictures and sent them to Laurel.

Back in my office I found chaos. On the corner my desk was a pile of records concerning the history of the Blue Dogs that had come from the archives. The various gang members were either dead, incarcerated, or too old to be considered active in activities. The last known Blue Dog crime was a sale of pills to an undercover USDA agent nearly twenty seven years before. It seemed like the new Blue Dog gang, if it existed, had nothing to do with the old one. I spent a little time on the computer and found nothing substantial on the new Blue Dogs other than some FBI and DEA reports that were written in such a bureaucratically obtuse way that one could reasonably expect dogs and the color blue to be selling drugs. And none of those reports were newer than six months old nor closer than two hundred miles to Paragon. Was Owen on a fishing expedition or had he sent me on a fishing expedition to see how I worked? Anyway, I sent him a note to say the requested archived data on the Blue Dogs was ready to be sent over to him and he should have it in a day or so.

Jane Morris did not answer when I called but thirty seconds later she was calling back. "Sorry, I was taking care of some things for my mom. I called her this morning to tell her not to come. But first I called Scott this morning. He was very hung over. He says he loves me but said he is getting cold feet about the commitment. He admitted that he should have picked me up at the airport or met me at the church. I let him have it about his stupidity and then I told him the wedding is off."

I did not know what to say in response but managed to mutter a 'wow'! I wanted to ask her about the listening devices Ayce had found in my bedroom but did not. There was something about her that was too good to be true. She sounded a little too cool for the situation.

"I'm supposed to meet with his mom to return the wedding ring at four." Her voice had a slight amount of sadness in it. For a moment I wondered what her game was and if it was somehow connected to the missing suitcases full of money. She was the most logical one to plant the listening device. Or could someone else have done it?

I took a deep breath, "I have to go to a meeting and will be done about half past five. Will you have dinner with me?"

"Some place with good drinks?" She had suddenly perked up greatly.

"Yes, ma'am." It took me a moment to figure out where to go that would be perfect. "It's a place called Darwin's Revenge. Can we meet there at six to give me some time to clean up?"

"Perfect," She said. "See you at six."

Chapter 15

The County Commissioners Court was made up of seven residents who had a mixed set of reasons for public service. Two wanted a better place for their families to be raised. Two were going to use it for stepping stones to high political office. One was feeding her ego and another was in over his head but was determined to see out his commitment. And then there was my step-grandmother Willow Montgomery McDavey who just seemed to enjoy gently torturing the other members of the board. The members of the County Commissioners Court were traditionally called judges and Willow obviously loved that title. Not only was she the majority landowner in the county she was one of the bigger tax payers. Plus she had connections, memories and friends galore to ensure she was the queen of the court. Being called a judge was like the maraschino cherry on the banana split for her.

Once a week the judges met to run the county and my attendance was required most of the time. But it was hard to judge before a meeting if I would just sit in the cheap seats and fight to keep awake while they discussed sewer rates or road repairs. Or if I was going to be in the hot seat answering complaints or explaining why my department was spending so much on gasoline. But this time I had a hunch that it was my time in the barrel.

"Sheriff, we have some questions for you." Willow sat with the other county board members behind a long table that sat on a foot high riser. First they asked about Dolly Wood and took my assurances that the perpetrator was in custody and not likely to get bail. So they proceeded to the next most urgent need. "Will you have enough staff for the upcoming 10K race?"

"Yes, ma'am. Three deputies, six volunteers, and the scout troop are all ready to go." The course circled the campus of Paragon High School and was very easy to contain the runners and redirect traffic. "The only difficulty I can foresee is that we are running short on patrol vehicles and I cannot order replacements until the new budget year."

Willow smiled and said, "Every other department is feeling the budget pinch. And like every other department you will have to wait a few more months for the new fiscal year. Would it help if we got some overtime for the motor pool out of the general budget to help repair what you have?" She was the bitchy ice queen when running the board meetings.

"Yes, ma'am. We do have one hanger queen we can rebuild. A drunk driver the other night took out another patrol unit will mean a reduction in service." It was not the time to mention that the head mechanic was thinking about leaving or that I had a few other vehicles that were verging on being unsafe. I was glad that the majority of county revenue no longer came from speeding tickets but what we did bring in that way was still a large chuck of the operating funds.

She pursed her lips. "And what about these rumors about a car being pulled out of a creek?" I told her and the rest of the council members about the mustang and that the forensics team was working the case.

"And did you ever find out the identity of the dead man from the rest stop last week?" Willow has a way of smiling like the Cheshire Cat that lets you know that she knows more than you know and that you are about to walk into a trap. Before I could answer I felt a light tap on my right arm. Lizard was there and whispered into my ear. I looked back at Willow and said, "Ma'am, if you will excuse us for just a second."

"We might as well recess for today," Willow said, dismissing me and the others. "By the way, I am sorry you lost your house. We have a spare room if you need it."

"Thank you, ma'am." As I walked out of the room, Lizard took me by the arm. Lizard took me away from the council chamber and out into the hallway where a pimply faced kid of undetermined gender stood with a computer under one arm. Lizard asked, "Any place where we could have some privacy?"

"My office across the street?" I said. The three of us walked across the street and into the Sheriff Department but the kid with the computer balked when we approached my office. The kid tapped his own right earlobe and nodded into my office. Could my office be bugged? It seemed like a long shot but it was still possible. We headed to a spare office where supplies and paper for the printers were stored. After the door was closed, the kid opened up the laptop and started typing with the laptop balanced on a pile of boxes.

Lizard said, "Your dead man from the car at the rest stop was not much of a creative thinker, thank God. I know the Feds grabbed the case but it rankled me. J here did some digging for me and found something useful." I was not sure if the name of the kid was the letter J or Jay or some other variation but let it slide. "The self-storage place down on Victory Hill had one new rental to a male in the last month. Victor Humberto Green. Not Verde which is Spanish for green but Green." She motioned to the kid and J swung the laptop around. On the screen was a video of the dead man from the rest stop using a cart to wheel four large and heavy suitcases into the U-Store-Ur-Stuff Storage Center. The man stopped at a small garage like unit and fumbled with a lock before opening the door. Above the door was a small plaque that read C-1017. The camera was angled not to see into the particular storage unit but you could view the man as he put the suitcases into the unit. The man shut the door and affixed the lock. The man maneuvered the cart and placed it before another unit before leaving. J played with the laptop and another video from a different angle that showed the mystery man getting into his car and driving away. Green did look a little woozy and I remembered the rest area was off the same exit as the storage units. I was looking at the live version of the dead man from the car in the rest stop in the last hour of his life.

He had been alive and had stashed the luggage. I still did not know who wiped down the car, took the car keys, or killed Victor Humberto Green. But I knew where and when he had stashed the cash and hopefully the log books.

J said in a whispered, thin voice, "I pulled it from the cloud. I will give you the address. Each time a customer visits the storage locker their visit is recorded and put in the account folder. It is all straightforward. But I can't be a witness."

I asked, "Why not?"

For a second he looked as if he was considering not telling me but then the words burst out 'of him. "I am not supposed to be here, in this country. I am a US citizen and all that but my former … employers think I am somewhere else." J gave me a crooked grin. "Not being where I am supposed to be keeps me alive." I was not sure if he was bragging or trying to impress me but it did seem likely that he was being direct and honest with me.

I sent a patrol unit to park outside of unit C-1017 while I wrote up a request for a search warrant. Judge Judith Kempe was in her office and she eyed my request suspiciously but said nothing critical. She used her computer to generate the warrant. I called Laurel Hardy to come along with me to help collect any latent evidence. And just over two hours since I found out about the storage locker I was using a pair of bolt cutters to cut the lock off the particular storage locker. The day manager of the facility stood to my left and Laurel was on my right. Laurel put the lock in an evidence bag and I carefully opened the door to the storage unit. The unit was supposed to be five feet deep and ten feet wide. But the back wall had been removed and there was a gaping black hole behind the C-1017 unit. The back walls seemed to have been pieces of drywall sandwiched between sections of chain link fencing. Someone had unbolted the brackets that held the fencing and pivoted the wall into the unit behind. There was a dark void beyond C-1017 that looked ominous.

I used a flashlight to peer into the darkness and just as I was about to take a step forward Laurel cried out for me to not move. She was down on her hands and knees peering at something. I moved my flashlight's beam and caught a faint flash of brilliance. She said, "Tripwire."

It felt like it took an hour but it took a few minutes for Laurel to find where the trip wire was anchored on one side to the wall and where it headed to an ordinary looking cardboard hidden away in the corner. The box was balanced on a corner so that the slightest jolt would pull it over and signal that someone had passed. She quickly unfastened the anchor and then pried open the box. Inside the box was nothing. I had feared a mercury switch connected some explosives wrapped in nails. But Laurel said the empty box was more devious as it would be damned near impossible to replace it exactly as it had been.

Why would anyone use extremely fine gauge wire, almost invisible, and tie it to an empty box? Laurel suggested it would be an obvious marker if someone had entered the storage unit. And it would be hard to miss that you snagged the trip wire or could assume the breeze of someone walking by would cause the unbalanced boxes to fall. It was a cheap but efficient tool. Stepping over the tripwire, I was as nervous as a long tailed cat walking around in a room of active rocking chairs.

Overhead was more chain link fencing that revealed an open area for air circulation. It also meant any fire would almost instantly spread to all the units. I swept the beam of the flashlight across the floor looking for more tripwires and evidence until I got to the opening of the second unit. The two storage units were back to back and I was willing to bet my next paycheck that the unit opposite C-1017 would not have been under the eye of a security camera. The manager had provided me with evidence on the units around the storage locker in the video. He said the unit behind was for long term storage and he guessed that since it was empty there would be no rental records. And no rental meant no need to have a camera on it. So Green had used the second unit as a pass through or dead drop. There were no other tripwires. Or Suitcases.

The manager explained that he had been on the job for only a few weeks and had no idea about how often gate access codes, unit audits, or other activities took place. But he knew for sure the units on the backside were all unrented.

I was beyond frustrated and Laurel looked exhausted. It took very little convincing to send her home and went back to my truck for a replacement lock that I had brought along. The manager scampered off as quickly as he could waddle away. I grabbed a copy of the warrant to leave in the storage unit as prescribed by law. I carefully balanced the warrant and one of my business cards on the box as not to disturb the delicate position of the box. I took one last look around. And that I when I noticed the right hand wall was not square to the others.

I gave that wall a gentle nudge and it swung open. Someone had set it up so that it was a hidden passage to the next stall. I popped on my flashlight and peeked around the door/wall into the next storage niche. There sitting on the floor were four large suitcases made of black plastic and a backpack. Bingo. A dead drop within the larger dead drop. Victor Green was devious.

Since I knew where the camera was, I pulled my unit around to block the view into the unit. I used a blanket from my truck to cover the suitcases and the backpack to frustrate anyone watching, either live or on video before replacing the moving wall. Then I double checked the search warrant was in place as I closed up the storage unit with the new lock in place.

Down the road I radioed in and said I would be
unavailable. Then I turned off the radio, shut off my cell
phones, and made certain nobody was following me before
heading off to a place I knew I could store the suitcases
properly. After the suitcases were secured, I went through
the backpack but I could not make heads or tails of the
ledger book inside. The diary read like an appointment
book of a very business executive. 'Mar. 2nd Sales - 15K R.
Unser, 2115 Hawthorn Apt 103, 10k L. Uvalde, 14122 2nd
Ave.', 'March 4th Bought 150k (75 w, 50 m, 25 c) Zeno',
'March 4th – Invest 600k Launderia Especial Todos, M.
Martin'. I was pretty sure this was a full trace of the
dead man's money flow. In the back were enough details,
addresses, and a running tally. There were also phone
numbers with names and numbers. And of course Ayce was at
the top of the alphabetical list. Carl Owen's name was
there too.

There was a small stack of twenties, some debit cards,
and Victor Green's driver's license. I pocketed the cash
and stored the backpack with the suitcases.

Lizard was not too shocked when I put the ledger and diary on the desk in front of her along with the backpack. "You found them? I will not, must not ask where." She started to ask another question and stopped herself. "You need someone to watch your back."

"No shit, Sherlock."

"The suitcases! Did you find them …" She stopped and shook her head. "Strike that question. Are you taking these with you to Oklahoma?"

"Could you arrange copies for me? Preferably digital and placed somewhere where I can access them with a password over the internet? And maybe send a few pages to the Federal DA in OKC?"

"As part of a proffer or anonymously?" She warned me I was tap dancing in a minefield and that she would be a better go between. I told her I wanted her clean of things at this point. So she asked again. "A proffer or anonymously?"

I said, "I am not sure. If it is a proffer they will want me hooked at the hip with Owen and his cohorts. Anonymously would give me no leverage but keeps me clean. Or at least cleaner." I certainly did not want to have to spend most of the next several years being interviewed, deposed, questioned, prepared for court, waiting in court, and answering post trial questions about DDA Owen. So I found myself in a damned if I do and damned if I do not situation.

She nodded. "I will get them copied and put on a website. I will send you the details later, on the burner phone. Write the info down in block letters and then toss both the pen and the phone. I will put the originals under lock and key. And then we can decide about the email."

Her father arrived and looked through the ledger. "I feel like the guy in the story who found the magic lamp, polished it, and when the Genie popped out the only thing he could think to wish for was to be left alone."

I nodded. "I could go for that."

Chapter 16

Jane Morris was dressed in snug jeans and a blue silk halter top. Her hair and makeup were perfect but she looked a little uncomfortable on spiked heels walking across the parking lot. On a scale of one to ten she ranked somewhere in the mid-twenties. She gave me a warm kiss. We had met in the parking lot of Darwin's Revenge. "So what is the story behind the name of this place?" We stood on an asphalt parking lot next to an old barn. Vehicles drove in and out of the lot around us but her eyes were locked on the building. Mainly she seemed focused on a cartoon of Charles Darwin astride a bucking beagle with a pork rib clamped firmly in his jaw.

I was wearing relatively clean jeans, boots, and an untucked polo shirt to cover the H&K 45 tucked into the top of my pants. The clothes were a spare set from the office locker. Something made me a little unsettled, edgy, and I fought to keep that from showing. But I could not pinpoint the source of my discomfort and I will admit it was a target rich environment. From the moment I had found out about the storage unit I felt as if I was teetering on the lip of a precipice. I had made sure that I had not been followed since I left the storage unit but something primal in my brain was sending signals that some sort of predator was lurking nearby and salivating at my presence. I smiled at her and forced myself to relax. "Long story. Are you sure you want to hear it?"

"William Darwin taught chemistry at the University of Texas down in Austin. He was fascinated with barbeque sauces, the types of woods used, and the assorted processes from a chemist's standpoint. After a complete chemical analysis of many restaurants, he submitted a tongue in cheek research paper. The paper was published and a national brand of barbeque sauce sued him for divulging the recipe for their product. Dr. Darwin said providing a mass spectrometer report would not give anyone the means to reproduce the sauce. They took him to court and he stuck it to them. It also came to light that the company was using a recipe found in a Betty Crocker cookbook. One of the retired chefs from the company did testify for Dr. Darwin. The judge found for Dr. Darwin and awarded a nice chunk of change, Doc Darwin returned home, refurbished the family barn, and sold more of his sauce

than the company that sued him." We walked to the front
door. I glanced at the sky and saw lazy white clouds
forming to the North. The drought had been long and hard
and these were the first serious cirrus clouds in months.
Out of the corner of my eye I spotted a man out of place;
his clothes looked wrong, sunglasses were a little too
large, new jeans, well-worn but polished black tactical
boots, light blue untucked button down shirt, and a new
Dallas Cowboys baseball cap was pushed too far down on his
head. It wasn't hard to guess that the untucked tail of his
shirt was covering a pistol. The clothes looked brand new
but the boots were worn but in a well-cared for condition.
And despite his sunglasses I could tell that he was
watching me out of the corner of his eye.

        I pretended to answer my phone and took a quick
snapshot of him. I said, "Do you know the guy over to the
left in the blue shirt and baseball cap." I kept my voice
low and Jane surreptitiously looked at him.

        "No," She said. "He does not look comfortable in those
clothes, does he?" She was cool and did not break stride
as we entered the barn. Em Darwin, granddaughter of the
restaurant owner greeted us and took us to a booth in the
back of the dining area. I asked Em about the guy and she

said he had been out there for at least twenty minutes. She had placed us so that my back was to the wall but the front door was in my line of sight along with the man in the blue shirt and baseball cap. And the guy in the Cowboys hat was working very hard to act like he was not watching me.

After Em took our drink order and disappeared into the kitchen, Jane Morris said, "Nice young lady." There was a small amount of frostiness in her voice.

I nodded. "High school junior, straight A student, champion barrel racer, Judo Nikkyu, and ran a two hour fifty five minute marathon last spring. She wants to either be a chemist like gramps or a lawyer like mom or do legal stuff for chemists. Her grandmother was my high school math teacher."

Jane seemed to relax a little and settled into her chair. "My high school math teacher told us in class that the state lottery was impossible to win. The odds were worse than being attacked by a polar bear and then a brown bear on the same day. We bought him some lotto tickets as a gag gift for the last day of school. Three point four million bucks! The bastard took the money and never looked back. Or thanked us." She laughed at her story and then calmed herself as our pair of ices teas arrived. "What do you recommend here?"

There was a commotion at the front door and I slid my hand down my back to feel for my own pistol. Scott Fisher bounded through the door and straight to where we were sitting. In his wake was his sister Jennifer and his lawyer, Westmorland Heart. "What the fuck is goin' on, Sheriff?!" His pudgy face was red and his hair had started to recede since I had lost sight of him. I kept my trigger finger on the trigger guard but kept the gun behind my back.

He did not seem to recognize nor notice Jane Morris, which no longer puzzled me. Heart gently moved Scott Fisher out of the way. "Please elucidate us on why the minor children of the Fisher family are currently locked in your jail?" He had a great theatrical voice and most of the folks in the restaurant had turned to watch his performance. The man came across to me as a pompous, self-inflated jerk but certain people loved that in their lawyers. And I would not put it past him to create a scene in public to poison the potential jury pool. And I wondered how Scott and crew knew where to confront me publically.

I kept my voice low and calm. "I understand that both the young ladies in question were caught shoplifting, then made terroristic threats against the shop, and then battered one of my deputies. Since both are on probation for previous similar offenses, my office has asked their probation officers to consult with the district attorney before their first appearance on this case. That means no bail or release on their own recognizance due to having their paroles revoked provisionally. That is the standard protocol for cases like this."

"I want my baby out of that jail NOW!" Jennifer screamed. Her brother told her to shut up and Heart urged her to remain calm. Heart looked like he had a bad case of indigestion and tried to placate his clients while trying to focus on me. The lawyer tried to filibuster me but I raised my hands in surrender.

Heart forced a smile, "Surely, we can come into some sort of accommodation considering the two young ladies are so … so young." He flashed his polished smile as if his charm and bluster would convince me to change my mind on releasing the young shoplifters.

I forced my own smile, "Are you asking for special treatment for your clients, counselor?"

"Only in light of their young age," He said with enough syrup in his voice to induce adult onset diabetes in an otherwise healthy individual.

"In light of their previous convictions and the battery, my hands are tied. Sorry." The contents of a glass of ice water from another table appeared in my face, tossed by Jennifer Fischer-Mosher. I turned to Heart, "You get out of here, all three of you, or I shall press charges. Got it?" Heart damned near put his clients in headlocks to march them out before they could do more damage. A busboy appeared with dry towels which I gladly accepted. "Sorry, about that," I said to Jane Morris.

"Does that happen all the time," She asked.

"No too often." It had never happened to me before. I have had people throw punches, spit, curse, threaten, and cajole me but never had a glass of very cold water with ice cubes come my way in the middle of a restaurant.

Then she made her big goof. "Who were those people?"

"The man in the good suit is Westmorland Heart, Attorney at Law. The woman is Jennifer Mosher. And the man is your former fiancé, Scott Fischer." The look on her face was part surprise and shame. "So who are you, really, and why are you making such an effort over me?"

She stood up and opened her mouth to say something but then thought better of it. Very quickly Jane Morris or whatever her real name was marching out of the restaurant. I put some money on the table to pay for the tea and prepared to walk out in my soggy clothes. My work phone chirped and I pulled it out of my pocket to read a text message. Janet Polk had identified the suspicious man by the front door of the restaurant. He worked for Federal Deputy District Attorney Carl Owen as an investigator named Matt Schottenheimer.

A moment later I caught movement out of the corner of my eye and was extremely surprised to see my grandfather approaching with his wife. Willow smiled and said 'Hello'.

The old man said, "Mind if we join you for a few minutes?" He then sat next to me and my step-grandmother sat across from us. Both seemed not to notice I was soaking wet. "Very impressive. You handled that perfectly."

Willow said, "It is rare to see a man handed his own balls with such style." I was not sure exactly whom she was talking about -- West or me. I did not feel very proud or happy with myself.

The old man swiveled his head to look at me, "Through the grapevine I heard that you got a warrant for the storage place off Fourth Street."

I shook my head. "Why are you interested?"

Willow said, "My brother took some items that belonged to my mother that I inherited and he bragged that he had them locked up there. I was hoping that we could persuade you to let us inside the storage facility."

The old man said, "If the warrant is broad you might be able to peek in his locker."

"Do you know the number?"

He said, "B-155." I was very happy inside that it was not in the C Block.

I said, "I'll see what I can do." My step grandmother thanked me and invited me over for Sunday lunch. I promised that I would try to make it Sunday and they departed. Sitting in my wet clothes I felt like my world was rapidly drifting downstream towards a waterfall with sharp, jagged rocks at the base.

Outside in the parking lot, I spotted Matt Schottenheimer and walked over. The investigator was puffing on a cigar as he sat on the bumper of a Ram pickup truck. He wore a sweat soaked blue shirt and removed his baseball cap. His voice was a buttery purr, "Sheriff, I have some papers for you." With those words spoken, he handed me a subpoena. He then started coughing and I knew he was my mysterious caller and had sent the pictures of Ayce and Green.

"Okay if I read it?"

He smiled, "My work here is done so I really don't give two shits if you read it or not."

I quickly read the subpoena. "I thought you worked in Dallas District? This is from Oklahoma City."

He shrugged, "Transferred."

"Were you following Owen's CI? The one we found dead in the car park. How did Owen miss the suitcases?" I made sure not to say 'how did you miss the suitcases?' The effort it took to try to look and sound calm was all that I could muster.

"Part of the reason I put in for the transfer. That and he was billing my hours against background checks. He and his crew were claiming to work for some black project, strictly hush-hush, and needed to know only stuff. But the accountants kept bitching. I was draining the budget line for background checks and that they were not drawing from a special project." He smiled, "I complained to Owen and your buddy Ayce running roughshod over me and they got me suspended for insubordination. I was notified of my suspension from a phone call while I was watching CI. After he left the storage unit I went home for three days of unpaid vacation. But I am safe in a new district and they cannot cause me any more problems." He was now grinning happily at me. "But my new boss is being asked by his boss about why you were digging into the old Blue Dog group and why you are interfering with one of his investigations. Into one of his peers. So that is why he wants to talk to you."

So my looking into the Blue Dogs was noticed. "Hypothetical question. You just pulled your best field agent and you want to corral a confidential informant but have limited field skills. Or maybe rusty field skills. How would you take down that CI gracefully?"

"Hypothetically? Well, strictly hypothetically, I would arrange for a meeting with the CI in some place innocuous. Maybe a MacDonald's or an In-N-Out or a Whataburger. Some place public and open but quiet enough for a one on one, face to face meeting. Demand he bring his money, tell him it is marked and has a RFID type tag that can be tracked remotely with readers stuck on highways over passes and railroad bridges. Tell him you want to see the books. And you will swap all his marked money for clean, unmarked bills in suitcases without tracking devices. But you show up late, buy him a soda accompanied with some very salty French fries, and break the news to him that the money is up the road at a rest stop. Or the money is on the way to the rest stop and you'll down the exchange someplace less public. You tell that CI you will see him in twenty or thirty minutes and off he goes not knowing his drink has been spiked."

"So at the rendezvous he would be groggy and easy to manage?"

Matt Schottenheimer grinned at me, "Beats getting physical especially if you are a pretty woman, say someone like one of your former FBI classmates. Only she doesn't realize dosages can be tricky. Or the CI has heart problems. All hypothetically speaking."

"But he, the hypothetical CI, just happened to have a safe drop nearby and decides that he wants to make sure he is not walking into a trap. He does not want to lose the money or his 'get out of jail free' log book.

"So I am taking pictures of the hypothetical CI and the hypothetical FBI agent when the call comes that I am to stand down." He winked at me, "See you next Wednesday at 10 sharp in OKC, Sheriff McDavey. And hypothetically, I would have a hell of a bonfire if I ever found those hypothetical suitcases and that logbook. My mom was old school Sicilian and believed that evil transferred to money if it was made from evil activities."

"And how does one get all this hypothetical information, hypothetically speaking?"

He said, "Well, you get stuck on a conference call and get told to hang up after giving your report. But something tells you to fake hanging up to hear the others give their reports. And that is how you learn the goose that was laying the golden eggs has stopped handing over the eggs. Besides the egg layer has been busy documenting each and every egg with great detail as an insurance policy against potential problems. And, hypothetically, you hear your boss offer up his very potent cough medicine to his female right hand man and the female right hand man promise to use her feminine charms to use that cough medicine to get the goose sedated."

"So, in your humble opinion, just how screwed am I?"

He smiled, "I think you are about to get a Federal gang bang and it will be under a sealed order so nobody will ever know about it. The military term is BOHICA – Bend Over Here It Comes Again."

"And what if your former boss was using the Blue Dogs and their name as a smoke screen to mislead your current boss? Someone knew that old gang name would set off alarms."

294

He smiled. "I know, you know, and very soon my new boss will know. Some knowledge you can share and some knowledge requires you to jam two fingers up their nose and drag them over to see."

I felt like I was a million years old and badly needed a nap. "Recommendations?"

He moved so that he was standing close enough to me and put his hand over his mouth so no lip readers could see what he was saying and to muffle the sound a little. "Let me tell you how the Feds work. You find some schmoe you don't like and make him defend himself in court so that even if he is innocent he will be broke and broken at the end of the process. You end up with a win that you show to your bosses, those bosses show that that win to their bosses, and the big boss shows Congress that they are getting wins. Even if the schmoe stays out of prison his life is shit. You win on a technicality but you are broke, have a shitty reputation, and pretty much unemployable. You sir, have landed in that zone where you may not be guilty but others are going to make it quite clear to everyone else that you may not be innocent. Now in your job reputation is the key. They will dip you in the shit and claim you are one hundred percent shit. Now it is there shit but you are the one the public sees and they will just pack their personal belongings and move to another office or a private practice. And sadly no matter how good you are they will scrap you. Now my *new* boss realizes he has some associates in the district to his south that are problematic and can clean them up by using you. But he will be using you. And he will score a big win."

I sighed and thought for a moment. "My dad told me a story about a baby bird born early one spring. While the parents were out getting worms to feed him, a wind came up and knocked him out of the nest. The little bird was freezing and was almost dead when a cow passed by and dropped a load of manure on him. Suddenly the bird was warm and he knew he was not going to freeze. But then a cat appeared and started digging at the edge of the cow patty to get to the baby bird. The moral of the story is that all that shit on you are not your enemy. And all that try to help you out of the shit are not necessarily your friend. So, which are you?"

He grinned, "Well, I never before wanted to say that I hope I am the shitting cow." He stubbed out his cigar on the ground. "You never heard this from me but the Blue Dogs were being investigated only because the granddaughter of

one of the former gang members who wrote an article in a
college paper that claimed the FBI back in the day were
racist pigs who targeted the Blue Dogs only because of
their race. Just the FBI checking its tracks to head off
potential embarrassment from our J Edgar Hoover influenced
past. It was a coincidence that made a nice red herring to
get you to spend time on it and I am sure Owen used the
recording of you two talking about the Blue Dogs to help
get some sort of warrant, after some careful editing." He
walked off happily and climbed into a little white car.

Detective Ben Mentzer climbed out of an unmarked
patrol car with a shit eating grin on his face. "I thought
we'd lose signal when you got doused with water but I was
able to get it all recorded. I have all the video feeds for
the restaurant's security cameras copied too. And, as I
said to you recently, you do have a way of pissing people
off, Sir. A unique way."

-

After my sojourn to Florida, the FBI sent me to an
area of South Central Los Angeles. My computer skills were
needed to add some additional equipment to cell phone
towers. There are a number of devices coming into use with

names like Barracuda, Rhombus Primer, Fleisler Signal Processor, and a few others. Essentially they copied the signals from cell phones as they bounced off cell signal towers. Most of the devices you find on cell towers take the messages and repeat those messages to the cell towers neighboring that tower. And they are called 'repeaters'.

But these new devices had more programming and parts so that these 'repeaters' would send copies of some cell phone traffic to special computers, or watch for certain credentials from a wireless device for extra processing.

Installing the devices required climbing the cell towers, finding a suitable location, and bolting things into place. I was lucky that an old phone line worker did most of the installation work and my job was to test the communications software. The hard part was that most of the towers we were adding gear to was along the 405 freeway. They do not set up cell towers in the back yards of upper income areas and it is cheaper to put them in what was euphemistically called lower income higher density areas. This meant that the majority of the towers were on real estate contested by various gangs. And the gangs were very interested in what was happening to things on their turf plus they were suspicious that what was happening was part of a conspiracy to watch, control, and contain them. I was very aware that I was being watched at all times. And unlike the John Ford western movies where the Apaches watch from high on the mesa the cowboys below, there would be no seventy cavalry to save my bacon just before the credits roll.

"Well, I'll be damned," Gus, the phone line technician said on a wet afternoon as we prepared to install a new device. Gus was not his real name. We had a device called a Sync Sponge – a box two meters by twenty five centimeters, according to the mounting guide – that was supposed to be the latest, state of the art, tool to intercept cell tower traffic. "Somebody must have put this install on my list wrong."

"Why do you say that?" He pointed to another Sync Sponge that was already in place. He thought, since the Sponge was the latest and greatest, that another lineman had recently installed it and we had a duplicate work order. But from the dirt and grime, it was obvious that this Sponge had been in place for several months. I checked the manufacturer's plate and wrote down the serial number, the MAC address, and the other details. I used a small screwdriver to pry open the access port and used a cable to connect up a laptop computer.

"Do you know the password?" Gus looked nervous as he alternated from watching a pair of gang bangers down the street watching us through a set of binoculars and peeking over my shoulder.

"It is the default. Whoever installed it kept the default password," I said. The log files told the history of six months of operation. I scrolled through a series of menus until I found the network address of the two computers receiving the information this older sponge was soaking up for half a year. I then checked the installation notes I had been given and the computer addresses were from the same computer subnet. "I thought these sponges were only a few months old. This one has been up for half a year. And it's been sending data to one of our slash twenty four networks all that time."

"Ours is not to reason why, ours is to install crap," Gus muttered. "Do you ever wonder why the fuck an old bastard like me, long past retirement age, is climbing towers to install crap with a wet behind the ears academy grad? Basically, it is because I have no life. I went through a series of wives, drove off a small tribe of my own kids, and managed to spend a decade after I was supposed to be retired on a job because I am good at my job. Being good at my job includes not poking my nose past the boundaries my bosses have set. What you are doing is treading on very thin ice with shoes that are burning hot." He paused a moment and said, "You will not get me involved in your crap. Do you understand me on that point?"

We installed the new sponge, I used my laptop to make sure it was set correctly, and climbed down from the tower. The gang bangers were standing a dozen yards away, glaring at us. They had no idea exactly what Gus and I had been doing but they correctly suspected it was not for their benefit. Gus and I drove back to the office and I was quickly called on the carpet. The SAIC, Special Agent in Charge, of the Los Angeles office wanted to know why I tapped into a secret device. A device I was not authorized to access. Gus had tattled on me.

"Sorry, Sir. I thought the Sponges were brand new on the market. Seeing one in place that had been there for several months seemed odd."

"Damn it. It was a prototype. I applaud your initiative but you cannot just poke your nose into everything." He told me there was a certain way he expected me to act and that while my breaking into the sponge showed initiative, he was not a fan of people working for him having initiative.

"So the others are ours too?"

He blinked at me. "What others?" There were three other sponges up there and I handed over my notes on the other three. The four other sponges, other than the one I help installed, had been in place for a minimum of two months. Two of them reported to a computer is an IP number range for an internet service provider in San Antonio and the other to a business in Idaho. "Maybe you should stick your nose in everything."

The next day the SAIC's boss tore me a new asshole before asking me to determine to whom the other Sponges belonged to. So I learned that I pissed my bosses off but they in turn used the information I came up with for their benefit. For a moment I was their pet rogue.

For my 'initiative' I was rewarded by a new assignment with Gus. We climbed over two hundred cell towers documenting the soak sponges we did not know about as well as some other odd devices. Eight months later I was reassigned to a desk job and kept away from all computers.

Chapter 17

There were gray clouds in the sky when I left the restaurant that were reflecting the reddish hues of the setting sun. They had a heavy leaden color that promised rain to the parched ground. But with the drought lasting so long the actual prospect of any precipitation was next to none. Good things had bypassed us so often I sincerely questioned if anyone in the county hoped to receive any precipitation until the winter storms hit and most were predicting a weak mild winter at that. But I was already wet from the glass of water that had been thrown on me so I doubted that I would notice a sudden baptism had erupted from the sky. The evening seemed to be going from bad to worse when the first of two phone calls came to my phones.

"Do you have my earrings," She asked in a sultry tone. "I think I left them the other night at your place. And I am sorry I got mad and stormed off like I did." She was speaking in a low voice, almost a whisper which made me think she was with others but was out of earshot of them. There were somewhat muffled conversations in the background and light jazz music. I guess she had at least a pair of very strong adult beverages under her belt.

I said, "Yes, I have them with me now if you want them. Want me to bring them to you?"

"Oh, hell no. I'm at dinner with some people from Austin and will be stuck with them all night. I only noticed the earrings were missing when I was getting dressed and I remembered wearing them the other night. Thank goodness you have them. They are my favorite pair," she said before covering the phone with her hand. I could hear through the muffled connection that she was making someone named 'Earl' a promise that she would be right inside in a minute. "I've got to go. I wish I could visit you tonight." She let out a sigh that sounded painful, "By the time I get out of here and get my husband settled, it will be way too late for me to visit you. And before you ask, yes I am giving him yet another chance. Another trip around on the old Merry-go-round." She paused and I heard the sound of her licking her lips before she said, "Maybe I can talk him into leaving early."

I started to tell her not to bother when she interrupted. "By the way, you are being Silver Plattered to the SAG."

"What?"

"I was talking to Sadie Evans in the State Attorney General's office at lunch today and said the new Federal ADA in Dallas thinks you lifted evidence and they are working on proving their case. Sadie told me because she knows I live in McDavey County and wanted some background on you. I let her know that you were the last person to convert case evidence. She doesn't like that new ADA and she is here with me telling me she told her boss to pass on the investigation. The ADA has a lot of sloppy circumstantial evidence and is promising to have your head, or at least your balls, on that proverbial silver platter Monday morning. So you need to take care. Owen is the guy who tried to railroad Virginia Cooper a few years ago and got his hand slapped for it before they promoted him to the Southern District of New York. He got a lot of bad press for that fuck up. And to get your hand slapped and promoted means he has a patron high up in the ranks."

"Did you hear they burned down my house? The FBI also has torn up the domiciles of a third of my deputies?"

"Your house is gone?" She then said she had to run and hung up before I could respond. I made a mental note of the name Virginia Cooper for later just to see how the game was played in the past.

I had just put my personal phone back in my pocket when my work phone rang. Janet Polk wanted to let me know Ruiz and Vince had both handed in their resignations and Lilly Greeves had just asked if she had an example resignation letter. "We're shorthanded now before losing these three. With them gone we are going to be hurting," She said. I asked her to call out volunteer reserve officers, usually cops from other areas that were semi-retired but still wanted to keep their status active by working a few hours a week for me if any of them could step up. Janet said she would and was going to leave a message for the Country Human Relations manager to run an ad for deputies.

I climbed into my vehicle and was just putting my work cell phone away when the burner phone I had been given in Lizard's office vibrated. There was a text message letting me know an adult beverage was waiting for me and the location of where it waited. The location was in Longitude and Latitude and I had to plug those numbers into my phone to find out where I had to be.

Next was a quick stop by a store to buy some civilian clothes. I bought a cheap set and a good set to replace what had burned. Changing out of my wet stuff in the dressing room, the cheap set fit fairly well and I paid cash.

Back in the truck I looked up Virginia Cooper and found out she had been a twenty eight year old graduate of Columbia Law School who had committed suicide. Her family claimed that the Federal prosecutors hounded her to death, caused her to lose jobs, and finally felt she had no option but to swallow enough sleeping pills to kill a horse. Like a good lawyer she kept a contact log and six months before her demise Carl Owen asked her for details on one of her clients and told her and her managing partner at the law firm that Owen needed some privileged information on a client. Said client had an uncle who was connected to the mob and Owen wanted to start a racketeering case against the client and uncle. Cooper balked and brought in her managing partner into the meeting who said she was right to

tell Owen to go to Hell. That night the partner was
hosting a dinner party for his friends when Owen arrived
with a search warrant and proceeded to tear a very nice
Brooklyn brownstone apart. The partner was embarrassed
when it was announced that he must be part of the
racketeering since he refused to hand over the materials.
The next day the managing partner fired Cooper to provide a
space between them.

Cooper found another position a few weeks later and on
her second day Owen arrived demanding she testify on the
case from the old job since she no longer had client-
attorney privilege. Her new bosses did not want to upset
the Department of Justice and promptly fired her.

When she got back to her apartment she found it
swarming with FBI Agents who had cleared the place out,
frozen her bank accounts, and were telling her landlady
that Cooper was suspected of being a shady lawyer who ties
to the mob. She was evicted on the spot. With no money,
no place to live, and no prospects for a future, the young
woman went to the local pharmacy for a slightly early
refill on her sleeping pills.

She recorded a video with the details of what happened and posted it on the internet as she waited for the drugs to take effect. The video went viral and Cooper's sister in Atlanta took things to the press. It was that week's messy national scandal and it turned out the suspect client had never actually had any dealings with the mobbed up cousin since their first communion together. The mobbed up cousin gave the Westchester County prosecutor's office some evidence on cigarette smuggling before going into the witness protection program. Eventually a large undisclosed sum went to the sister. The scandal was blamed on the rising tide of white collar crime and eventually the press moved on to the next horror story. And Owen got a promotion for his diligence.

If I had disliked Owen before, I now had a burning hate for the man. His superiors probably loved the results but the damage in his wake was immense.

I traded the patrol unit for an older enduro motorcycle the department used for back country trail work. I fished my two derringers from my office safe and loaded one with 380 shotgun shells and the other 38 rounds. I grabbed a black jacket from the gear room as I wondered what the Hell Vince wanted. It took me half an hour to get the location.

Vince Izzard handed me a tumbler generously filled with a smooth single malt. His text message had provided me with the coordinates of his deer lease and I arrived at the rendezvous site. He took the property from a client as payment on legal bill and Vince made sure nobody hunted on the lease. He liked having some place that was very private and admitted he did not think he would enjoy waiting in a blind in order to blow away some poor passing deer. He claimed that sitting out in the middle of nowhere let him reflect on his life and thoughts. When I arrived Vince was waiting in one of two folding chairs and tending a small fire in front of an old deer stand. The stand was a small shack on spindly stilts that had seen better days. Sparks from the fire danced upward in the dark night as if they were going up to join the stars. His dogs, large mastiffs, eyed me with suspicion until he clucked at them. At Vince's feet was the paperwork I had found in the storage locker. He clicked his tumbler with mine and said, "Mazel tov." He waved a hand to indicate I should sit in one of the lawn chairs by the fire.

"What did you find out?"

Vince smiled. "It is like the old good news, bad news joke where the fortune teller tells the beautiful woman she is going to be named a beauty queen in five years. The bad news is that she is going to be living in a leper colony." I didn't laugh and after a moment he sighed in disappointment. He glanced up at the night sky and took in a deep breath. "What you have here is a calendar, a diary, an address book, bank records, and other items of data from a very anal, precise record keeper. Either he knew the ax would fall and needed a way to save his neck or he wanted to double cross the folks he was working with enough weight to save his own ass. The stuff in the backpack is the legal equivalent of a hand grenade with a very loose pin in the hand of someone with the shakes."

His cell phone chirped and after a quick glance he put it back in his pocket. "Herself found a tracker in the rear bumper of your patrol SUV. And she said two vehicles kept creeping past your place, or what is left of it." I explained that Jane Morris had been some sort of plant and that I had been served a warrant by an investigator from the Oklahoma City Federal DA's office at the restaurant. Then I told him about the Fishers, Heart, and the glass of water. Then, sadly, I was told that the investigator or the Oklahoma DDA had previously had been working for Owen but now worked for the OKC DDA. Vince shook his head, "Shit." He produced a bottle full of a fine single malt and ordered me to take a refill.

A few minutes later Lizard arrived driving a Polaris Razr off-road buggy. In the passenger seat was an impressive looking K-98 Mauser rifle with a scope that looked like it picked up everything but cable TV in the reticles. She was wearing all black and tossed something that looked like a hockey puck at me. The puck had a sticky side so I think it was the tracker from my Yukon. Wordlessly she pulled a black balaclava over her head and slipped off into the dark. I said in a mock British accent, "So whom are we expecting."

Vince smiled, mouthed the word 'whom' with a smile on his lips, and handed me a piece of paper folded in half. The exposed half had a picture of a male Hispanic about fifty from a mug shot. "Michael Archuletta. Our hacker friend found out he was the one who rented the car you found at the rest stop."

"But this is not the driver."

"No, but he was the best friend and former roommate of the guy you found. This guy is right now he is in a cooler in the Travis County Morgue. Seems he was eating at a food truck when he dropped dead. They are waiting for a toxicology report but his lips were cyanotic and his stomach looks like someone walked in there while wearing track spikes. My guess is that he was working with the guy from the rest stop that you found. He was the grip for the Sinaloa cartels and was rumored to have a golden government shield on both sides of the border covering his ass. However recent rumors are that he, for some unknown reason, has fallen from favor with his employers." He took back the piece of paper and dropped it into the fire where it quickly crumpled into a black ball. Another folded piece of paper was offered and this time it had a picture of Green, the driver of the car found at the rest stop. In the photo he wore a dark blue suit, crimson necktie, and a white shirt. It was a professional photographer shot like for a real estate salesman or car dealer.

"That's the DB." The features were a little crisper than when I saw him but it was the same guy we found in the car at the rest stop. I said, "What are his particulars?"

Vince then handed me another photo. "Edward John Wayne was his birth name. Never trusted a defendant with three first names when I was in court. Also known as Ed Green, Victor Green, Edwardo Verde, and Ed Verde. Mom's maiden name was Verde, Spanish for the word green. He was working for the Assistant Federal DA who was running operations from El Paso under a variety of names. He graduated third in his class at Georgetown Law, clerked at the New York State Supreme Court, was going to be a third generation trust fund management lawyer, and then he was drawn to the dark side. The Department of Justice hired him to review financial audits of Fortune 1000 companies and he was a superstar at that work before he got tempted. By the way he and Owen were tied at the hip."

"Dark side?"

"He was asked to handle confidential and secret paperwork for covert operations. One of his classmates evidently begged for a favor and he found the excitement more to his liking than the tax codes of the state of New Jersey. It seems Mr. Wayne actually bloomed as a person from dealing with the shady side of the law. It seems it was like a drug for him and he kept taking on new responsibilities. He took the stuff like a duck to water."

"How do you know all this?"

"Lawyers like to hear their own voices. The one in charge of collection for burial of the body of Mr. Wayne, got a few drinks in him and let his mouth run. Someone who owes me a few favors was on the receiving end of the story and had to suffer along hearing about the costs of an undertaker who could make the body look good before handing over the body to his family and the difficulty of forging supporting documents." He grinned at me, "So now that your house is ashes, where are you staying?"

"They are renting me one of the cabins at the nudist resort but I also rented an apartment off the square. Considering all that I own is in the locker at work or the clothes I bought today at Walmart, I still feel like I have way too much to carry."

One of the dogs stirred, sniffing the air. The other dog was soon up and growling. Vince gave a command and the dogs slipped silently into the darkness. A vehicle appeared, shutting off the headlights but it kept approaching. "Whatever you do keep in your chair until I tell you to move." He then muttered something about the next time he retained me it would cost me more than a buck.

The vehicle was a black Chevy Suburban with heavily tinted windows, like the kind often used by government agencies. I had seen that Chevy before. The front doors opened and Carl Owen stepped out of the passenger side. Ayce Huggins got out from behind the wheel. Vince stood between them and my position. He called out to them, "You are trespassing on private property Mr. Deputy District Attorney."

Owen laughed, "Oh, I have a search warrant, of a sort." He nodded and Ayce drew a pistol, aiming it at me." A split second later the red light of a target laser lit up the center of my chest from an angle off to my right. The red beam led from my chest out into the woods. Not to the barrel of Ayce's pistol. Lizard had me dead in the sights of her Mauser.

Vince was incensed. He said, "You do something stupid and your fall guy gets blown to bits and the folks watching the video I am making will think it was you doing it, not me. So, young lady, put away your gun and we will talk like adults. Or this will look so bad the Department of Justice and the Federal Bureau of Investigation will be the first government bureaucracies ever shut down."

Owen nodded and Ayce holstered her pistol. The red aiming light stayed centered on my chest. I tried to keep calm knowing a large caliber round could slam into my sternum any moment. There was no way to get out of the lawn chair easily. I took Vince's warning to stay put to heart.

Vince returned to his folding chair and pulled some papers out of the stack. One of the pages tumbled into the fire, "Oop-sies, my bad." I have been reading this crap and I must say to Mr. Owen that your original idea was good. Very good. It did not scale and too many cooks shoved their way into your kitchen when they saw it was a success. And they certainly wanted their turn at the money teat. But working around budget constraints by cutting yourself in on the smuggling action was brilliant. You set up some poor dirt farmer in Mexico to run drug production, take a cut of his profit for help getting it across the border, set up a Federal operation to shut him down when the earnings plateau, arrest the farmer, and then start again with some other poor farmer. Meanwhile you get dealers you control to sell the product for full street value with no worry of getting caught. And then you partnered with the smaller cartels to avoid having to deal with the farmers directly. It is like cultivating a crop.

Nearly thirty seventeen million with nearly fifteen of that left in several banks since you started. Kudos."

I noticed Ayce glance at Owen as if she were surprised. She then looked at me and I could sense frustration on her face. Her hand was flexed as if she was planning a fast draw of her pistol.

"Those are classified documents belonging to the Department of Justice and you will hand them over immediately. And you will also hand over the evidence in the suitcases." Owen had puffed up like a peacock trying to show his non-existent tail feathers.

"I asked a friend of a friend to look into the official files. There is no record of Operation Bezerker online, in the files, or the collective memory of the field operations folks. So you cultivate the business, bring in the money, spread the cash around your bosses on the sly, and just happen to forget to tell your bosses that you are skimming off the top." Vince sprinkled another piece of paper into the fire. "And from what I can tell your predecessor in your current position who had been reporting to you had just one set of records of who did what and to whom with what bank account numbers." He dropped yet another piece of paper into the fire.

"Stop that! What do you want?" Owen was very upset and barked out, "What do you want you motherfucker?"

Vince nodded at me. "First, McDavey is no longer your fall guy. I do not care who you stick this on as long as it is not him or one of mine. Second, you shut down Operation Bezerker. At least in this area. Move it west or move it East but not around here. Third, well, third is a favor that I will want later, kind of like in pro sports when they get a draft choice later. Do we have a deal?" He reached down and had some sort of remote control joystick that he jostled. The buzzing noise that developed over my head had to be some sort of drone but I could not see it.

"Deal," Owen said as he too looked for the drone. At the moment there was a streak of something near Ayce and suddenly she was down on the ground. A figure in black stood over her. Another figure in black was holding something to the head of Carl Owen. "What the fuck!"

The dogs appeared near Owen with saliva dripping off their fangs. The dogs had a deep, rattling bark that boomed out into the night. I guessed that Owen was about to become a chew toy shortly.

Vince nodded to me and said, "You can get up now." The laser pointed at my chest had blinked off for good. He walked over to where Owen was being trussed up like a roped calf ready for branding. The unconscious body of Ayce was dragged to a position next to Owen. The anger on Owen's face was clear but he kept his mouth shut.

The black figure who dropped Ayce spoke and I realized who it was when Lizard's voice came out from behind the black balaclava mask. "The javelinas will be here soon." She patted Ayce down and came up with a spare magazine for the pistol. Owen had his wallet, a cell phone, and a fat wad of cash. "We need to be gone before they cross down to the river or they won't come near the bodies."

Owen looked shocked. "What bodies? What is a Java-whatsis?"

I decided it was my time to talk, "They are most likely feral hogs and not Javelinas. They really are wild pigs that like all sorts of food, especially fresh food. A pig that goes feral takes on the traits of a wild pig in just a few months. I think my legal council plans to leave you here for the hogs to discover. The big ones have razor sharp tusks to tear flesh and jaws that can snap the femur of a bull like a matchstick. A truck hit a five hundred pound one a year ago and destroyed the front end of the truck but the pig just trotted off into the bush. They devastate crops, trash heaps, and anything they can digest. They are very messy when they eat. In Wise County they got to two dogs chained up in a backyard and the security camera footage of what they did was pretty gruesome. They toss parts all over the place and soon there are only traces left. It is like a three hundred pound chainsaw hitting a side of beef. And what they do not get, the hawks and buzzards and bugs will spread over a ten mile radius."

Vince said, "And your family and friends, assuming you have any of those, will never know what happened to you. They will wonder until the ends of theirs days what the fuck happened to old Carl. They will ask each other 'did he run away' or 'did he die alone out in the middle of nowhere' or 'maybe he just went on a drunk and died in a gutter somewhere'. A week from now the best forensic scientists could sweep this area and not find anything useful. Wild pigs are amazingly destructive and make your average buzzards look like a picky eater. Skin, hair, bone, clothing, shoes all consumed only to be crapped out over a very wide area."

Carl Owen had started to look frightened. For a moment I thought he might whine or cry. But then he got control of himself. "What do you want to set me free? Name your price. I can get as much as your heart desires but let me go."

Vince used one of his feet to poke Carl sharply in the belly.. "'Me'? Not us? You hear that honey?" He was looking over at Ayce who had regained consciousness and was paying attention very carefully. "The DDA has already sacrificed you without hesitation..."

"You can do this to us," She said. Her eyes locked onto mine. "You are not a murderer." Desperation clouded her face and I could see tears welling up in her eyes.

"Technically, it is not murder. I did not stun you. I did not tie you up. And how was I to be certain that wild pigs would come along?" I squatted down to face her. "You came to me with threats. Threats to me and threats to those who work with me and threats to my friends and threats to my family. You knew my history and tried to use our past association to wheedle something out of me. Something you got illegally. When that did not work you went to threats.

You tracked me like an animal. You had my house and all my possessions burned. You have ruined the lives of the folks who work for me. And not a few minutes ago, you pulled a gun and aimed it at me. Tell me Ayce, how much sympathy should I have for you?"

Owen snarled and tried to break his binds. "Let me go. I am ordering you as the ranking law enforcement official on scene. You have sworn to uphold the law."

I shook my head. "Well, the sheriff is the ranking law enforcement official in his county bar none. I could arrest you, bring a case with the evidence I have, and see you spend years playing games in court without paying your dues. But you have tainted my office, tainted my deputies, killed your informant, probably killed your predecessor, and did a litany of nasty stuff with this fake drug operation of yours. You are the type of scum that would make a mockery of any trial and you probably could trade on some old favors to get things to lean your way. It would be best for you to pass into history, through the bowel of a pig."

Vince smiled. "Oh, by the way the papers I was burning were one of the copies I made of the materials your money man left behind as a guarantee. I guess he did not trust you and those materials were his 'get out of jail free' card. So somehow you frightened him into fleeing to what he hoped was a sanctuary. But you managed to get him drugged and you killed him before he could hand over that evidence."

I wondered why the dead CI had left the documents and money behind. Was it because he suspected Owen and Ayce? Or did he leave them for someone else to come along later and collect? Was there someone else working with the dead man? I wanted to ask questions of Owen, Ayce, and now Vince but I kept my mouth shut.

"It was only enough to knock him out," Ayce said. "I gave it to him at a fast food joint down the freeway. He showed me a few pages copied from one of his diaries and said he was going to bring down the entire system but he wanted me to turn myself in with him. He thought we would get some sort of deal with immunity. And he had some lame ass romantic feelings he had for me. He was tired of the work and wanted out of the game. He said that if we did not let him go he had put his diaries on a webserver and it would go live if he did not check in to reset something or other. That information would be dozens of people in the

DOJ ruined, thousands of cases thrown out, and a fuck load of criminals turned lose on the street."

Lizard said, "So you let him drive off and you tried to follow in your car until the accident?"

"Accident?" I was greatly surprised at that news.

Vince nodded. He said, "Our digital friend was looking at all the security camera footage up and down the interstate. He found the dead man leaving a Waffle House down in Fort Worth but then noticed a silver Camry that left right afterwards. But in her hurry she had a fender bender with a family backing out of a parking space. Dumb using your own private vehicle." Ayce told Vince to go fuck himself. "And then you called old Carl here to say you were stuck and your CI was heading north. Lucky for you he was down in Fort Worth according to his cell phone tower tracking records."

Lizard said, "If she had showed up in a big Suburban he would have known he was in trouble. So she used her private vehicle to make the meeting. Put him at ease. He probably asked her to help support him when he went public with the information. He must have got cold feet being the guy responsible to supply dirty cash to you and your buddies."

"So the poor bastard drives down the road, feels weary and pulls off for a quick forty winks. I guess he was heading to Oklahoma to talk to their new Federal DA. My counterpart has hated my guts for years and I knew he had been asking questions. Anyway I thought he was going to take a quick nap and then back on the road with enough time to make a ten AM meeting. But during the nap he died. Overdose or the dose was good but not with an underlying heart condition. Or our good buddy Carl here finds him and makes sure he is dead." I forced myself to speak slowly and keep my voice calm. The puzzle pieces that had been fuzzy and amorphous were suddenly sharply defined as they dropped into place.

"He was dying when I found him. Hell, I broke speed records trying to catch him on his way to Oklahoma City. I saw him as he was pulling off the freeway to get to the rest stop. I thought he needed to pee but he never got out of his car. So I walked over to his car and tapped on the window. Diaphoretic, difficult respiration, and incoherent. I think he expected me to take him to a hospital. I searched him, searched the trunk. Nothing. I wiped everything down and took anything he had," Carl Owen said. "That fucktard."

"I could not figure out why you took the car keys," I said. That was the biggest clue that said it was a murder. Having no fingerprints was weird but no car keys meant someone had to have taken them with them after they locked the car.

"I took the keyring out of habit not thinking that someone with half a brain would wonder what happened to the car keys." Owen said quietly. "I was surprised later when I realized that I still had the keys. Then I thought maybe it was better that I had them. I hoped one of the other keys on the keyring went to a lock somewhere useful."

"So your latest cash was gone, your money man was gone, and you had to cover things up," I said.

"That is a good summary," Owen said. "But I really wanted the log books, not the money. He said he kept the bank accounts in there and who bought what when. Some of the names on the list are pretty big. We worked with folks who wanted to help, who wanted investors but did not know we were the FBI. The money got laundered and they got a cut. Most of them wanted drugs so I made sure that they got the top rate product, for a top rate price."

Lizard said, "But how did all this get started?"

Ayce rolled onto her back and said, "You know how tight our budgets are. Feast or famine. One day we can get all the equipment we need and the next we are recycling paper clips out of the gutter. One day we had a little extra cash on hand from an undercover drug operation and Owen said it was too bad we could not use it to help make other cases. We knew we could run the drug business better than the crooks and we could cover our asses. We could use the criminals to fight the criminals, as long as we did not get too wild with arresting our clients. The money flowed in and we were able to use our success to insulate ourselves. No more cost accountants and budget trimming crusaders looking over your shoulder all the time asking 'why does this cost so much', 'this needs to go out for competitive bid', and 'your need to scale back', and all that shit that really goes too far in fucking up ongoing operations. We skimmed some money from another case and got the idea into play. We came up with our own budget source. And we did and it worked for a long time."

I said, "You cannot run that sort of hustle indefinitely."

She gave me a malevolent look. "My boss there let his mouth waggle to some of the wrong folks. When certain people hear about what was going on they get upset. And then they threaten to shove their greasy hands so far up your ass that you will feel like a ventriloquist's dummy. That is until you cut them in. A lot of big players demanded into our little money factory as we got more successful. "

Vince prodded Owen, "Just you two and Archuletta knew about all this at the beginning?"

Owen nodded and said, "Yes, at first. My bosses were suspicious but did not want to know where the money they were enjoying was coming from. They knew we were doing something odd but they did not know the details. But they loved it when we were able to help them out, from time to time. And they will come snooping when the money they are used to receiving stops coming." I doubted him that others did not know about what he had been doing.

I said, "Then the blond calling herself Jane Morris was a figment of my imagination?"

"She did not know any details. She is a private eye from Baltimore my ex-wife used in our divorce. Her real name is Evelyn Short and as you know she is really, really good. She was supposed to shadow you but then got the idea it would be easier to do if she was in your pants. Only Ayce and Archuletta and Wayne knew the real details of the operation."

"And the dear departed Mr. Wayne," Lizard laughed. "Impossible. Someone would have noticed you doing things without all the required paperwork."

Owen said, "Archuletta took care of all that. He started off as a contract accountant from the Department of Justice, a cost accountant. Then he started asking to go on a raid. He and Wayne were similar asshole types who liked walking on the wild side. Wayne actually was adopted and managed to get a set of ID under his birth name of Verde and then another set as Green. It was lucky for him that he turned out that he was good at counting cash. Then one night after work, we are all gathered around a taco stand and he mentions how easy it would be to skim the recovered money and the skim to cover operations. I just need to figure out how to work that angle from within the system." I did not like the tone here as they were now blaming things on a dead man when I was sure Owen, Ayce, and others had been running things their way.

"Did you ever think he was skimming you? He was." Vince was now squatting on his haunches. I could see into the chest pocket of the shirt he was wearing and there was a little red LED light glowing on some sort of a device. Was he recording all this? "Or that you were being set up?"

The look on Ayce's face was that of shock and Owen looked confused. He said, "There is no way …" Owen looked at Vince, "What is in the diary?"

"Enough to have got your mail forwarded to Florence Supermax prison permanently. But it is the stuff not in the diary that would make you a good prison wife."

"What stuff?!"

"Your accomplice has a type of computer account to store video, audio, spreadsheets, and stuff like that. All encrypted. The data is encrypted but files have interesting unencrypted names like 'SanMarcosDrugBuyMay02.mp4', which they tell me is a movie, and 'ListOfCashSerialNumbersApril22.pdf'. Did you check to see if the bills were marked? You may not have been marking him but he was. And they don't have to put a physical mark on the bills anymore and sometimes just recording the serial numbers is enough." Vince stood up and added, "You were being played by one of the best. By the way, the reason he was driving to Oklahoma City was to give evidence for a proffer to your counterpart, the Federal District Attorney for OKC, like you suspected." It was obvious to all that the guy keeping the books was not only documenting everything in the very illegal game that was being played but he had created for himself the ultimate 'get out of jail free' card.

Owen began to gag and Vince stepped back just in time to avoid being splashed with the vomit. Vince nodded for me to follow him out of earshot of the two tied up on the ground. Lizard and the still masked stranger stood guard. Vince kept his voice low, "Where is the money?"

"Safe," I said. I received an incredulous look from the old man that he was frustrated that I was not more forthcoming. "Wasn't it Saint Augustin who said something like with enough temptation even a saint would sin?"

"You point being?"

"I trust you and Lizard with my life. But that much money is too much temptation. Even for you." Or the recording device in his pocket.

"You're probably fuckin' right. Next question. And remember that as a lawyer that I usually never ask a pointed question that I do not already know the answer. You know if you arrest them they will have to go to the feds and the federal government will bury this deeper than we can imagine. This story will be quashed, the money confiscated, my life will be made Hell, Lizard will suffer, and you will end up so tied up with this case that you spend the rest of your life giving depositions, testifying, and having everything in your life minutely examined. I think we scared them enough with the story about the hogs."

"So, councilor, what is your recommendation?" I said those words knowing what the answer would be. I reached into his pocket to find his cell phone and that cell phone was recording the audio. I turned off the application and replaced the phone.

"We leave them for the hogs," He said. "Those two assholes on the ground are scum and will not be missed. From the grapevine I heard that they pretty much isolated themselves and they will not be missed for a week or more from the office. If they played things as close to the vest as they claim, it may be a month or more before they are reported missing. And there is no way either of them told someone in their office where they were. Put their cell phones on a freight train car and, if someone checks on them, they will travel all over Hell and back."

He was right. Letting Owen and Ayce go was not going to stop what they were doing. They might shift their operation to another area but they would still be ruining the lives of others. After trying to find another way out of the problem, I nodded my acceptance of his plan. The scam had to be stopped in its tracks and Owens & Ayce needed to be removed totally. I said, "Who is the other person in black."

"You do not want to know," Vince said. "You know those two have ruined your career and probably the careers of everyone who has worked for you. Every two bit lawyer will know about the search warrants and will use those searches as grounds for dismissal or to attack you and yours. You may get re-elected but you'll not get further."

I nodded my head sadly. "A lot of things end tonight, or at least, they start to end tonight."

I went back to Ayce and patted her down. Lizard had patted her down but I knew Ayce and Lizard did not. I turned up a knife and a handcuff key tucked under the belt of her clothes. In one of her boots I found an old straight razor with an obsidian handle that must have been an antique. Owen came up clean when I patted him down. I exchanged looks with Lizard and she looked tired. I said, "You three clear out before the pigs come. Take their shoes and belts as the pigs will not eat the metal parts."

Lizard said, "We can stay." But the tone of her voice told me that she knew I was right.

I said, "Better that I do this alone." I did not need her, her step father, and whoever the Hell was in the black hood being able to say 'Yes, I saw Sheriff McDavey let these two federal employees get killed by wild pigs'. Vince packed up his belongings and doused the fire. Lizard took the Suburban Ayce and Owen had arrived in. Vince and the person in black left in the Razor dune buggy. I moved the motorcycle so the pigs would not smell it and then double checked on the two trussed up on the ground.

The breeze picked up and a sour smell in the air began to get stronger. I checked the two guests and said, "Not long now. And screaming or yelling is not going to bring anyone to the rescue. You're on a ninety two acre tract of land that has no neighbors. And the noise will bring the pigs faster." I climbed up into the blind and was thankful to find Vince had left some bottled water and a blanket. Through a slit in the wall, I could see Ayce and Owen on the dusty ground. For a while they trashed around until they were exhausted. From the height of the blind I could see the animal tracks from the wooded area to the nearby watering hole.

I caught a whiff of hogs close to two hours later. Several large sows with piglets in tow. They would head down the creek for water and root by night before heading back to the woodlands with the daylight breaking. In the moonlight the hogs were sleek black forms darting from shadow to shadow. The largest sow sniffed Owen and he cried out. The pig startled when he cried out and she slashed him with her tusks. The coppery smell of fresh blood and meat brought the others pigs in a feeding frenzy. Twenty minutes later the last of the juvenile pigs followed the others on the way down to the watering hole. There were patches of bloody ground and a few strips of clothing left of what were two humans. A coyote dashed out from the brush to grab something with her jaws before trotting off into the shadows.

I climbed down and retrieved the motorcycle. The headlight caught a skunk hurrying away with a bloody strip of something in its mouth as I left. A deep rumble shook the air and the trees were suddenly dancing in a stiff breeze. Large raindrops spattered on me as I headed down the road. The sound of rain on the road sounded like a sizzling steak on a griddle. My clothes were soaking wet as I pulled up to the gate for the nudist colony. I had managed to rent a small cabin which was pretty Spartan but it was a palace compared to the ash pile that had been my home. I pulled off the wet clothes and replaced them with dry stuff from a pair of Walmart bags.

The drought was over the raindrop pounding on the top of the cabin sounded like a snare drum. I dropped my wet clothes in the kitchen sink and headed to bed. And somehow I slept peacefully that night.

Chapter 18

Three days later Vince Izzard was in the hospital after a stroke that left his left side useless. Lizard said it was probably caused by the stress of the last week but did not go into detail to anyone but the look she gave me told me it was probably from his activities at the deer blind. She made sure to tell me that she did not blame me and that Vince knew he had been on borrowed time for a year or two. A second stroke the next day made things worse and the doctors followed his expressed wishes on file medical orders for no resuscitation or extraordinary measures to extend his life.

Laurel Hardy called me to look at a three dimensional view of the female skull from the sunken Ford Mustang. Her lab was spotless except for the pictures that I had provided and she was uneasy. "I hope you do not want me to say that with any confidence that it is the same woman." The computer generated face looked somewhat like Rachel. And more like a million other women. There was no way to tell if the girl underwater for so long was Rachel. I told laurel I was actually happy with the results because I was.

Lilly Graves had taken a few days leave to clean up her house after the search warrant. The FBI would eventually pay for the repairs and acknowledged their fault after Lizard started a lawsuit on her behalf. Lilly said that on a sleepless night she reviewed her life and decided that she no longer wanted to wear a badge, carry a gun, or anything to do with a uniform. She told me that she had once felt proud to have worn the uniform but that feeling was now gone. I wished her well.

Carl Owen was actually missed much earlier than I had hoped. A secretary from his office called to say she saw an appointment in his calendar to speak to me but he was unavailable and she did not want me waiting on his call. His cell phone was duct taped to the frame of an intermodal storage unit on the back of a trailer at a truck stop and went who knows where. Ayce's cell phone ended up the hopper of an empty coal carrier of the Burlington Northern and Santa Fe Railroad heading towards Oklahoma. The truck the two of them had used that night had been left at the rest stop that started it all with the keys in the ignition and a few hours later it was gone too.

Lizard called to say she was selling the bar and taking the insurance money from her stepfather's estate to travel the world. "What are you doing of value? Come with me, what do you have here? Janet can run the Sheriff's Department even if she is reluctant and she has basically run the place anyway. We have nada here, cuz, so let's go." I refused her offer but could not answer her second part of the question. What did I have here?

I drove up early for my meeting with the Federal D.A. in Oklahoma City. On the record I said I knew nothing. Off the record, I handed him a thumb drive with the digitized records from the backpack and let him know I had no idea of the content but was assuming that there were other copies hidden on the internet just ready to be embarrassingly revealed if more problems came my way. It may have sounded like me making a threat but I honestly had no idea if the dead man from the rest stop had something rigged to appear on the internet.

I called and asked the old man to meet me. He tried to beg off but I said I really need to talk to him. He said to meet him at Cross Creek, where the old Mustang had been drug out of the mud. But with the recent rains the creek was not a glorified mud puddle but a quickly moving stream. The old man had a fishing pole in hand and made large, lazy casts when I arrived. He eyed me as I approached, "Remember when you told me you were running for sheriff that I was not exactly thrilled at the prospect?" I said that I did remember that he was not exactly happy when I announced my candidacy. "A sheriff is like the parent of a county. The disciplinary parent. The one that hands out the spankings and gets cursed. Not the popular parent either. You are the shoulder to cry on and that bastard who pulled someone over for a DUI rather than see them drive into a freeway abutment or head on to someone other poor fucker. Sometimes to keep those you need to keep safe you end up doing things you do not like." He cranked the reel of the fishing rod absently, "You run off a child molester to keep him away from the daughters of his new girlfriend who has no idea the new man in her life raped a four year old or the new neighbor has a large collection of kiddie porn featuring babies getting raped. Or you slow walk an arrest warrant to help someone with a bogus charge from twenty years before you avoid extradition in a case you know some overworked junior prosecutor will not take to court. And you lose good people who work for you over stupid stuff. And then there is the always all-consuming and rapidly growing bureaucratic demons that make everything harder to do."

I began to wonder if the forth figure from the deer stand was my grandfather. But my better judgement told me it was not him. But the idea nagged at me. I watched him cast the line again back to the same spot. "Right before I retired, I was heading home after a long night. Suddenly there was a woman, naked from the waist down flagging me down in the middle of the road. I stopped and she scrambled into the car. A moment later a man came out of nowhere with a shotgun leveled at her."

"So what did you do?"

"I hit the gas and drove over the son of a bitch. He was trapped under the oil pan, which was burning his face. I let him bleed out and then called for an ambulance." He grimaced, "I probably could have saved his life if I had moved the car and called EMS right away. But I made a decision that the woman shivering and crying in her car did not need to be beaten and raped by her husband every time her husband got mad at her or mad at the world. She was too traumatized to remember the car running over her first husband. It was reported as a hit and run, unknown driver, and unknown vehicle. She never saw him with the shotgun or even noticed that I ran over him. The push bar took the collision without a scratch. She was in shock. I hand washed the car to get the blood and burned flesh off the underside. But the next day someone found the man's body on the side of the road and it was written up as a hit and run."

I was unsure if he knew about Owen, Ayce, or the suitcases. Had he been at the deer blind? I was still uncertain. "So what advice do you have for me?"

The old man chuckled. "None, really. You're a good sheriff and you are doing a great job. The one … suggestion … is that you need to groom Janet Polk to take over for you. With all the shit you've taken the past week you should take some vacation and let her run things. That way you have someone good to replace you if you ever want to step down. Or if something else happens to you. You do not want your last thought to be wondering who the Hell is going to run things when you are gone." He was tugging on the fishing pole and the pole bent over at the recalcitrant fishing line. The old man gave an extra pull and the line came free. But there was something on the lure that was heavy but not fighting like a fish. He reeled in what looked like a clump of wet weeds. I grabbed the line with one hand and went to unhook the mess. Then I noticed that there was something under the weeds and there was a dull metallic color. When Dolly Wood had told me about the Cross of Santa Cruz I assumed it was three feet high and very ornate but the object in my hand was barely a foot tall. But it was a very simple cross and very definitely made of gold. The old man laughed, "Dolly's been talking about that damn thing as long as I have known her." I cleaned the last of the muck off the cross and almost didn't hear the old man. "You know, if Rachel had wanted to find you she would have."

Those words hit me hard. "So, she is alive?"

He shrugged and recast his fishing line. "I honestly do not know. When you were running around with her I was worried that her husband would shoot one or both of you. I don't know if he ever knew. I heard that she kissed you at your high school graduation and wondered if you two were going to do something dumb. So I had a talk with her."

I was dumbfounded.

The old man continued. "I saw her at the grocery store buying what we called feminine hygiene products plus some things for a road trip. I took her to the side and asked her if she was planning on getting you or her killed? Her husband would have been the kind to plug you both. She said she was leaving him and walked away."

My heart was pounding in my chest. "We were planning to head to California that night. She was going to pick me up at the old train depot but never arrived. I assumed that she left without me."

He reeled the line in and then cast again. "If she is still alive and if she had wanted to contact you again, she would have done so by now." His saying it a second time hurt just as much as the first time. But this time I realized it was her life and her choice.

"But what about the girl and the guy that were in the car over there in the creek. If it is not Rachel, then who is it?"

"You know some cases you just can't solve. One girl under water for years is pretty much like the others." With that he put a hand on my shoulder, gave me a stern look, and then walked away. How many unidentified bodies in unmarked graves are there in this country, this state, this country that will never be known? I'd hate to have to dredge any of the big lakes in the state and do the paperwork on the bodies I would find." He looked at the cross and told me to take it away from him.

I took the golden cross to Dolly Wood in her hospital room and she was overjoyed to see it. Her old wrinkled fingers caressed the cross and a look of awe was painted on her face. "So it is real!" She then told me she had to go to a nursing home as her injuries were too severe for her to live by herself anymore. Her nephew would take her dogs and would help sell off her belongings. Tears spilled down her face. The joy of life that had filled her spirit had now departed and she seemed to be waiting for the grim reaper to come for her. I gave her a gentle hug and let her know the cross was heading for the county museum until legal ownership could be determined.

Late that night in the cabin I occupied while arguing with the home insurance company a dream hit me hard. I was back hiking to the old train depot with a duffel bag over my shoulders and the guitar case in hand. As I passed the old creek I noticed a ripple from the water. The sun was setting and the air took on an odd chill. The water rippled a second time but the little wave grew larger. Not sure if it was a water snake or a turtle due to the fading light, I walked closer and found it was Rachel stepping out the water. She was naked save for a thin coat of dark mud covering her. Her eyes had been closed as walked out of the muddy water but opened to fix on me intently. "Why do you think I am stuck in the mud? You are the one stuck in the mud." Then I was awake with a pounding heart and diaphoretic.

-

Three weeks later I was far away from home and parked down the street from a small bungalow in Culver City, California. Lizard had written down the address on a Post-It note for me. She had told me that I had better not ask questions on how she got the address as she handed it over. I took a few days of vacation, bought an airline ticket, and rented a car at the airport. I waited in that rental car but not for too long.

A new Ford Mustang GT convertible pulled into the driveway and parked under a carport. A slender woman with dark hair climbed gracefully from the car. I could not see her face as her back was turned to me but my heart was beating hard enough in my chest to cause bruising from the inside. After she went into the house, I started the rental car and drove up and parked in front of the bungalow.

I knocked on the door and heard a woman call out, "Just a minute!" After a short pause the door opened and there was a woman wearing sunglasses. Her black hair was beginning to pepper with gray. But I could not tell if she was really Rachel. Time had changed her or maybe this woman looked sort of like Rachel. I could not tell if it was her. She wore a flowered sundress but no shoes.

"Sorry to bother you ma'am, but I am with the sheriff's department." I did not say it was not the local sheriffs and that I had no jurisdiction. I was hoping she had little or no knowledge of how the Los Angeles County Sheriff's Department operated. "I am looking for a Rachel Marie Lopes." Her face had no reaction at all and I still could not tell if it was her or not. After all these years it could be her. Her lack of reaction disappointed me.

"Rachel Marie Lopes? I haven't heard *that* name in years." She pulled the door shut behind her and stood on her front step with me. "She was my cousin. I came out here from Louisiana to be an actress and Rachel was already out here getting small roles on TV. She helped me get a good agent, warned me about certain producers, and was just wonderful to me. Neither of us had much luck in front of the camera and we both waitressed more than our fair share. Then about two years ago she found blood in her stool and it was stage four cancer. I have a copy of the death certificate if you need it."

I felt rocked to my core. Rachel was dead, really dead. "No, ma'am. But thank you."

She gave me a smile and slipped back into the house. She poked her head out the door and smiled. A hand was raised and her sunglasses came off. And there below the left eye were golden flecks in the shape of a pyramid. "I don't know if this will make a difference to you but she did have a happy time out here and had a pretty good life. And she hoped you were having a good life too, Will." Will? I had not said my name! Like a turtle withdrawing into its shell, her head went back into the house and the door locked in her wake. And I had to admit that Rachel had become a pretty fine actress. My fears that she had been stuck in the mud all these years evaporated.

"Thank you," I said before I headed off back to Texas.

www.ingramcontent.com/pod-product-compliance
Lightning Source LLC
Chambersburg PA
CBHW032137190626
46814CB00005BA/1734